Kari is a loner. He's lived alone with his father for his entire life, and he wants that to change because his dad deserves better. That's why he's taken it upon himself to get rid of the evil men in the Allegheny forest, and he's finally managed to convince the council to put him on the team that will help the carriers obtain their freedom.

Calder has been fascinated with Kari ever since Kari confessed he was the one who caused the death of Oscar, one of the council members who were abusing carriers. Kari is slippery and has kept his distance, so Calder is surprised but eager when Kari plainly tells him he wants him in his bed.

Kari hasn't told Calder he's a carrier. He doesn't plan to, at least until the condom breaks and he ends up pregnant. But Kari doesn't want people to know he's a carrier, because too often carriers are protected, not sent out to save people from their abusers.

Will Kari have to choose between building a family with Calder and continuing the work he's been doing for the past months? Or is there a way for him to have both?

Let Love In
Copyright © 2019 Catherine Lievens
ISBN: 978-1-48742-708-5
Cover art by Angela Waters

Published by eXtasy Books Inc or
Devine Destinies, an imprint of eXtasy Books Inc

Look for us online at:
www.eXtasybooks.com or www.devinedestinies.com

LET LOVE IN
ALLEGHENY SHIFTERS BOOK 5

BY

CATHERINE LIEVENS

CHAPTER ONE

Everyone was yelling, or at least that was what it sounded like. Calder wished he could leave, but he was a council member, and that meant his presence was needed at this meeting—if he could even call this a meeting. Right now, it felt more like it was about to transform into a wrestling match.

"They're loud," Abel lamented from his seat beside Calder.

"Did you expect anything different? You knew this wasn't going to go down well."

"I hoped everyone would behave like adults."

Calder snorted. "Behave like adults? Sometimes, I wonder if they *are* adults."

But of course, they were, and they were *dangerous* adults. They were council members, and they made the laws for the shifters who lived in the Allegheny forest—which was one of the reasons people were yelling right now. The good guys finally had the majority in the council, and that meant they could pass laws that should have been passed decades ago. That meant that the council members who wanted to keep the carriers in slavery weren't happy, which explained why they were yelling.

Abel looked at his watch, and Calder knew precisely why. He leaned closer to his friend and knocked their shoulders together. "How are Philip and Myron?"

The smile that bloomed on Abel's face transformed his expression. "They're good. Myron is starting to teethe, so we haven't been getting a lot of sleep, but we're dealing with it."

Calder wondered if it was too soon for Myron to teethe, but

1

it wasn't like he had a lot of experience with children. "I'm happy to hear that. That you're dealing with it together, I mean, not that Myron isn't letting you sleep."

And he was.

Philip had been through so much, and he deserved everything he now had with Abel. Abel would treat him right, and that was exactly what he needed. It was time for the carriers to have normal relationships and lives, although of course, that would only happen if the rest of the council members stopped yelling and finally sat down to talk.

"Are you even listening?" someone snapped.

Abel jerked, but Calder limited himself to arching a brow at Miriam, the raccoon council member. "I would listen if you all stopped shouting and behaving like children."

Miriam straightened her back. "We're not behaving like children."

Calder could see he had touched a nerve. "Looks to me like you are. We're here to discuss the new laws for the carriers, yet most of you are yelling at each other because you don't want to talk about it."

"We can't change traditions—"

"Of course we can. Why should we continue following a tradition that hurts people? Besides, that's exactly what your bunch did when you passed a law that all carriers had to be handed off to the council."

"Carriers aren't like the rest of us."

Abel jerked as if Miriam had slapped him. This was a touchy argument for him, since he and Philip had just gotten together and Abel was so entirely in love with his man, although Calder supposed it was a sore spot for all of them who weren't monsters.

"Carriers are humans and shifters just like us," Abel said through gritted teeth.

It was obvious that he was restraining himself, but Calder

had no such problem. "The difference between you and them is that they're not all assholes like you."

Miriam's eyes widened. "How dare you!"

"How dare I? You want to keep human beings, shifters like you and me, in a state of slavery. You want to be able to sell them, to abuse them, only because they are men who can get pregnant. How can you not see how wrong that is?"

"The traditions—"

"Fuck the traditions. We shouldn't follow them if they're hurting people, which they are, and you know it. Didn't you talk to your alpha? Don't you know he had to move your raccoon carrier because he was afraid the man would get hurt?"

Miriam's cheeks flushed. "I don't often talk to him."

"Obviously." Calder had enough. He wanted to get out of there. He'd already known that the half of the council that was now outnumbered wouldn't be happy about this and that they would try to stop it, so even though he hated the yelling, he wasn't surprised by it.

Just like Miriam and her traditions, a lot of council members and alphas wanted to keep things the way they were. Calder didn't know if it was because they genuinely thought it was for the best or because they were profiting on the backs of the carriers, and he didn't care. He wasn't going to allow the trafficking and abuse to continue, not when he finally had a way to change things. He knew Abel and the other council members on his side agreed, which was why they'd called this meeting. He wasn't sure what he'd have to do to make people listen to him, but he wanted to go home and for the yelling to stop.

"You're going to regret it if you do this," Miriam said through gritted teeth.

Calder couldn't help but think about the carriers at the Bishop house. They were there because they'd had to flee their homes when the council had passed a law that all of them had to be handed over. They were there because they'd been abused and rescued. They were there because they didn't have another place to go, not a safe one. The lucky ones had been brought by their alphas because they were worried the council would take advantage of them, but the unlucky ones like Philip had been through hell and back, and they deserved to be able to make their own decisions. They were men, fathers in some cases, not objects or incubators.

Calder leaned forward, and he was glad to see Miriam move back. "I don't think so. I don't know about you, but I'm on the side of life that doesn't want people to be abused and raped. I honestly couldn't care less about what you want or think about this, not as long as we have the majority. So shut your mouth, vote the way you want, but know that you're going to lose this time."

Miriam's face flushed even redder, but Calder was done. He pressed back against his seat and linked his fingers together over his stomach.

"Was that necessary?" Abel asked in a whisper.

"Didn't you have enough? Because I did."

"Of course I did, but you won't gain anything by antagonizing her or any of the other council members."

"Maybe not, but I'm done walking on eggshells around them. They're the ones in the wrong, and we all know it. The only reason they want to keep up with these bullshit laws is that they gain from it, and I'm done."

"You're right, but still. This won't work if we don't try to find common ground."

"Of course it'll work. We finally have the upper hand, and just like they didn't care what we thought when they created the carrier laws, I don't care what they think right now."

Abel sighed, but Calder knew he was on his side. He always would be. He would have been even without Philip, but now that Abel and Philip were an item, Abel wanted to start their life together. That wouldn't happen until Philip was able to leave the Bishop house, and *that* would only happen when the laws were changed. As it was, if any of the carriers at the house tried to leave and someone found them, they'd have to be brought to the council. Calder and the people on his side had the majority now, but that didn't mean the carriers wouldn't be hidden or trafficked.

Calder wouldn't allow that. He might not be a carrier himself, and he might not be in love with one, but he'd watched his alpha's children grow up, and two of them were carriers. Calder was older than they were, and he wasn't close to them, but that didn't mean he wasn't aware of the fact that they were human beings just like he was.

He should probably be one of the council members yelling right now. Most of those were the ones who wanted things to go on the way they had like Miriam, but a few were fighting back, yelling even louder. Calder didn't like yelling, and he knew nothing good would come of it. He supposed he should wait until everyone yelled themselves out, then present the law he'd written for the carriers—which wasn't complicated. It was only a few lines that said that carriers were human beings and shifters just like everyone else in the forest and that they should be treated as such. He'd added a clause for a council team to be created and that the team would be allowed anywhere in the forest to check in on carriers and make sure they weren't trafficked or abounded, but that part would be harder to pass, even though the team was already a reality. Thomas and his allies were choosing members right now, and it would be ready to go in a few days.

Not everyone would see things the way Calder did, but as long as something was done, he didn't care.

They could go fuck themselves.

This meeting felt never-ending. Kari was getting bored, but he couldn't leave without being sure that something had been done. He needed this new law to pass. His father needed it.

He wiggled his weasel ass, trying to find a more comfortable position in the ceiling. He was used to spending time as a weasel and to watching people when they didn't know he was there, but he wasn't used to yelling. He didn't like yelling. His father never yelled at him, not even when Kari had been a child and misbehaved. Kari wasn't a child anymore, and his father couldn't stop him from doing what he was doing, but he still couldn't wait to go home and tell his dad that they were both free men.

Of course, to be able to do that, the people in the room under him would have to stop yelling and actually *do* something.

"Are all of you done shouting?" one of the men who'd already pointed out that most of the people in the room weren't behaving like adults asked. His voice was loud enough to shock the yellers into silence this time.

Kari peeked into the room. Things were finally moving, or at least, he hoped so.

"How dare you?" a woman asked. She sounded angry, and Kari wished he could see who it was.

"Oh, shut up, Jacqueline. We all know why we're here and shouting at each other, and being indignant isn't going to change that."

"You should never have been made a council member."

"Would you look at that? I think the same thing about you. Now shut up, sit down, and listen. All of you."

Kari liked that voice. He liked the man it belonged to. Calder had always struck Kari as a good man who was dealing with this situation the best he could. Now that Calder and the people on his side had the majority, Kari hoped that meant this freaking law would pass. He wanted to take his father away from the cabin in the woods where they'd lived most their lives — or in Kari's case, all his life. His dad deserved everything the other carriers in the Bishop house had and more, and Kari had been working toward that for weeks.

"We are council members just like you. You can't talk to us that way," a man said.

Kari was pretty sure it was the bobcat council member. He didn't like the man, and he was grateful the bobcat alpha wasn't like him. The alpha's father had chosen the council member, and Alpha Wiley hadn't been able to get the man to step down yet.

Some of the council members were so old that they'd been chosen by alphas who were now deceased. They needed to be replaced, but of course, they wouldn't go without a fight.

"I'm sorry for hurting your feelings. Wait, no. I'm not. Shut up, Drake, and listen." There was a pause, then the sound of paper being moved. "I already wrote a new law. I'm not asking for us to vote on it right now, but you should at least all read it. It's straightforward, and I have nothing against amending it if it needs to be, but I want it to be voted on during the next meeting."

"This is outrageous." That was Drake again. Kari couldn't help but wonder why he hadn't yet killed the man.

"No, what is outrageous is the way you and your friends have been treating carriers. You didn't ask our opinion when you passed the law that all of them have to be handed over to the council. At least *I'm* giving you a chance to help shape this new law."

As long as they didn't try to change it entirely, Kari didn't care. He wished the council would vote right now, but he understood that it might not be possible. Waiting another few days or even a week wasn't going to change anything, at least not for him or his father.

But the carriers who were still in the hands of the alphas

abusing them needed to be helped, and Kari would make sure that happened. It had nothing to do with this new law. The carriers could be hidden just like the others had been in the Bishop house in cete territory.

"This law, as you call it, is outrageous," Drake continued.

Kari rolled his eyes. Of course Drake thought that.

"I don't give a fuck what you think. Read it, take notes, and be here to vote. If you're not, we'll vote anyway, so don't try to come up with an excuse to avoid the next meeting." Calder rose from his chair, and Abel followed him out of the room.

It was time for Kari to go.

He wiggled his way out of the ceiling, once more grateful that his animal form was so small and agile. His clothes were where he'd left them, and he rushed through dressing and fixing his hair. He didn't care if he looked like he'd escaped prison, but he knew Abel was a sensitive man, and he didn't want to spook him more than he already would.

Calder and Abel always stopped to get coffee on their way out of a meeting, so Kari had more than enough time to sneak into Abel's car. He settled in the back seat and made himself comfortable, keeping an eye on the entrance to the council building.

It was only ten minutes before the two men appeared. They were talking with their heads close together as they sipped on their coffees. Kari couldn't hear what they were saying from where he was, but he had no doubt they were talking about how the meeting had gone. He was going to have to ask Abel and hope the man would answer. He'd heard a lot, but it was different from being in the room and seeing and hearing everything from there. He might have missed something.

He slid down the seat to make sure neither Calder nor Abel would notice him and watched them as Calder patted Abel's shoulder and left. Kari couldn't help but watch Calder walk away. He'd noticed the man the first time he'd seen him. He'd made a point of learning as much as he could on every council member, and Calder was the only one who still fascinated him.

Calder was gorgeous. He was older than Kari by more than a decade, but Kari didn't care about that. What he *did* care about was the fact that Calder wasn't into one-night stands, which was the only thing Kari could offer. He couldn't have more, not right now, probably not for a while. No one knew he was a carrier, and he wanted things to stay that way. He wouldn't be allowed to go out there and fight the abusers and traffickers otherwise.

A lot of shifters in the forest—most of them, in fact—viewed carriers as precious. Kari thought it was ridiculous, but he couldn't change that. They'd try to coddle him if he came out, which meant he wasn't about to do it. Of course, that didn't mean he couldn't have sex, but Calder wouldn't want a friends-with-benefits arrangement, which was a pity. Kari had never talked to him, but he had eyes, and Calder was hot. Kari couldn't help but want to run his hands in Calder's messy brown curls that always looked a second away from getting frizzy.

And that ass. No one should be allowed to have an ass that looked like Calder's.

The sound of Abel trying to unlock the car jerked Kari out of his thoughts about what he would do to Calder if they ever shared a bed. Abel slipped into the driver seat, and before he could drive away, Kari popped up from the back seat. "Hi there."

Abel jumped, one of his hands flying to his chest. "What do you think you're doing? I almost had a heart attack."

"And we can't have that since you have a family. I'm sorry. How did the meeting go?"

Abel rolled his eyes. "As if you don't already know."

"You're right. I *do* know how it went, which isn't well."

"That doesn't matter. We already know we have the votes to pass this law. Asking the other council members to read it over is only protocol."

"Good. The sooner you pass a law, the better it will be for everyone. Do you remember your promise to make me a member of the team that will go in the territories to rescue the carriers?"

"Of course I do. You know everyone agreed with it."

"Good, because I know of at least another two carriers who are being abused as we speak."

The small smile that had been playing on Abel's lips faded. "Really?"

"Yes." Kari always did his best to find carriers, but even he couldn't find all of them. It was a pity, but he did what he could. He needed help, and he hoped he'd found it.

"All right. Let me talk to the others. I know Thomas asked the other alphas to pick one member of their pack to add to the team. If they know there are carriers to be rescued, I don't doubt they'll rush through it."

"As long as you remember the promise you made me."

"I will. Don't worry about that. I keep my promises."

Did Calder? Kari couldn't help but wonder what life with Calder would be.

He shouldn't think about that, though. It hurt, and that wasn't something he needed right now. He couldn't allow himself to take his eyes off the goal of every carrier in the forest being safe.

CHAPTER TWO

Calder could have done without another meeting, but at least this one was with people he liked — mostly. He knew no one would yell and tell him he was a disgrace to all the shifters in the forest.

"Have you heard from the other council members?" Thomas asked.

"Unfortunately. A couple of them have been texting and emailing me threats and insults, but I expected it. They're not happy we have the majority and that nothing they can do will help keep up the carrier law they voted for before."

"Any idea when you'll have another meeting to vote this law in?"

"I'm giving everyone another two days before calling one. I don't care who comes. As long as we have the majority, the law will pass."

Thomas relaxed. "That's good."

Even though both his carrier sons were married, it didn't mean the council wouldn't have eventually gotten their hands on them if things hadn't changed. Besides, he'd agreed to take on all the carriers who needed a safe place, and he wanted to make sure they were okay. The Bishop house was far away from the edge of cete territory and isolated, so the council probably didn't know about it, but the sooner the law passed and the carriers were free to go, the better it would be for everyone.

"So we're just going to wait until it passes?" Ambrose asked. He was the opossum alpha, and he'd been one of those who had brought his carrier to the cete.

"I think that's the best thing to do. Right now, we'd be in the wrong if we barged in another alpha's territory to take his carriers."

"Actually, we wouldn't be, not the council, anyway," Abel said.

Everyone turned to look at him, and his cheeks flushed, but that didn't stop him from explaining what he meant. "The law right now is that all carriers who aren't married have to be handed to the council, right? That means that if an alpha has unmarried carriers in his territory, they should give them up. We would be in our right to go in and take them since the law hasn't changed yet."

He was right. Calder had been so focused on writing this new law and making sure that anyone who would abuse and traffic carriers once it *was* law paid for what they did that he hadn't realized they could save the carriers still in the hands of their abusers already.

"We have to be sure of it, though," Ambrose said. "We all know who the alphas in this case are. They're not going to step aside as we go in and take what they view as theirs. Even if this new law were already a thing, it wouldn't make things easy for us."

Since the council had always tried to stay out of the business of the different groups of shifters in the forest, Ambrose was right. No one had ever barged into a territory that wasn't theirs, and the alphas weren't going to be happy. It didn't matter, because Calder and the others wouldn't wait and let them do what they wanted, but it would make things harder on everyone.

"You can amend the law," Thomas said.

"Such as?" Calder asked even though he suspected what Thomas meant.

"Add a line that the council is allowed to send in their team if they suspect abuse is being carried on in the territory."

"I already did that, but you know the council members against us and their alphas are going to be pissed and that they'll do whatever they can to make sure it doesn't happen."

"Of course I do. But like you said, we have the majority."

Calder wasn't sure his majority would hold if he insisted on making this part of the law, but it was worth a try. All the council members on his side realized that things couldn't go on like this. Carriers had been abused for decades. They'd been hurt and trafficked, and no one had cared about it. The council had been put in charge to keep the peace between the different shifters in the forest so that the humans would stay away, but that didn't mean they couldn't have a more active role. They were supposed to protect people, and they hadn't been doing that.

"Kari says he knows of at least another two carriers," Abel said.

Calder swore. He might not have been sure about Kari in the beginning, but so far, nothing the man had said had been wrong. Calder had no idea why Kari was in this, but he didn't think it mattered, not when people's lives were in danger. "Where?" he asked.

"He didn't tell me. He wants us to make good on the promise we made for him to be part of the team we're building. He'll tell us if it comes to that, but I don't want to betray his trust. We need the information he can give us. We need *him*."

Calder hated the thought of putting Kari or anyone else in danger, but the man knew what he was doing. That much was obvious. "Like I said the first time, I don't have anything against him being part of the team."

"We still don't know if we can trust him," Ralph, the bat alpha, said.

"He hasn't done anything that proves we can't," Calder pointed out. "Besides, I don't think we have another way to do this. He knows where the carriers are, and even if he tells us, I don't want us to betray the promise we made him. People trust us for a reason, and I don't want that to change."

Ralph raised his hands. "That's all right with me. I know the carriers aren't in my territory and that they're not bat shifters."

Odds were that the carriers were part of one of the abuser alphas groups. That left the rodents, the coyotes, and the skunks. The rodents had been trying to convince Calder and the others that they were on their side, but after what had happened with the old alpha and Seamus, Calder wasn't sure he could trust them. The new alpha was an asshole, no matter how hard he tried not to look like one.

"Does everyone here have someone to add to the team?" Thomas asked.

That wasn't Calder's area of expertise, since he was more used to meetings than to building teams that would barge into other alphas' territories and save people, so he stayed out of it. He trusted his alpha implicitly. Thomas was a good man, as everything he'd done in the past months had shown. Calder already knew that, of course, but Thomas wanted to help all the carriers in the forest, not merely his sons. That was one of the reasons he and Calder were friends and that Calder respected him as much as he did.

The alphas put their heads together and threw out names that Thomas wrote down.

Things were taking shape. The law would pass before the end of the week, and Calder hoped that line about the council having the authority to go into alphas territories to make sure no one was abused would pass along with the rest of what he'd written. The alphas were putting together a team that would eventually answer to the council, and that would save the people who needed them, but not everyone might see things that way.

There was nothing else Calder could do. No matter how much he might want to, he wasn't trained to go in with the team. It wasn't his job. No, his job was to stay behind a desk, at least part of the time, and to make sure the council did everything they could to keep the forest calm and out of sight of the humans. The last thing they needed was for the humans to step in. They already had more than enough problems as it was.

Kari's phone didn't usually ring. His father had his number, of course, but he knew better than to call Kari. Besides, they were both at the cabin, so he wouldn't have to even if he needed Kari.

The only other person who had Kari's number was Abel.

Kari swallowed and answered. "Yes?"

"Kari? It's Abel."

"I know. What's going on?"

"We have a team."

Kari released the breath he'd been holding. He'd suspected this was why Abel was calling. He couldn't be sure Abel and the others would want him on the team, no matter what they'd said.

"Kari? Can you hear me?"

Kari shook himself. "Of course. So you have a team. Am I on it?"

"Of course you are. I already told you that. As long as you give us the location of the carriers, you're with us."

"I would have given you to location even if you'd decided you didn't want me." Kari wanted to be able to help more than he already had, but he wouldn't have put the carriers' lives in danger because of that. He wanted them to be free and safe, whatever that meant for him. Still, he was relieved Abel was keeping his promise.

"What about when they're rescued? Will you keep me on the team, or will you kick me out? Is it a one-time thing?"

"I know how important this is for you, so no, it's not a one-time thing. You're welcome to stay on the team for as long as you want, as long as you follow orders."

That would be the hardest part for Kari. He wasn't used to following orders. He'd always worked alone, moving through the various territories and sticking his nose where it didn't belong. Being a weasel shifter had helped him to find out where the carriers were, because no one had ever noticed him, but being with the team would get him noticed. There was no way around that, but it didn't matter. Kari couldn't be sure, but he thought these two carriers were some of the last ones who were being abused in the forest. If there were others, he'd find them, or he hoped so, anyway.

"I will." He'd keep that promise. Even with all the known carriers safe, the team Abel and the others had put together was needed to *keep* everyone safe. Kari wasn't an idiot. He knew that the alphas weren't going to be happy at having their carriers taken away, but most of all, at having other shifters invaded their territory. They were going to strike back, and if things escalated, it was possible that an outright war would happen. Peace wouldn't happen for a long time, but there was no way out of it.

"All right. When can you come?"

"Right away, if you need me to."

Abel chuckled. "I'm not even surprised you're this eager to do this. Come around to Thomas' house. I'll tell him to expect you."

"Now?"

"Of course now. It's no use to wait, especially with two carriers still being hurt. We're going to do this as soon as we can, and we need you."

That made Kari's stomach churn. He'd never been needed,

not really. His father needed him sometimes, but Julian could have survived on his own easily. If anything, Kari needed *him*. And maybe the carriers he'd found and tried to help on his own had needed him, but not anymore. The only thing Kari had that could help them was their location, and once he handed that out, he wouldn't be needed anymore. "That's not true."

"Maybe, but that doesn't mean you won't be a valued member of the team. Just come here, Kari. This is what you wanted all along, and you finally have it. Are you really going to say no?"

Kari wasn't.

He and Abel hung up, and Kari stared at the wooden wall in front of him. The cabin he'd grown up in had been tiny in the beginning. His father had been lucky he'd managed to build it in the first place, and once Kari was older, he'd helped his dad expand it so they now each had a bedroom and the kitchen area was separated from them. He'd answered the phone in his bedroom, but he suspected his dad had been able to hear the conversation. The walls weren't exactly sound-proof.

"Dad?" Kari called out as he left his room.

"I heard," his dad said when Kari stepped into the kitchen. "When are you leaving?"

"As soon as possible. Abel wants me to go right away."

Kari's father nodded. "Does that mean you and the rest of the team are going out now?"

"I don't know. The sooner we go, the sooner we can get the carriers out of their abusers' hands, but I'm not the one in charge."

Kari's father put down the carrot he'd been peeling and turned to face him. "Maybe you should be."

Kari couldn't help but smile. "You only say that because you're my father."

His dad shrugged. "Maybe, maybe not. What I do know is that you've been haunting this forest for years and helping people however you can. No one else has done that."

No one had helped Kari's father, that was for sure. He'd fled the weasel gang at seventeen, and he'd never gone back, even though they still lived in gang territory. No one had found them, though. No one had ever suspected they were there, and as far as Kari knew, most of the gang didn't remember they existed. That was a good thing, even though he couldn't help but wonder if his dad was lonely sometimes.

Kari's father spent most of his days alone. Kari tried to be home in the evenings, but he didn't always manage. His dad understood, and he agreed with Kari that this was important, but people weren't made to be alone, not as wholly as Kari's father was. Kari needed to get him out of this house, of this forest, and he needed it to happen soon. His dad was still young, young enough that he could make himself a life that didn't keep him alone in the forest. He was only forty-two. He could still give Kari siblings, although that wasn't something Kari liked to think about. He didn't want to think about his father with a man, let alone children, not because he was jealous, but because it was *weird.*

"You promise to be careful?" Kari's father asked.

"Always, Dad. You know that."

"I do, but that doesn't mean I'm not afraid for you."

"Just like I'm afraid for you when I'm not here." Kari reached out and grabbed his father's hand. "I promise this is almost over. I'm going to make sure you can leave this place and never see it again." Maybe Kari should make it a condition of joining the team and giving the carriers' positions to Abel.

No. He couldn't do that. He couldn't put other people's lives in danger just because he wanted his father out of the cabin. His dad was safe here, no matter how isolated he was.

He wasn't risking his life, not the way the carriers where.

Kari's father looked around. "I think I'm going to miss it when it happens."

"Maybe, but you'll have a house, a real one."

"But we built so many memories here."

Kari couldn't deny that. His father had raised him alone, and that meant *really* alone. Kari had only had his father until he'd been old enough to leave the cabin. But now he wanted both of them to have more, and that objective was almost close enough for him to taste it. "That's true, but it doesn't mean we can't build more memories in the new house. I want you to have a better life, Dad."

"My life is already perfect the way it is. I have you. That's all I need."

Kari smiled. "Maybe all you need, but not all you want. Think about it. You could have a home with actual walls and electricity. You could have a bathroom, and you could use real soap. You can make friends, maybe find yourself a boyfriend."

His father's cheeks flushed. "Let's not talk about boyfriends. That's something *you* have to think about, not me."

Kari shook his head. "Not right now. I have to focus on this."

His father squeezed Kari's hand. "Keep telling yourself that. Love has a way of finding you when you least expect it to. Don't close yourself off because you think you don't have the time or that it's not the right time to deal with it."

Kari nodded, but he knew it was a lie. They both did. Kari was going to focus on rescuing the last carriers in the forest, and he was going to build a better life for himself and his father. That was all he could allow himself to focus on.

Abel was too trusting. That was the only reason Calder had

wanted to be with him when Kari arrived.

Or at least, that was what Calder was trying to convince himself. If he was honest with himself, he knew the main reason he wanted to be there was that the man fascinated him. He wasn't sure why, considering he'd only seen Kari once or twice and they hadn't had the time to talk, but there was something about the man, and Calder wanted to know more. He could tell Kari was prickly, though, and that trust didn't come easily for him. The man was a mystery, and Calder wanted to understand him. Why he wanted that didn't matter.

"I hope he won't freak out," Abel said, peering at the driveway.

Calder leaned back in his chair on the porch. "Why should he freak out?"

"Because you're here. I didn't tell him you would be."

"I don't see why that should be a problem for him. It's not like he expects to be part of this team and keep to himself."

"Maybe, but you know he's not like us."

For some reason, those words made Calder bristle. "Why isn't he like us?"

Abel rolled his eyes. "That's not what I meant, and you know it. It's just that he's isolated, and whether or not it's something he wants, it doesn't change that fact. He's not used to being with groups of people, and he'll have to adjust to that. I just wanted to make things easy on him, at least in the beginning."

"He's going to have to get used to that as fast as he can if he wants to be part of your team."

Abel's cheeks flushed. "It's not *my* team. We're all working on it."

"Maybe, but it looks like Kari trusts only you. Maybe it'll be your team member. What kind of shifter is he?"

"I have no idea. I don't think anyone knows."

And wasn't that strange? Calder didn't know every single shifter in the forest, of course, but when he met people he didn't know, they usually either told him what kind of shifter they were, or he could smell it on them. He hadn't been close enough to Kari to find that out, but he hoped things would change today. He still wasn't sure he trusted the man, no matter what Kari had told them about the carriers.

"You know, I understand why you don't trust him," Abel said.

"I never said I didn't trust him."

"You haven't, but it's obvious. That's why you're here, isn't it?"

Calder grinned. "Maybe I wanted to spend more time in your company."

"You can do that anytime you want." The blush on Abel's cheeks was still there, going strong.

Calder bumped their shoulders together, then rose when he heard the sound of footsteps coming from the side. They hadn't expected Kari to arrive by car, but they'd still decided to wait for him on the porch of Thomas' house. The others were inside, still talking, but Abel was right. Kari was used to being on his own, and Abel didn't want him to be overwhelmed. Calder wasn't sure that was possible, considering what he knew of the man, but he hadn't protested. He wanted to see Kari, and the fewer people were around what had happened, the less probable it was that he'd humiliate himself in some way.

Neither of them was surprised when Kari appeared walking around the side of the house. He was dressed, but the only way for him to have come from where he was coming from was to have been in his animal form. The fact that he'd managed to sneak by the guards patrolling the territory made Calder smile instead of worrying him. Kari was the only one who'd ever been able to do that, and Calder suspected he was some kind of small shifter. It was the only thing that made sense.

Abel got up and stepped toward the porch stairs. "Kari. I'm happy to see you."

Kari blinked. "You are?"

"Of course. I want to go find those two carriers just as much as you do."

Kari's expression went blank. "That's why you're happy to see me. You want to know what the carriers are. Of course. I have a condition."

Abel frowned. "I thought we'd gone over this. You have a place on the team as long as you respect the team leader and listen to him."

"And I'll do that. I'd give you the names and their positions even if you say no to this, but I have another request."

Calder wasn't surprised. He had no idea what Kari's life was like, but he suspected the man was as lonely as he appeared. Maybe he wanted a house in cete territory, or with the deer. They'd probably give it to him if that was what he asked for.

"I'm listening," Abel said.

Calder could have talked to Kari instead of Abel, but for some reason, Kari had reached out to Abel that first time, and neither of them wanted to push him away, not with the knowledge he seemed to have.

Kari cleared his throat. "I know about the Bishop house."

Of course he did. Was there anything in the forest Kari didn't know about? The man seemed to be able to sneak into any place he wanted to without anyone noticing him.

Abel nodded curtly. "And? We're not going to give you a carrier, no matter what you're offering in exchange."

"That's not what I was going to ask for. What you take me for, a monster? My father is a carrier, and he's been living alone in the forest since he was seventeen. I'd like him to have a place at the Bishop house. I want him to finally have a real home and be able to make friends. He's had only me for most of his life, and that's not fair."

That wasn't what Calder had expected. "Your father is a carrier?" He'd thought they knew about all the carriers in the forest, although of course, Kari had shown them just how wrong he was about that with the two new names he had. It looked like he had a third one, though, one no one had known about.

Kari glared. "Yes, he is, and his life hasn't been easy."

That seemed to be a sore spot for Kari. Calder raised his hands in what he hoped was a gesture that made him look harmless. "I was just surprised. You're what, twenty? Twenty-one?"

"Twenty-five."

"And your father's been living on his own since he was seventeen? In the forest?" It was a miracle no one had found him.

"Yes, he has, and no one knows about it. That's why I want him to go to the Bishop house. He doesn't deserve to spend the rest of his life alone in the forest."

"You're right. No one deserves that, especially not for something they can't change."

Kari relaxed. It was subtle, but Calder noticed. "He had to leave when he was seventeen. His alpha raped him, and when he realized he was pregnant with me, he knew he couldn't stick around. He left his people because of me. He wanted to keep me safe, and I've been doing my best to keep *him* safe and happy ever since I've been old enough, but it's been hard, since he won't leave the forest. He's afraid of what might happen to him, even though the man who raped him isn't the alpha anymore."

"Of course we'll take your father in," Abel said.

Calder would have said yes, too, but he wanted more

information. "I'd like to talk to him first," he said.

He expected Kari to protest, but Kari nodded. "I suspected you'd want to. I didn't tell him about this because I didn't want him to get his hopes up, but I can take you to our cabin if you want. Or I can have him come here, but if you're going to say no, then I'd have to take him home, and I don't want that."

"If he's a carrier, we'll take him, no questions asked. We both know how dangerous being a carrier in the forest is right now. I'd just like to meet him before taking him there. I have no doubt you've already been to the Bishop house, so you know how many people are hiding there. We need to know your father is safe and that he won't run to, I don't know, the coyote alpha to tell him where everyone is." Calder could think about a few men who weren't alphas anymore and who might be Kari's second father, and the coyote was one of them. That would be the worst-case scenario, of course, and Calder had no way to be sure the dead man was Kari's father, but even though he knew they'd take Kari's father in, he wanted a few reassurances first.

Kari was nervous, but he knew that was nothing next to how his father would feel when he got home with Calder. The only person Julian had had any contact with for the past twenty-six years was Kari. He hadn't needed anyone else once he'd settled in the forest, and he still didn't. That didn't mean he shouldn't have friends, maybe a boyfriend one day, although that wasn't something Kari wanted to think about. But he wanted his father to be happy, and he knew that wouldn't happen if his dad couldn't leave the cabin.

Kari knew he should have approached the new alpha. The one who had raped his father, who had impregnated him, had died ten years ago. His beta had taken his place, and he'd been as bad as the alpha. But now, the alpha's son — his *other* son — had taken his place. The man was only twenty, younger than Kari, and they were brothers.

That was why Kari hadn't reached out to him. He'd observed the gang, of course, and he knew his half-brother was doing his best to repair the damage their father and his beta had done. But he'd only been alpha for a few months, and Kari didn't know if he could trust him with his father's life. He hadn't wanted to risk it, and he still didn't. He wouldn't talk to his half-brother until he was sure his father was safe.

"Where do I go?" Calder asked.

He was the only one who'd come with Kari, since Abel had wanted to go home to his boyfriend and their son. Kari wished Abel was with them, but not because he was afraid of Calder. No, he feared not being able to resist the man. Of course, his father's presence would probably help with that.

"Turn here."

Calder was driving, since Kari had never learned. They'd crossed bear territory without anyone stopping them, which wasn't surprising, since the bears and the badgers were allies. The sons of the alphas had gotten married and had a son, and that linked the two groups more than any kind of promise or deal could.

"Ah. Weasel territory."

This was inevitable. Kari had kept what kind of shifter he was a secret until now because it was useful for him. People didn't look for weasels or rodents in general when they were doing something they shouldn't. They didn't think about it, and that had always worked to Kari's advantage. He didn't think Calder and his friends would use it against him, but he was still wary. He didn't trust people easily because people had never given him a reason to trust them. "Yes," he said curtly.

"You're a weasel?"

"I am, and so is my father."

"Good. I half expected you to be a coyote."

Kari grimaced. "Yeah, no. I'm relieved I'm not." Everyone in the forest knew how bad the coyotes were. Kari didn't know if all the members of the band were like their old alpha and the new one, but he didn't want to risk it. He was sure some of the coyotes were okay people, but so far, he hadn't met any of those.

"The fact that you managed to remain hidden is a small miracle."

Kari was aware of that. "I think it's because we're close to bear territory. My father didn't dare to cross into it, but he stayed as close as he could, in case his alpha found him."

"That was smart."

Kari couldn't help but smile. "That's my father. He's smart, smarter than a lot of people thought him to be back then."

"I'm sorry about what happened to him."

Carey shrugged. "He's not the only one in the forest who had to go through that. Hopefully, that won't happen again now that the council finally sees how wrong it is."

"We'll do everything we can. You should know that. Not everyone is like the alpha who raped your father. We want carriers to be safe and happy just like they deserve."

That was the only reason Kari was making himself and his father vulnerable. He knew Calder and Abel, and the other alphas and council members who worked with them, wanted the best for everyone in the forest, including the carriers.

"What can you tell me about your father?" Calder asked.

Kari blinked. "What do you mean?"

"Well, I know he's a weasel shifter, just like you are. I know he's been living in the forest for the past twenty-five years, since you're twenty-five, and you said he left when he realized he was pregnant with you. I know that pregnancy didn't happen because he wanted it."

"My father has always loved me," Kari snapped.

Calder glanced at Kari. "I never said he didn't. He wouldn't have left the gang if he didn't love you and if he didn't want something better for you than what he could give you there. I'm sure making that decision was hard and that he wouldn't have been able to go through with it if it weren't for you."

Accepting that he was a child of rape had been hard on Kari. His father had explained everything to him as soon as he was old enough, and Kari had spent months hating himself. He didn't want to be his sperm donor's child. He didn't want to have been created in hate and pain and humiliation.

But he couldn't change what happened, and he'd come to terms with it, mostly thanks to his father. His dad hadn't allowed him to focus on the way he'd come into this world. It had been hard, but nowhere as hard as Julian's life had been. Kari had no right to obsess over it, not when his father had managed to get over it.

"I'm sorry," Kari said. "This is a touchy subject for me."

"It would be for anyone. But I have to say I'm impressed and in awe of your father's strength. You said he left the gang when he realized he was pregnant with you, and that means he had you on his own in the forest, right?"

"He did." He'd told Kari about it, of course, and Kari knew how dangerous it had been. It had still been better than going back to the gang and risking the alpha taking Kari away and raping Julian again.

"But he didn't come out when the old alpha died."

"Well, his beta was just as bad as him, and the man was effectively the alpha for almost ten years."

"He's not anymore, though."

"No. The alpha's son became the alpha a few months ago."

"Your brother."

"I don't know if I'd consider him my brother. We share the

same father, but that doesn't make him family." The only thing that would make him family was if he was a good man and they got along, and Kari didn't know if they would since he hadn't talked to him. "I don't know if he's safe, and I won't put my father in danger by going to him until I'm sure of that."

"You're right to do that. But I've talked to Milton, and as far as I see, he's a good man. He's hesitant and unsure of his role as the new alpha, but then, he's only twenty. He has more than enough time to grow into it. He does look like he's trying to make the right choices for the gang, and I'm sure that if he knew you and your father were part of it, he'd do right by you."

"Maybe I can try talking to him once I know my father is safe."

"You should. But if you need someone to be with you when you do, you can ask Abel or me. You're not alone anymore, Kari. I know it must seem strange to you and that you don't trust us, but things are changing."

Kari wanted to believe him. He wanted to trust him, and not only because he thought Calder was hot. He'd watched so many people going on with their lives, being happy and building families, working, and going home. He wanted that, too, both for himself and his father.

CHAPTER THREE

Calder was in awe of the strength both Kari and his father had shown. They hadn't had a choice, and it was evident that Kari had grown up without having to follow the laws that governed the forest and its inhabitants, but things could have gone so much worse for them. Besides, no matter what Kari did, it was for the right reason. That didn't excuse killing people, but Calder couldn't deny he was glad Kari had.

The people Kari had killed, like Oscar, the porcupine council member, meant that things were changing in the forest, and they were changing for the good. Besides, it was the law of the forest. They weren't human, and they didn't follow the same rules. If someone betrayed them, put others in danger, trafficked carriers, and hurt them, so they deserved to die. Calder couldn't find it in himself to be angry or to view Kari as nothing more than a killer.

He'd killed, but he'd done it for the right reasons. That was all that mattered.

Kari was fascinating. Calder had been intrigued by him ever since he'd first heard of him, but it was getting out of hand. In the beginning, he'd thought Kari was nothing more than a killer, but that wasn't true. Kari loved his father so much that he was ready to do just about anything for him. It had to have been hard to trust people the way Kari was with the person who meant the most in his life.

Kari was full of contradictions. He was hard and didn't hesitate in front of difficult decisions like killing people to protect others. He was caring, and he loved his father so much that he was doing all of this for him. He was harsh and soft at the same time, hateful and loving. Calder wanted to get to know him, to find out everything about him. He knew it was probably a stretch, since Kari didn't trust anyone but his father, but maybe now that Kari would be part of the team who would save the carriers still in danger, Calder could get closer to him.

It wouldn't be easy. Calder knew that, and he didn't care. He didn't want easy. He wanted Kari.

"Turn again."

Calder sneaked a peek at Kari, but Kari was looking straight ahead. He had to, because Calder would never have seen the tiny road—if he could even call that a road—to their left.

He turned, but he had to stop the truck after only a few minutes. They were surrounded by trees, and nothing more. The road was gone.

He turned the truck off and looked at Kari. "What now?"

Kari grinned at him. "Now, we walk."

So they did. Calder wasn't surprised. Having a road stop near their cabin would have put Kari in his father in danger of being found. They'd managed to survive twenty-five years in the forest without anyone noticing them. They were smart, and they knew what to do not to put themselves in danger.

Calder had expected a tiny house made of wood, and to be fair, the cabin they finally got to *was* made of wood. It wasn't small by any means, though. It was a decent size for two adult males, and even though Calder doubted they had electricity or running water, it looked welcoming and homey. There was a yard with vegetables growing in front of the house, and Calder could see colorful curtains hanging in the windows.

"You go into town regularly," Calder said.

"I do. Now that I'm an adult and I know to be careful, I've been able to bring more food and other things to my father."

Calder wished Kari and his father had left this place a long time ago, but he understood why they hadn't. They could have snuck into bear territory, and Morris would have welcomed them as part of his sleuth. Kari should have realized that when he'd started spying on them, and maybe he had. He hadn't been willing to put his father in danger, though, and that showed how much he cared for him. His love was also the reason he was trying to convince Calder to move his father to the Bishop house. Things were changing, both for Kari and his father.

"This looks like a home," Calder said.

Kari glared at him. "That's because it is. You know how long we've been here. What did you expect? That we slept in the trees or something?"

Calder barked out a laugh. "No, but I didn't think you were this organized." Although, of course, they had to be to live for twenty-five years in the forest with barely any contact with the outside.

Kari paused before opening the door. "I know I don't have to warn you not to hurt my father. You won't. But we've been alone for twenty-five years, and he hasn't seen anyone but me in all that time. I wouldn't be surprised if he's afraid and if he shies away from you. Don't be offended."

"I won't be." Calder suspected Kari was right, but it didn't matter. He was there to get to know Kari's father and to take him to the Bishop house. Kari's father didn't have to become his best friend.

Kari nodded and pushed open the door. "Dad?" He called out.

"Who's that with you? Why did you bring someone? Kari, what's going on?"

Kari's father was freaking out.

Calder remained by the front door, but he stepped in. Kari's father looked a lot like Kari—he had the same hazel eyes, and his hair, although streaked with white at the temples, was brown. He was older, but even though his life had been hard, he was a gorgeous man.

Kari raised his hands. "It's okay, Dad. I promise. Calder is one of the men I'm working with."

"Calder? You mean the badger council member?"

"Yes. I talked to him and Abel, and they both agreed you should move to the Bishop house."

Kari's father knew what Kari was talking about. He didn't ask what the Bishop house was or why he should move there. Instead, he looked around, and Calder thought he knew what he was thinking.

Even though he'd been forced to live here on his own for most of his life, this was still his home. It was the place where he'd had his son and where he'd raised him. Leaving was probably hard for him, even though it was the best thing he could do right now.

Kari's father looked at Calder. He straightened his shoulders, and Calder's surprise, he stepped toward him and offered him his hand. "I'm Julian."

Calder took Julian's hand and shook it. "As you know, I'm Calder. It's a pleasure to meet you, and I am incredibly impressed with what you've done with this place."

Julian cocked his head. "Kari told you what happened to me, didn't he?"

"He did. He had to. No offense, but we had to know if you could be trusted." Calder realized it couldn't be easy for Julian to face people who knew what had happened to him. He hoped Julian understood it had been necessary.

"Why don't you tell me about the Bishop house?" Julian said. "I can make some tea or coffee."

"Of course." Julian needed to be reassured. He trusted his son, so he probably trusted Calder, too, at least in part, but he wouldn't leave his house—his *home*—without being sure it was the best thing for him.

"The Bishop house is deep into badger territory, toward the edge of the forest. It's impossible for other shifters in the forest to get there without being seen," Calder said. "Except Kari, of course, but he seems to have a way of sneaking around without anyone ever seeing him."

"The rodents could. Their territory borders the badgers'."

Calder couldn't help but smile. "You're right, they could, but I'm sure you know they're not organized enough to do it. Besides, the Bishop house is far from the edge of their territory. It's closer to the foxes, but the fox alpha is on our side. Even if he wasn't, he couldn't get to the Bishop house without being seen. I promise you that." It would have been safer if the place where they kept the carriers had been in fox territory toward the edge of the forest were no other territory bordered, but things were the way they were. They couldn't move the carriers.

"Why do you keep the carriers there? And I know you don't just have badger carriers."

Calder sat at the table. "You're right. We have at least one carrier of almost all the groups in the forest. The alphas trusted us with them when they couldn't trust the council. We've been keeping them safe, and while I know you don't want to leave your house, we can do the same for you. That's why Kari came to us. He wants you to be safe while he saves the world."

Kari snorted. He couldn't help it. "Save the world? What are you talking about?"

Calder grinned at him. "You're trying to save the carriers and to make this forest a better place for everyone. I call that saving the world, or at least, our world."

It was ridiculous, but Kari couldn't help but feel pleased.

The only person he was trying to save was his father, but if he managed to make the forest a better place for everyone like Calder had said, he was okay with that.

He hoped he wasn't making a mistake by trusting Calder and Abel with his father's life. He knew that once his dad was at the Bishop house, he couldn't just sneak him out and take him back here. Calder knew about this place now. He could come back and drag both Kari and his dad back to the house if he thought that was for the best.

He wouldn't do that, or at least, Kari hoped he wouldn't. He wanted to trust Calder, but it wasn't easy. He'd never trusted anyone but his father.

"I'm glad I'm not the only one who sees Kari's potential," Kari's dad said.

Kari rolled his eyes, but he didn't say anything. His father was relaxing, and that was what Kari had wanted. His dad needed to trust Calder and the others to be able to live at the Bishop house.

"Oh, I think everyone saw it when he killed Oscar."

Kari looked down. His father knew what he'd done, of course, and while he didn't approve, he understood it had been necessary. Kari wouldn't change it, but he didn't want his father to think ill of him.

"It needed to be done, from what I know," Kari's dad said.

"You're right, it did. Without Oscar's death, we wouldn't have the majority in the council, and we wouldn't be about to change the carrier law that has been passed recently."

Kari's father leaned back in his chair. "Why should I move to the Bishop house if you're going to change that law? Unless it's not a law written to protect us."

Kari gritted his teeth. Calder didn't know he was a carrier like his father, and he wanted to keep things that way. People always looked at you differently when they knew you were a carrier.

Kari was as capable of fighting and using a gun as anyone else—probably even more so than most people. He knew what would happen if Calder or one of his friends found out about his status. They'd move him to the Bishop house, and they wouldn't let him help. He didn't want that to happen. He'd earned the right to make the forest safe for his dad.

"Well, we *are* going to pass that law, but it's not as easy as it should be. The minority in the council isn't happy with us and will do what they can to make sure we don't do this. They can't do anything to stop us, but it doesn't mean they won't push back. Besides, even with the law, we both know some alphas won't respect it. The council can't go in their territory, and they can do what they want there. We're trying to include a clause that the council can go in the territories if they suspect someone is in danger or being abused, but there is going to be some push back. We want to be sure the carriers are safe until the situation calms down. You're welcome to stay here, of course, but I know Kari would feel better if he knew you were with friends and that nothing will happen to you while he's out with the team."

Calder was reassuring. Kari could see his dad trusted the man, and he did, too.

God, he did. He wanted to push Calder onto the table and have his way with him, but of course, even without his father present, he couldn't do it. Kari couldn't have a relationship. He was too busy for that, and he couldn't allow himself to be distracted, especially not by Calder. He had to think about his dad—about making him safe.

Besides, he knew how people treated carriers. Even if they thought carriers were like everyone else and should be able to choose how to live their own lives, they were still treated with a deference Kari hated. He didn't want to be treated differently. He was just like everyone else in the forest except he could get pregnant. His biology shouldn't make people think he was weak or strange — or different.

"I'll come."

Kari blinked, and it took him a second to realize what was happening. "You'll go to the Bishop house?" he asked his father.

"Of course I will. I would have agreed to it even without Calder reassuring me. I know it's what you want, and I trust you. You know what you're doing. I can't say I'm happy to leave my home behind, but we both know this wasn't going to last forever."

Kari took his father's hand and squeezed. "You should have more. You *deserve* more." The weasel alpha had taken so much from Kari's father. He'd forced Julian to run, to leave his family behind. He'd forced him to live alone in the woods and to have a baby on his own with all the risks that entailed. Now that Kari was an adult, it was time for his father to live the life he hadn't been able to live until now.

"As long as you're safe and happy, I have everything I need," Kari's father told Kari.

Kari knew he was serious, but he wanted more for his dad. That was why he'd been doing all of this. "I'll be happy once you're at the Bishop house. I'll even help you pack."

His father chuckled. "Of course you will. But I don't need a lot of things."

They hadn't accumulated much over the years, just enough for them to be comfortable. They left Calder in the kitchen with a cup of coffee and headed to the bedrooms.

"Will you continue living here?" Kari's father asked.

"For now."

"You could move in with the badgers. I don't like thinking of you alone here."

"I suspect I'm going to spend more time with you at the Bishop house than here anyway."

"Then we should pack your things too. We don't have to

tell Calder you're moving in if you don't want to. I know you're not eager for him or anyone else to find out your status."

Kari's father understood Kari like no one else did. "All right. We'll stick some of my stuff in your bags. But I can come back any time I want to grab the things I need, so don't worry about me."

His dad smiled softly. "I'll always worry about you. No matter how old you are, you're still my baby boy."

Kari huffed, but his father's words reassure him. Their lives were changing in a way they never had before. Neither of them could be sure what waited for them once this was over, and it made Kari nervous. They could do it, though. They *would* do it.

It didn't take them long to pack. Since they'd been isolated, they hadn't accumulated a lot of things, and everything fit into two bags, even Kari's stuff. He was going to have to sneak into the Bishop house every night to sleep with his dad, but he didn't mind. With things changing the way they were, he needed to feel close to his father, and he suspected his father felt the same way.

Calder was where they'd left him when they went back to the kitchen. He got up when he noticed their bags and smiled. "Ready?"

Kari looked around. He wasn't sure he would ever be ready, but he nodded anyway. "I'll come back to get the vegetables." He knew his father wouldn't approve if they let the food go to waste. "I'll finish packing up the kitchen and bring everything to the Bishop house so you can use it. I'll also close up the cabin." Maybe one day they could transform it into a real house where his dad would live. They'd have to get the permission of the new gang alpha, and it wouldn't happen anytime soon, but it was a goal to look forward to.

There were leaving, but it didn't have to be forever, not

unless they wanted it to.

Calder was relieved when he finally parked in front of the Bishop house. Kari and his father had spent the entire ride in the back seat with their heads close together as they whispered. Calder didn't mind—he knew the two of them had lived together for Kari's entire life, and they were about to separate since Kari couldn't stay at the Bishop house—but he'd felt oddly isolated. He realized it was selfish, but he wanted Kari's attention on him.

He really was an asshole sometimes.

"We're here," he said.

He heard Kari and his father moving around behind him, but he left the car instead of staying with them. They probably needed a few minutes to themselves.

The front door of the Bishop house opened, and Calder smiled at Jacob. He was one of the badger guards who stayed with the carriers twenty-four-seven, and he was in charge right now. Calder had called him to tell him he'd be coming in with a carrier and Kari, but he hadn't explained everything. He'd wanted to get Kari's father to the house quickly before someone noticed where he'd gone and found Julian. Calder wouldn't put it past some of the people in the forest to sneak up on Julian and drag him away from his home. It kind of was what Calder had done, but Calder wouldn't hurt Julian, and he hoped that Julian would be able to go home if he ever wanted to. But right now, he would be safer here with the other carriers and the guards.

"I was surprised when you called," Jacob said.

"I didn't expect to find another carrier in the forest," Calder said.

Jacob's gaze moved behind Calder. "You didn't give me many details."

"I didn't have the time. You've heard of Kari?"

Jacob's lips curled into a smile. "Of course I have. I'm pretty sure everyone here has heard of him. He's the one who killed Oscar, right?"

"He is."

Jacob nodded. "Good. I like him already."

Everyone was touchy when it came to Oscar because of Philip and what Oscar had done to him. No one had cried over Oscar's death, and Calder wasn't surprised Jacob was okay with what Kari had done. "He's a nice man. I didn't know his father was a carrier until now because they stayed hidden for the past twenty-five years."

Jacob's eyes widened. "Twenty-five years?"

"Trust me, I was as stunned as you. I'm amazed that no one ever found them in the forest."

"And why is Kari's father coming out now?"

"Kari is worried." They all were, even though they tried not to mention anything in front of the carriers. "He wants to be sure his father will be protected when he goes out with the team."

"Well, he won't have to worry about that anymore."

Kari and Julian stepped closer, and Calder gestured at Jacob. "Jacob, this is Kari and his father, Julian. As I already told you, Julian is a carrier. He's not used to sharing a home with this many people, so if you have a single room available, I'm sure he'll be grateful to have it."

Julian's cheeks flushed. "I don't want to bother anyone."

Jacob gently patted Julian's shoulder. "You're not bothering us. This is your home now, and it's going to be for a while. You might as well make yourself comfortable. No one here will mind if you take a single room. You won't be the only one. Philip has a single room, too. Why don't you come in? You can take a walk around the house, meet some of the carriers and the guards who live here, and see the room where you'll sleep. We still have a few bedrooms available, and if Calder and his friends finally get that new law passed, I'm sure a few more will empty."

Some of the carriers probably couldn't wait to go back home, but Calder thought he was going to miss them. Shifters didn't usually mix the way they'd had to in the Bishop house, especially not carriers. They were kept a secret, and with good reason. Even if one didn't believe that the sons and daughters born from carriers were stronger than those born from a woman, they were still some of the most abused people in the forest. Not because they were weaker, but because it was so easy for people to gang up against them. Here in the Bishop house, they were safe, and they could make life decisions they otherwise wouldn't be allowed to make because of those stupid laws.

"So this is how it works," Jacob began, reaching for Julian's bag. "The guards have twelve hours shifts. There are always four of us on duty, two badgers and two bears. Of course, even the guards who are not on duty live in the house, so you'll see them around. They're allowed to leave the house, and some of the carriers have taken to asking them to buy them things at the grocery store or whatever. Feel free to do the same. If you feel more comfortable coming to me, please do."

Calder followed Julian and Kari, who followed Jacob inside the house. Calder wanted to give them space. Kari wouldn't be allowed to say for much longer, since it was getting late, and Calder couldn't help but wonder if he was supposed to go back to the house he shared with his father. It was his home, but it was so far away from the Bishop house, and Calder doubted Kari would want to stay away from his father.

The first thing they saw when they entered was Chris bouncing down the stairs. He beamed at Jacob and kissed his cheek on his way to the kitchen, stopping when he noticed Julian and Kari. He cocked his head and said, "You're new."

Kari took a step back, leaving his father to face Chris and a few other carriers who were already drifting to the entrance. It had to be hard for both Julian and Kari to deal with this, but they were making an effort.

Julian rubbed the back of his neck. "I am. My name is Julian, and I'm a weasel shifter."

Chris nodded and offered his hand. "Bobcat. You're a carrier?"

"I am."

"You're married?"

Calder had to suppress a smile. Chris wasn't known for his diplomacy, something he would have to learn if he ever wanted to take his father's place as the alpha.

Julian cleared his throat. "I'm not. I never was." He licked his lips and looked around. "I was raped when I was seventeen, by my alpha. When I realized I was pregnant with Kari, I ran away. We've lived in the forest since then, so I am not used to being around other people. I apologize in advance for any misstep I might make."

Chris' eyes widened, but thankfully, he didn't say anything Julian might find offensive. Instead, he gestured at the house and the other carriers who had gathered in the entrance. "You're not the only one with that kind of story, and you won't find any judgment here. We're all friends, well, except Calum, but that's because he keeps to himself. You're welcome to do the same thing, of course, but I like to think we're a family, even though we're different shifters. I think becoming friends would be useful to all of us once we leave this place."

Chris could be overwhelming, but Julian seemed to be able to deal with him. He nodded slowly, and his gaze drifted to the other carriers again. Calder thought he saw it linger on one of them in particular, and he wondered if Julian had ever met Kaspar. He doubted it—Julian had never left his home since he'd fled there when he was seventeen, but maybe it was worth exploring.

"Kaspar, why don't you take Julian up to the bedrooms so he can choose one?" Calder suggested.

He didn't miss Julian's relieved smile, and he knew he'd done the right thing. Julian was overwhelmed. He probably needed ten minutes on his own to breathe, and he'd have that soon enough. "Kari and I are going to leave. Kari is welcome to come around during the day if he wants to, but only the carriers and the guards live here. I'm sorry."

Julian frowned and looked at Kari, who shook his head. "I'll be okay, Dad. Don't worry about me."

"You're sure?"

"Of course I am. I'll see you soon." Kari waited until his father had disappeared up the stairs, and everyone else was gone to turn back to Calder. "Thank you for this."

"You don't have to thank me. The Bishop house is open to all carriers in the forest. You should know that, since you've been spying on us."

Kari smiled.

It transformed his expression. He always looked so severe and dire, but the smile was a pleasant surprise, and it made him look softer.

"You're right, I have," he said. "It's a nice way to discover things about people."

Calder laughed. "Well, I don't know what you discovered about me, but I know I don't have any secrets. Are you going home? Do you need a ride?"

Kari crossed his arms over his chest and cocked his head. "You'd drive me back to the cabin?"

"I would, although I suspect you'd rather stay closer to your father."

"I was thinking about staying in your bed."

Calder blinked. He was sure he'd heard that right, and he didn't want to assume anything. "In my bed?"

"You heard me."

"With me in it?"

Kari rolled his eyes. "Of course with you in it. What would be the point otherwise?"

What would be the point, indeed?

Kari knew what he wanted, and he wasn't afraid to ask for it. He'd learned to do that when he realized no one was ever going to help him and his father, not of their own volition. Asking for sex wasn't any different.

Kari was an adult male, and he was horny. He usually kept his sex light and uncomplicated, sticking to clubs and bars, so this might be a mistake. It probably would end up creating more problems than he could afford to have right now, but he couldn't resist. He didn't *want* to resist Calder.

Calder was right—Kari *had* been spying on him and almost everyone else in the forest. He'd been watching Calder for a while now, trying to understand if he was one of the good council members or not. And even once he'd realized Calder was a good man and could have stopped spying on him, Kari hadn't.

Calder fascinated him. He was a good-looking man, twelve years older than Kari, with perpetually messy brown hair and brown eyes. Kari thought he'd even noticed a hint of freckles on Calder's nose, but he'd never been close enough to make sure of it.

This was his occasion.

He was relieved that Calder didn't balk in the face of his straightforwardness. Life was too short to hesitate, and sometimes, even to think things through. Kari might regret this come morning, but at least his body would be sated. Besides, he wasn't planning on hanging around for long. He'd told his father he'd come back so they could spend the night together, and he wouldn't go back on his promise. His father needed him, and if he was honest with himself, he needed his father.

The only person Kari had ever been close to was his dad. Both their lives were changing, and Kari desperately wanted to cling to his old one. It felt safer, comforting.

Calder stopped the car in front of his house. "This is it, although I'm pretty sure you already knew that," he said.

He'd taken the knowledge that Kari had spied on him surprisingly well. Kari had expected him to be angry like most people would, but he wasn't. Actually, he seemed to find it amusing, something that puzzled Kari. He wasn't going to try to analyze his feelings about it right now, though.

He had something better to do.

He hopped out of the car and gestured at the house. "Lead the way."

Calder grinned. "Right to the point."

"Always. I hate when people waste time for no good reason." He especially hated it when people wasted time when he was trying to get fucked.

"Let's go, then."

Kari followed Calder to the house. Calder didn't bother flipping on the lights downstairs, something for which Kari was grateful. Most people would have asked Kari if he wanted something to drink, or if he wanted to see the rest of the house, but Kari cared about none of that. He wouldn't stay around long enough to use any room that wasn't Calder's bedroom. Of course, Calder didn't know that, so he was probably planning to offer Kari food and drinks later.

Kari wouldn't be around by then.

Kari had never entered Calder's house. He might have been spying on Calder, but he hadn't wanted Calder to feel violated. The house was Calder's safe place, and Kari had wanted it to stay that way, just like the cabin had been his. Still, he'd spied enough from the windows that he knew what Calder's bedroom looked like. He wasn't surprised to find it a bit messy, with the blanket still pulled down and a dirty sock peeking from under the bed.

Kari ignored all of that and leaned down to untie his boots.

"You don't waste time," Calder said.

"Why should I? We both know what we want. Why should we dance around each other when that's the case?"

"I can see your point. I guess I'm just not used to things going this fast with men."

Kari straightened and grinned. "You better get used to it if you want to get into my pants." And with that, Kari grabbed his jeans and pushed them down.

Calder blinked. "No underwear?"

"It's a bother when I have to shift. What are you waiting for? I thought we were going to fuck."

"We are."

Kari turned his attention back to the bed. He took his shirt off and dropped it to the floor, then climbed under the blanket. "You have condoms and lube?"

"Of course." Calder sounded nonplussed, but to Kari's relief, he finally got naked.

Kari stared. He wasn't ashamed to say he'd wanted to see Calder naked ever since the first time he'd noticed him. He didn't see a reason for him to act like he wasn't interested. He hoped Calder wasn't self-conscious, because he had no intention of looking away.

"You're very direct," Calder said as his shirt hit the floor.

"I don't understand why everyone isn't. It would save a lot of time and create so much fewer problems."

"You're probably right, but I suspect you're the only one who can get away with it."

Kari shrugged. "That's fine with me. I'm not here to make friends. I'm here so that my father can have a good life, a life he deserves after everything he's been through."

Calder finally stood naked in front of Kari, but his words distracted Kari from the sight. "That's why I like you. You love your father, and you're ready to do anything to give him what he deserves."

"Now that we've talked, can we get to the point?" Kari wrapped his fingers around his cock and tugged on it a few times.

Calder chuckled, and Kari was relieved when he finally moved. He walked to his bedside table and took out the condom and lube, which he dropped on the bed. Kari snatched the lube, ignoring Calder's amused glance. He didn't care if Calder found him funny as long as he also found him hot and was ready to fuck him.

Kari quickly stretched himself. He ignored the sting of pain and discomfort because he knew what was coming would be good. He couldn't afford to savor this moment, to take the time he so much wanted. He couldn't afford to have feelings for Calder, which was exactly what would happen if Kari allowed himself to think about this moment.

"You know, this wasn't what I was thinking about when I thought about sex with you," Calder said.

Kari looked at him to find that he was rolling the condom on his cock. "You thought about sex with me?"

Calder rolled his eyes. "Just like you thought about having sex with me, clearly. I'd hoped we could take things a bit slower."

"You're hard."

"I know I am. I'm not saying it isn't pleasurable to watch you stretch yourself for my cock. But we haven't even kissed yet."

Of course Calder would be the kind of man who wanted to

kiss. Kari should have known that.

Kari sighed and took his fingers out of his ass, cleaning them on the sheets and ignoring Calder's glare. "Come here."

Calder kneeled between Kari's legs and aimed his cock toward Kari's hole, but Kari shook his head. Calder wanted to kiss him, and to be honest, even though he wasn't the kissing type, he wanted to kiss Calder, too. He'd think about the meaning of that later, because right now he was busy, and he didn't want to waste even one second obsessing over something he had no control over.

Calder arched a brow, but he lowered himself on top of Kari. He felt good there, solid and heavy, pinning Kari to the bed. Kari puckered his lips, and Calder huffed a laugh. He kissed Kari, though, and Kari closed his eyes, losing himself into it.

He'd been kissed before, although not often. The people he had sex with didn't tend to want to waste time kissing, and Kari didn't either, usually. Kissing Calder was an experience, though. His lips were warm and a bit chapped, but he kissed like he knew what he was doing, and from Kari's point of view, he did. Calder's tongue was slick and pressing into his mouth, and Kari opened for him.

"This is better," Calder murmured, and this time when he reached for his cock, Kari didn't stop him.

The first push was always the worst one. Kari felt incredibly full, too much so. He gritted his teeth against the sensation of being invaded and kissed Calder again to distract himself. It worked, and when Calder moved back and thrust in again, Kari found himself relaxing.

This was what he'd wanted for weeks, maybe even months. He'd been watching Calder, imagining how this would be, and it was even better than what he'd come up with. Calder was a gentle lover, but not so gentle that Kari would think he was coddling him. No, Calder made him feel wanted, like he *needed* to fuck him—and fuck him hard.

Kari lost himself in it. He didn't usually let go like this because he never trusted the men he fucked, but for some reason, he trusted Calder. He trusted him to make sure he was okay, not to attack him, and more importantly, to make him come.

Which Calder did easily. He continued pushing into Kari as he kissed him and somehow wiggled a hand between them to grab his cock. Kari would have done that himself—he usually did—but this was so much better. He didn't have to think about anything, be it making sure he came or that he was safe. Calder had taken charge, and Kari was able to let go.

It made his orgasm so much sweeter. Calder surrounded him, held him, and was inside him. Kari had never felt cherished the way he did right now, and he forced himself to focus on the pleasure and not obsess over something he couldn't have. He screwed his eyes shut and surrendered, pushing his head against the pillow as he painted Calder's stomach with his cum.

He was pretty sure Calder came, too, but he didn't have the energy to make sure of it. He kept his eyes closed as Calder retreated from him and momentarily left the bed, only to come back with a damp cloth.

That was new, too, and Kari regretted not being able to stay once Calder was asleep.

Kari rolled out of bed as soon as Calder was out, before he could wrap himself around Kari, and looked down at him. He wanted a world where he could stay with Calder, where he could snuggle against him and call this place his home.

But this wasn't that world, and Kari couldn't stay, no matter how much he wanted it.

He was pleasantly sore, but that wasn't a problem as he snuck out and hurried to the Bishop house and his father's bedroom, shifting into his weasel form and pressing his furry body against his father's chest. His dad stroked him, but it wasn't the same thing. It didn't *feel* the same. It didn't make sense, since Kari's father had stroked Kari's fur since he was a child, and that always made Kari feel better.

But Julian wasn't Calder, and that was all Kari could think about.

CHAPTER FOUR

Calder hadn't expected to be alone when he woke up. He'd had plans—make love to Kari a few more times during the night, maybe have a snack with him in the kitchen, or even in bed. Talk to him and get to know him because while the sex had been great, Calder wasn't a one-night stand kind of guy. He wanted more, but especially so with Kari.

Calder had no idea why. Kari was sexy as hell, and even though he did his best to appear hard and unyielding, there was a soft center to him, a place where his feelings for his father lived. Calder wanted to get to know that place, to explore it and see if he could make feelings for him grow there, too.

He rolled in bed and wrapped his arms around his pillow, since he didn't have anyone better to wrap them around. He needed to get up, but he wanted a few more minutes of wallowing. It wasn't like things with Kari were over. Calder had no idea where they stood, but he suspected Kari wouldn't say no to another meeting like last night. He also suspected Kari would do everything he could to keep some distance between them. Calder might be one for relationships, but he didn't think Kari was.

That didn't mean Calder wouldn't try to wiggle his way into Kari's life. Kari was a mystery, and Calder had always been curious. He wanted to explore Kari—and not only his body.

But all that would have to wait until later.

Calder pushed out of bed, leaving the pillow there. There was nothing he could do about Kari right now, and he had his job to think about. Today was the first day the new council team would meet, and Calder needed to be there. He also needed to talk to Thomas before he went, and that meant he'd have to leave his house in an hour, tops. He was hungry as hell since he hadn't had dinner last night—he'd been planning to eat with Kari, but that had gone out the window when Kari had left while Calder was sleeping—and he didn't have a lot of time for breakfast.

He managed to get to Thomas' house before the meeting started. Luckily for him, his house wasn't far from the alpha's. He smiled at Abel when he sat next to him in front of Thomas' desk, unsurprised to find his friend there. Abel might be a deer shifter, but he'd been spending most of his time in cete territory since he and Philip had gotten together. They were raising Phillip's son as a couple, and that meant Abel needed to be there.

"You look chipper," Abel said.

"I had a good night's sleep."

"Did you? I met Julian last night."

That was a weird change of topic, but Calder was glad he wouldn't have to talk about Kari with Abel. Abel wouldn't have anything to say about Calder sleeping with Kari, but Calder wanted to keep the encounter to himself a bit longer. He didn't know if Kari wanted it to be a secret, and in case he did, Calder had better keep his mouth shut. "He's a nice man, isn't he?"

Abel nodded. "I wasn't sure what to expect from Kari's father, but it wasn't Julian."

"Kari had to grow up strong and hard to make sure both he and his father were okay." And Calder wanted to do something about that. He wanted to give Kari the home he'd been fighting so hard for all his life and a place where he could rest and relax. He wasn't sure it was his place, but he wouldn't find out if he didn't push, which was why he was planning to do just that.

Thomas walked in, holding a mug full of coffee. He flopped into his chair and closed his eyes, breathing in and out a few times.

Calder frowned. "Everything okay?"

Thomas opened his eyes. "Yeah. I'm just tired. Levi left Evan with us last night. He wanted a date night with Dimitri."

Calder smirked. "Not used to having children around the house anymore?"

Thomas crinkled a sheet of paper and threw it at Calder's head. "You know I'm not. So, what's new? The meeting is still on?"

"It is." They were having this first meeting away from the council building in town because there was no way for them to know how the other council members would react. They hadn't passed the law that would allow the council team to enter the various territories to save abuse carriers and shifters yet. Calder wouldn't be surprised if one of the council members who were against this tried to stop them. No, it was better to have their first meeting here in cete territory to make sure they could do and say everything that needed to be done and said.

"Is there something I need to know?"

Calder bounced his knee. "There is. Kari approached Abel and me yesterday after he came to talk to us about his position on the team. He told us his father is a carrier. Julian had been living in the forest at the edge between weasel and bear territory for the past twenty-five years. Well, twenty-six if you count his pregnancy."

Just like Calder had expected, Thomas' eyes widened. "Twenty-six years?"

Everyone was always stunned at finding that out, and with good reason. "Ever since his alpha raped him, and he found out he was pregnant with Kari. The two of them have lived there until now, but Kari asked Abel and me if we could take in his father and take him to the Bishop house. I know I should have called you to ask your opinion, but after I found out Julian was all alone in the woods and had been for so long, I took it upon myself to say yes."

"I agree. That poor man. He's at the Bishop house right now?"

"Since last night. As far as I could see, he's already started blending in. Things will probably be awkward for him for a while since he's so used to being on his own, but he'll adapt."

"Good. The Bishop house might not be the best place for all those carriers, but right now, we can at least make sure they're safe. How many days until you vote?"

"Today, if things go the way they should. Kari gave us the two names he told us about."

Thomas put down his mug. "The carriers who are still being abused?"

"Yes." Calder took the bit of paper on which Kari had written the names out of his pocket, but before he could say the names out loud, someone else did it for him.

"Turner and Burnell."

Calder hoped that what he felt for Kari didn't show in his expression when he turned to look at the man. Kari was leaning against the open window of Thomas' office as if it were something he routinely did. He seemed perfectly at ease, but Calder was starting to be able to read him, and he didn't miss the way Kari's gaze jumped all around the room.

Thomas groaned. "Why don't you come in? It would be easier than talking to you through the window."

Instead of walking around the house like anyone else would have, Kari climbed through the window. He never looked at Calder has he moved, but again, Calder wasn't surprised. He fully expected Kari to ignore him until the next time he wanted to fuck.

"So, Turner and Burnell," Thomas said.

Kari leaned against the wall by the window and nodded. "Turner is a skunk shifter, while Burnell is a mink."

Thomas grunted. "I'm not surprised. Neither the rodents nor the skunks came to us for help with their carriers. I was hoping they didn't have any, but I suspected that couldn't be true."

"It isn't. They have carriers, or at least these two that I know of. I haven't been able to explore the territories fully, though. I have to stick to places where I can walk to because I don't have a car."

"You can have one if you need one. We'll supply it to you."

Kari shrugged. "Don't bother. I never learned to drive. Besides, since you guys managed to create this team, I won't need to explore the territories on my own. We'll be allowed to go in and do it as a team."

"Let's focus on these two carriers first. Which one do you suggest we help tonight?"

Kari sighed. "I wish we could get both today, but Turner is probably the one who needs more help."

"Understood. Since we all have things to do today, I suggest we get to work. The team meeting is tonight, and we'll go from there. I fully expect Turner to be at the Bishop house by the end of the night, though."

Kari was out the window before Calder could even move toward him. He didn't follow, because he had to go to the council building to set up the meeting there and the upcoming vote, but he was surprised at how much he wanted to.

Kari lingered by Calder's car even though he knew he shouldn't. He wanted to see Calder after the night they'd had, and he wasn't sure how to go about it. He didn't want to admit it, not to Calder, and possibly not even to himself, but that was how he felt.

"You didn't have to leave last night," Calder said from behind Kari before Kari could think better of it and run away.

Kari forced himself to face Calder. "Why should I have stayed?"

Calder arched a brow. "Maybe because it was the best sex I can remember ever having? Although of course, that might be just me."

It *had* been the best sex of Kari's life, but Kari didn't want to admit that. "It was okay."

Calder huffed out a laugh. "Only okay?"

Anyone else would have been angry, but Calder wasn't, and it confused Kari. Calder wasn't like most other people. He was a council member, and that meant he was a strong man who took his job seriously, but he was also playful and nowhere near as serious in his personal life.

Kari grinned. "All right, maybe more than okay. I enjoyed myself."

"Which is why you should have stayed."

Kari couldn't be sure why Calder had wanted him to stay. He hoped it was because Calder liked him, but so far, no one had ever wanted a repeat unless it was convenient. "Again, why?"

"Where did you go when you left? Did you walk all the way back to your cabin?"

That ruffled Kari's feathers. "So what if I did? It's none of your business, and it's not like I haven't been walking around the forest for a decade. I don't need your pity. You don't have to offer me a place in your bed just so you're sure I'm not outside at night."

Calder rolled his eyes. "That's not why, or at least, not only why. I'm worried about you going around alone at night, but I know you can defend yourself. You've shown that lots of times. Mostly, I want to have sex again."

Kari couldn't help it—he laughed. Calder never reacted the way he expected him to, and that kept him unstable. He was surprised to find that he liked it, though. Calder was the only one who could make him feel this way, and it made Kari curious more than ever. "That's good, because I want to have sex with you again, too."

Calder's smile widened. "Perfect. I like that you're unapologetic about wanting to be fucked."

"I'm not about to change for you." Kari eyed Calder's truck. It was parked in front of the alpha's house, but not so close that someone looking out the window of the house would be able to see the details of what was happening inside. Calder had left the truck under the trees, no doubt so it wouldn't be too hot because of the sun, but this might play to their advantage. "Do you have a condom and lube on you?"

Calder's eyes widened. "Why?" he croaked.

"Because I want to use them." Kari reached for the truck and opened the back door. Calder made a strangled noise behind him, but Kari ignored him until he finally followed him inside. Kari already had a hand down his pants, but stretching himself wasn't easy without lube to slick the way.

"You're crazy," Calder muttered as he settled in the seat and closed the door.

"I don't see you protesting."

"Someone could see us."

"That's why we're going to have to be fast. Undo your pants and give me the lube."

Kari pushed his jeans down his legs, toed his boots off, and dumped everything on the floor of the truck. He made sure Calder had rolled the condom on his dick before reaching for it and using the same lube he'd used in his ass to slick it. There wasn't time to make this slow like last night. Calder was right—someone could see them.

Kari straddled Calder's lap. He had to keep his head tilted

forward if he didn't want to hit the roof of the truck, but that wasn't a problem, especially not once he was sitting on Calder's cock.

Calder stretched him, although it wasn't as painful as last night. Kari had washed before leaving the Bishop house, but his ass still felt soft and yielding. Calder slid inside him as he if he belonged there, and for a split second, Kari wished he did.

Then he pushed away all those thoughts and focused on the pleasure.

He moved up and down, bouncing on Calder's cock and no doubt making the truck rock with his movements. Calder's hands clung to Kari's hips, helping him move up and down while Calder gently thrust his hips. He couldn't move any harder, since space was so restrained, but it was enough. Kari had been hard since he'd first thought of fucking Calder in the truck, and the lack of space wasn't going to keep him from coming.

Calder wrapped a hand behind Kari's neck and pulled him down. He kissed him, still moving inside him, and just like last night, Kari allowed himself to give up control. He might be on top, but Calder was in charge now. He made that obvious when he trailed his lips down Kari's throat and bit down, no doubt leaving a mark that Kari would have to explain to his father.

Kari didn't care, because the pain in his neck and the feeling that Calder was making him *his* pushed all the buttons that he hadn't known he had.

Calder continued nibbling on Kari's neck as he slid his other hand around Kari and cupped one of his ass cheeks. He teased the place where his dick was moving inside Kari with a finger, making Kari groan. Kari closed his eyes and burrowed his face against Calder's neck as Calder gently pushed his finger inside of him along with his dick.

Kari shuddered and rubbed his groin against Calder's stomach. The rough texture of Calder's shirt against the head of Kari's cock was enough to make Kari come. It was unexpected, and Kari clung to Calder has the pleasure swamped him. He could feel Calder push in and out of him with harder thrusts, then finally shudder against his body as he, too, came.

"This is crazy. *You* are crazy," Calder said as he kissed Kari's temple.

"Maybe, but you liked it," Kari muttered.

Calder gently pushed him away. "You're right. I loved it. But we can't stay here. Even if no one noticed what was happening, someone is bound to come outside when they realize my truck is still here. Besides, I have to go. I'm expected at the council building. It's a miracle Abel hasn't left yet, because he would have noticed us."

"Maybe he has. He doesn't strike me as the type of man who would have interrupted us."

Calder groaned and hit the back of his head against the seat. "You're right, dammit. Come on. As much as I like this position, I need to go."

So did Kari. He'd told his father he'd be back soon, and he wanted to spend time with him in his first few days at the Bishop house. He'd have to leave tonight, and he knew his dad was worried about that, even though he hadn't said anything. He wouldn't, because he knew how important this was for Kari, but that didn't change the way he felt.

Kari clambered off Calder. He didn't have anything to clean himself with, so he just pulled his jeans back on with lube still slicking his hole. He could feel Calder's hungry gaze on him, but he ignored it because now wasn't the moment. No matter how much he wanted to climb on top of Calder again, neither of them had time for it.

Kari grinned at Calder and quickly kissed his cheek. "Thanks for that. I needed it."

Then, without giving Calder time to say anything, Kari opened the opposite door and slid outside. He was gone before Calder could try to stop him, and he tried to ignore the feeling that he should go back.

He wanted to. He wanted to spend as much time as possible with Calder and fall in love with him. Hell, maybe he was already half in love with the man. It wasn't like he'd ever been in love before, so he had no idea how that felt.

But he knew he wanted to be with Calder, and that was worrying. Kari couldn't allow himself to feel this way. He needed to focus on his father and on keeping the carriers in the forest safe, and that wouldn't happen if anyone found out he was a carrier. He couldn't start a relationship with Calder without telling him the truth about himself, and now wasn't the right moment.

CHAPTER FIVE

K ari managed to ignore Calder, but it wasn't easy, espe-cially not after what had happened that morning. Even though he had to focus on the group of people in the room with him, he could feel Calder's presence and the man's gaze on him.

"A weasel?" one of the men asked. Kari was pretty sure he was a bat shifter, which was ironic, considering he thought Kari was too small and weak to be part of the team.

Kari crossed his arms over his chest and glared.

Calder cleared his throat. "Yes, a weasel shifter. Do you have a problem with Kari's presence in the team?"

There was a subtle *something* in his voice, an inflection that told both Kari and the bat guy that he was serious. Kari had no idea what that meant, except that the bat guy would be in trouble if he continued whining. Was this really the best the bats could do? Had they even taken the request seriously for someone who could help maintain peace and save people? At least the others in the room seemed more suited to the role. Kari knew Raven had been there when Philip had been taken out of porcupine territory, so he was pretty sure he was a good one. He had no idea about the others, though, and he hoped they weren't going to fuck this up.

Bat guy blinked. "Not a problem, but how useful is he go-ing to be to the team?"

Calder cocked his head. "How useful are *you* going to be to the team? As far as I know, bats are just as small as weasels, if not smaller."

Kari could defend his own honor, but it felt good to have someone else do it for him. It had never happened before. Kari knew his father would defend him against anything or anyone, but this was different. Kari was fucking Calder, and it meant something that Calder was defending him. Kari wasn't sure what, and he wasn't about to start thinking about it now because he had to focus on the situation, but maybe he could ask later.

Bats guy bristled. "I fly."

Kari had to resist the urge to roll his eyes.

"I hope you can, since you're a bat shifter. All of you are here for a reason—you were chosen by your alpha. You know what you're doing, and that's what we need to help these two carriers. We can't afford to have tensions in your group."

"But–"

"Enough, Alastair."

That was the bear shifter, Terrence. He was the team leader, even though they were meeting in badger territory. The bears and the badgers had become one big group since Levi and Dimitri had gotten married, so it wasn't surprising to see everyone wanted the team to stick close to the Bishop house. Besides, cete territory was more out of the way than bear territory.

Alastair glared, but thankfully, he kept his mouth shut after that.

Kari didn't want to have to kick his ass, but he would if that was what he needed to do. It was obvious even to him that he wasn't used to working with people. He had no idea how he was going to make this work, but he had to. This was important to him. He wouldn't have asked Abel to be part of the team otherwise.

Kari wanted all the carriers in the forest to be safe and treated as if they were normal shifters. He didn't want to leave even one of them in the hands of their abusers. That would only be possible if he was part of this team, and that meant he was going to do everything in his power to learn how to work with others.

Terrence looked at Kari. "Calder and Thomas told us you know where the two carriers we're looking for are?"

Kari didn't doubt Terrence already knew all about this, but clearly, he wanted the rest of the team to hear it, too. "I do."

"How?"

Kari curled the corner of his lips into a sly smile. "No one knew I existed until I killed Oscar. That gave me a lot of time to sneak around the forest and spy on people."

"You killed Oscar?" the fox team member, Sandra, asked.

Kari had thought everyone knew about that. "I did. Tampered with his brakes. The world is a better place without him in it."

She nodded in approval. "Damn right. You'll have to teach me how to do that."

"Planning to kill someone?" Terrence asked.

"You never know," Sandra said with a shrug.

Terrence turned his attention back to Kari. "You think going to the skunk carrier first is the best thing to do?"

"Only because he's in the worst shape. Honestly, if we could manage it, I think we should save both of them tonight, but I know it's not possible. We'll have to take Burnell out tomorrow, and no later. The rodent alpha is going to realize something is happening, and he might take Burnell away somewhere we can't reach him."

Calder cleared his throat. "I met with the rest of the council this afternoon. By only one vote, the laws passed. That means that tonight, this team is acting on council request. We'd rather not have you kill anyone, but you're allowed to if it's necessary. Otherwise, arrest anyone you find with Turner and take them to the council building. We'll keep them in a cell."

"And Turner?" Terrence asked.

"He'll go to the Bishop house until we can be sure no one in the forest is going to retaliate, both for what we're doing and for the new laws."

"So we're not doing this in the shadows. We can go to the alpha and knock on his door." Terrence didn't sound convinced.

Kari couldn't help but share his opinion. He was glad the new laws had passed, because it meant carriers were considered equals to every other shifter in the forest. That was a huge step forward, but it wouldn't work miracles. It would take a long time, probably generations, for carriers to truly be treated that way. Even with these laws in place now, the alphas who had the carriers and were abusing them would fight as hard as they could.

No matter how much Kari had snuck around the forest, he knew he didn't know about all the carriers in there. The territories were too vast, and with the trafficking going on, it was nearly impossible to tell who bought which carriers from whom. As far as Kari knew, there could be a rodent carrier in porcupine territory even now, and no one would be aware of it. They'd saved Philip from the porcupines, and the new alpha was a good person, but that didn't mean the old alpha's influence had been eradicated.

This was going to be a fight, for everyone, and things weren't looking good.

"Alpha Rhodes won't be happy to see you, but this is the way it has to be done. Now that there are laws in place, we need to do this the right way. We can't be on the wrong side of things."

Kari's first instinct was to act without caring about the laws, but he knew Calder was right. He might have gone around killing asshole council members, but he couldn't anymore, not when there was an alternative that would eventually work better.

"Besides, I'm coming with you," Calder said.

Kari's brain came to a halt. "You're doing *what*?"

Calder arched a brow at him. "I'm coming with you. We don't know if the presence of a council member will be necessary for Alpha Rhodes to let you in. Either way, I want to show him how official this is."

"Any of the other council members on our side could come instead of you." Kari didn't want Calder to get hurt. *Dammit.*

"You're probably right, but I'll be the one doing it. The situation with some of the council members and alphas is complicated, since most of the council members against us were chosen by older alphas, and the new alphas can't change them. That's something we'll have to deal with, but not right now. As it is, I contacted the other council members on our side, and none of them is available to come tonight. You'll have to make do with me."

For fuck's sake. How was Kari supposed to focus on rescuing Turner when he wouldn't be able to stop thinking about Calder and making sure he was safe?

Calder knew Kari wasn't happy with him. He hoped it was because Kari cared for him, but he wasn't convinced of it. Maybe Kari considered him a hindrance to the work they were there to do. Maybe he didn't care if Calder got hurt. There was no way for Calder to know without asking Kari, and now definitely wasn't the right moment to do that.

They were standing at the edge of skunk territory. It felt weird to be there, because most of the time alphas wanted other shifters to stay out of their homes. The way the bears and the badgers mixed was different from what happened in the rest of the forest.

"What now?" Terrence asked.

"Now we wait for the guards to come." Because there was

no way Alpha Rhodes hadn't sent guards as soon as he'd realized what was going on.

Sure enough, they only had to wait five minutes for the guards to appear. They looked like they were there to fight the team, but Calder wasn't afraid. He might be a council member, but that didn't mean he couldn't defend himself, just like the team members could. He wasn't even worried about Kari. No matter how Calder felt about him, Kari had shown that he was more than able to protect himself — and anyone else if he needed to.

"What do you want?" one of the guards asked.

"To talk to your alpha," Calder said.

"Alpha Rhodes is busy."

"Too busy to talk to one of the council members?"

The guard hesitated.

Clearly, he knew that going against the council wasn't done. The council was the last protection the shifters in the forest had against humans. If they fell, if they stopped negotiating with the humans outside the forest, it wouldn't take much for the forest to disappear, and all the shifters in it, too. "Tell him the badger council member wants to talk to him."

The guard who had spoken looked at the other three guards and nodded at them before disappearing back along the darkened street. Calder wished they'd done this during the day, but their day had been eventful, and while they could have waited until tomorrow, Calder wanted to get carriers out of their abusers' hands as soon as possible. Tomorrow would be dedicated to Burnell and any other carrier the team found with the rodents. Tonight was for Turner.

Calder wasn't surprised when the guard came back with Alpha Rhodes. He'd known the alpha would meet him. He also wasn't surprised to find that Alpha Rhodes was rude as hell.

"What do you want?" the man snapped.

"I'm sure you've heard by now that the council passed a new set of laws today," Calder said.

"Those bullshit laws. What does it have to do with me?"

"As I'm sure Kennedy told you, since he was at the meeting, they mean that the council team" — Calder gestured at the people around him — "can enter any territory to make sure no carrier is present and being abused."

"That's why you're here? To enter my territory?"

"Exactly. If you let us, no one will be hurt. We just wanted to take a look around."

"No."

Calder sighed. He'd expected this, too, but he wished Alpha Rhodes could see that there was no getting out of this. "The team has the authorization to enter, whether you allow them to or not."

"We're not going to stand aside while you break the laws that have always been in use in this forest."

"I was afraid you'd say that." Calder turned toward Terrence. "You and your team can go in."

They all knew they had a fight on their hands, so Calder stepped aside. He was just in time, because Alpha Rhodes gestured at his guards to attack.

They did. Calder might be able to defend himself if he needed to, but that didn't mean he was a fighter. He knew better than to try to intervene, especially with the team being experts at this. He watched them as they kicked the guards' asses, knocking them out or tying them to the closest trees. When the only one still standing was Alpha Rhodes, Calder stepped toward him. "You're under arrest. You should have let us in when we asked nicely."

Alpha Rhodes was outnumbered, and he was smart enough to realize what would happen if he continued to fight. He allowed Terrence to put cuffs on him, but he didn't answer when Calder asked, "Where's Turner?"

Calder turned to Kari. He'd been watching Kari while he fought, and even though Calder's first instinct had been to step in to help the man who'd barged into his life and wasn't going away, he hadn't. The only reason they were there was thanks to Kari, and that meant a lot. Besides, it was obvious Kari knew exactly what he was doing. He didn't need to be defended. He didn't need help. "Do you know where Turner is?"

Calder hated putting Kari in the spotlight with Alpha Rhodes still there, but they needed to be fast.

"Of course I know." Calder suspected Kari would have rolled his eyes if they'd been in any other situation.

"Lead the way, then."

Terrence asked two of his team members to stay with Alpha Rhodes and the fallen guards, and the rest of the team followed Calder and Kari deeper into skunk territory.

Their presence wasn't a secret, and people stood outside their houses watching them. The team wasn't there to hurt any of them, so as long as they stayed where they were and didn't try to intervene, everything would be okay. They had to know their alpha had been arrested, because otherwise, they'd probably have tried to stop them. They were smart enough not to try, and Kari led them away from the gathering of houses that made up the small village were the skunks lived. They passed what was obviously Alpha Rhodes' house, since it was bigger and nicer looking than all the others and walked deeper into the darkness.

"He keeps Turner here in the back. I'm pretty sure that at least part of the surfeit knows about him, but no one has ever done anything as far as I know. In my eyes, that makes all of them assholes."

Calder shared that opinion, but it wasn't like he could arrest all the surfeit members. They were already going to have enough problems after arresting their alpha. He didn't know if the beta was like Alpha Rhodes, and while the council had the power to walk into the territories to make sure no one was getting hurt, they still had no voice in who became the next alpha.

That was a problem they couldn't solve, especially not right now.

Calder wished he was surprised when Kari stopped in front of a tiny shed. There wasn't even a window, and no light came from inside.

"You're sure your guy is in there?" a member of the team asked. Calder thought it was Woodrow, the raccoon shifter.

As an answer, Kari quickly knocked on the door, then kicked it in. The sound was incredibly loud in the otherwise silent forest, and Calder jerked back.

"Turner? It's me, Kari," Kari said.

He didn't go inside the shed, but rather, he waited for Turner to step out. It was obvious they knew each other, because when Kari held out his hand, a small, dirty-looking hand came out of the shed and wrapped around it.

"That's my boy," Kari said.

"I'm not a boy," Turner grumbled. His voice was shaky. "I can't come out. He chained me to the ground."

Kari swore. "I'm coming in. Are you comfortable with that?"

"Of course I am."

Kari disappeared into the shed, leaving Calder and the rest of the team outside to wait for him.

"You're not jealous?" Woodrow asked.

It took a second for Calder to realize he was talking to him. "Why should I be?"

"You and the weasel have something going on, don't you?"

Calder didn't know how Woodrow was aware of that, and he didn't know what Kari wanted the others to know, but he wasn't about to hide what they had. He hoped it could become a relationship, and that meant going public. "So what if we do?"

Woodrow shrugged. "Nothing. Just that he and Turner seem to be close."

Calder knew it was likely because once Kari had found out about Turner and realized he couldn't do anything to help him, he'd probably come around to talk to Turner and maybe bring him food. He'd done his best to make Turner's life as comfortable as possible considering the situation. It wasn't surprising that Turner had latched onto Kari. "They're friends, and it looks to me like Turner needs all the friends he can find."

Kari carefully stepped over the door he'd knocked down into the shed. The place was tiny, just big enough for two people. That was a good thing, because Turner was never taken out of it, and it meant no one had raped him. There just wasn't a place to do anything like that in the shed. Of course, that didn't mean Turner wasn't abused and traumatized, but it could have been worse, and Kari was glad they'd gotten there before the alpha decided to marry Turner off or sell him.

Turner was pressed in the corner of the shed. Their hands were still linked together, and Kari crouched in front of him. "You're okay?" he asked.

Turner nodded. He was wearing a pair of sweats and a t-shirt, but his feet were bare and dirty from the earth of the shed floor. There was a cuff around one of his ankles, and just like he'd said, it was chained to a ring dug into the ground.

"I'm sorry I'm late," Kari said.

Turner chuckled. "It's not like we decided on a time, or even a day."

"You're right, we didn't, but I should have come sooner." He would have if he'd had a place to hide Turner.

He couldn't have risked taking Turner to the cabin with his father because he couldn't risk his dad that way. He could probably have taken Turner to the cete or the sleuth, but he hadn't been sure he could trust them until recently.

"The important thing is that you're here and that you're getting me out. You *are*, right? I heard other people out there, so I'm guessing you have help this time?"

"I do. I told you about the team some of the council members were trying to put together, right? The one that's supposed to go into the various territories to get you and the carriers out."

"They're here with you right now?"

"They are. They arrested Alpha Rhodes, so you won't have to worry about him ever again."

"And I won't have to stay with the surfeit?"

"You won't. I know we didn't talk about this in detail, but you remember the Bishop house?"

"The house where you said all the carriers are?"

Kari nodded. He pulled on the ring in the ground to see if he could get the thing out. "That house, yes. You're going to go there for a while, at least until we can be sure you're safe. I know it probably feels like exchanging one prison for another, but—"

"You're kidding me, right? It's a house. People live there, people who are allowed to move around, to open the fridge and take whatever they want out of it. It has nothing to do with this place."

He was right, but Kari wished he could give him more. He wanted to give Turner and the others everything—the possibility of doing what they wanted with their lives, to choose the people they wanted to spend the rest of them with. He wanted them to be free to move around the forest and be like everyone else.

But this was the first step, and it was a huge one.

"We'll have to get you out of here before we can take you anywhere, though."

"I don't know where the key is, but Alpha Rhodes usually has it on him."

"Okay. Getting the key will be easier than digging it out, so I'm going to go back outside and ask one of the team members to do that. All right?"

He didn't want to leave Turner alone, but he also didn't want to start yelling.

"Okay." Turner let go of Kari's hand, and Kari got up. Everyone was waiting for him outside, and he looked at Terrence. "He's chained to the ground, but he says the alpha has a key."

Terrence nodded. "Woodrow, go get it. You're authorized to knock the alpha around if he doesn't give it to you."

Woodrow whooped and rubbed his hands together. "*This* is why I signed up for this team."

He disappeared into the darkness before anyone could say anything, but Kari doubted the team would have. They might have been told not to kill if it wasn't necessary, but no one had mentioned not kicking asses. Kari almost wished the alpha would resist.

Woodrow's knuckles were bloody by the time he got back, looking triumphant with a key in his hand. He handed it off to Kari, who was now crouching on top of the fallen door so he could keep an eye on Turner while keeping the team in sight, too. Kari was quick, unlocking the cuff around Turner's ankle and helping him to his feet.

"Like I told you before, there's a bunch of people out there. They won't hurt you. They're here to help, and I promise they only want the best for you."

Turner looked wary, but he nodded. It would no doubt take him a long time to get used to his new life and to be able to trust people. Kari had never been able to get to that point, and he still distrusted most people instinctively. He was working on it, though.

Linking their fingers together, Kari led Turner out of the shed. Turner blinked at the group of people waiting for him, and he moved closer to Kari, but he didn't try to go back into the shed or to hide. To Kari's surprise, Raven stepped forward, holding a pair of slippers in his hand.

"I went into the alpha's house to get these. I don't know if they're your size, Turner, but it would be better than walking barefoot to our trucks."

Turner blinked at Raven and reached out with a trembling hand. "Thank you."

Raven nodded and stepped away once Turner had taken the slippers from him. "My name is Raven."

"Turner. Although I guess you already know that."

"I do. I wanted to introduce myself to you because I'm a badger, and I sometimes go to the Bishop house to make sure everything is okay. I work security for the cete. That means you'll see me around, and I didn't want you to be afraid of me."

Kari had no idea what to make of Raven's words, and he didn't care much. "We should get Turner out of here. I doubt he wants to linger in the place that holds this many bad memories. Besides, we should get him to the Bishop house. He needs food, a bath, and a good night's sleep in a bed." Kari doubted Turner had slept in a bed in the past few years. He looked to have been fed decently, probably because the alpha had known he would have a hard time getting pregnant if he wasn't, but that was where his care had stopped.

The way back to the trucks felt a bit like a walk of shame, but Kari kept his chin up and glared at everyone who dared to look in Turner's direction. He didn't know who had been aware of his presence there, and he didn't care. He was too angry. He knew Turner had once had parents, maybe siblings, but if they were here, they didn't try to stop him from leaving.

That meant they didn't deserve to have Turner in their lives. If Turner decided to come back once he felt better, it would be his prerogative. In the meantime, though, it was Kari's job to help him.

He stuck with Turner all the way to the Bishop house, ignoring the rest of the team and Calder. He heard them talking in the truck, but it didn't matter. They'd have to meet tomorrow before going to get Burnell, but Turner needed Kari now.

Calder stopped Kari as he was following Turner inside the Bishop house. "We're meeting tomorrow morning at eight. Do you need a ride home?"

Kari started shaking his head, but rescuing Turner had shaken him more than he'd thought. "To *your* home?" he asked.

If Calder was surprised, he didn't show it. "If you want. You're welcome to sleep in my bed."

"I'll come later."

"You'll have to walk there, unless you want me to wait for you."

"I just need some time to make sure Turner is settling in okay." But Kari could ask his father to keep an eye on Turner. The house was full of people, and Turner would always have someone looking out for him. But the presence of so many people had to be intimidating.

Calder nodded. "I'll wait for you at home, then."

At *home.* It sounded strange yet fitting. Kari wanted Calder's house to be his home, even though he had no right to it, even though he didn't have time to make it so. Calder didn't deserve to be used the way Kari was using him, but once Turner was in his bedroom, showered and fed, Kari found himself leaving the Bishop house and heading to Calder's.

He hadn't told Calder to wait up for him, and Calder hadn't. He was in bed, and Kari climbed next to him as soon as he was naked. Now wasn't the time for sex, even though Kari was naked. Seeing Turner that way had reminded Kari of what could have happened to him and his father. If his dad hadn't run away, they might both have ended up in a shed. Instead, they were free and safe, but that didn't help with the nightmares.

Kari snuggled against Calder's chest and breathed in his scent. Calder already felt like home, like safety, and while Kari wasn't happy about it, it was what he needed right now.

CHAPTER SIX

Calder woke up alone again. He'd hoped things would be different today, since Kari had snuck into his bed last night, and it hadn't been to have sex, at least not in the beginning. They'd both woken up early this morning, though, and they'd made love.

Because that was what it was. Calder wasn't in love with Kari, not yet, but he knew himself. It wouldn't take much for that to happen. And even if it didn't, this wasn't just sex. He liked Kari, and he wanted to get to know him, to see more of him.

That would be easier if Kari didn't run away every time they spent the night together.

Calder groaned and rolled to his side to grab his phone from the bedside table. He'd set the alarm so he wouldn't be late for the eight AM meeting, but he'd woken up a few minutes before it went off. He had more than enough time to get breakfast and shower before heading to Thomas' house. He'd hoped that shower would be a shared one, but with Kari gone, he'd have to make do on his own.

He was disappointed Kari hadn't stayed, but he hadn't really expected him to. Kari was prickly, slow to trust, and Calder had realized that having sex didn't mean trusting for him. His body was one thing, and his mind, his heart, was another. Calder wondered where Kari was staying, since he wasn't spending the entire night with him. Maybe sleeping a few hours here and there was enough for him, but Calder doubted it. Did Kari go home to the cabin every evening? Or did he have another place to stay closer to the Bishop house?

Calder supposed it was possible that Kari shifted and slept in the woods to be close to his father, but he didn't like that. Kari deserved a warm bed and arms wrapped around him. He shouldn't sleep in the trees or on the ground. Not that there was anything Calder could do for that. He knew Kari well enough to be sure Kari would tell him to fuck off if he ever suggested he move in. Still, Calder wanted to ask Kari where he was staying, and that would be easier if Kari was able to stay still for longer than the time it took them to fuck.

The meeting was quick. Kari was there, but just like the day before, he ignored Calder and focused on the topic at hand. The team decided they would get Burnell this afternoon, once Calder had gone to the council building to see what was happening there. They wanted to be sure they wouldn't encounter armed resistance. There weren't a lot of weapons in the forest, but Calder wouldn't put it past some of the alphas to have managed to get their hands on them and to use them against the team.

He left the team and Kari and headed into Northwood. He and Abel had arranged to meet in the parking lot, and Abel grimaced at Calder as soon as Calder got out of his car. "This is going to be a mess," he muttered as they headed toward the entrance of the building.

"You already knew that," Calder said. "You could have stayed home with Philip and Myron."

"And abandon you to face this on your own? I don't think so. I might only be a deer, but that doesn't mean I'm a coward."

Calder patted Abel's shoulder. "No one thinks you're a coward. But I wouldn't have been alone. I might not be as close to the other council members as I am to you, but it doesn't mean they're not on my side."

"Let's get through this. I want to go back to Philip."

Calder might not want to go back to Philip, but he wouldn't mind spending some time with Kari before they headed out to get Burnell. Besides, he wasn't looking forward to getting yelled at.

They heard the yelling as soon as they stepped out of the elevator. They looked at each other, and Calder grimaced. "It looks like it started without us."

"What did you expect? I'm pretty sure they've been yelling for at least an hour, if not more. You had that meeting with the team first, but they had all night and most of the morning to rile themselves up."

Calder wanted to turn around and leave, but he couldn't. This was his job, and he was used to fighting for the right thing. The fights the day before when they'd voted in the laws had been bad enough, but this was no doubt going to be worse."

Something hit the wall next to the door as Calder stepped through it. He blinked at the broken glass and looked up, not one bit surprised to see that Jacqueline had been the one to throw it. He didn't know if she'd been aiming at him, but either way, she was pitching a tantrum.

"They had no right!" she yelled.

She wasn't even the skunk council member, so Calder wasn't sure why she was screaming so hard. Of course, it could be because she and her new alpha were hiding something—like carriers. Calder wouldn't be surprised, but he knew that entering coyote territory wouldn't be easy, especially now that the alphas were aware of what was going on. Their council members might have warned them yesterday after the laws had been passed, but now they knew Calder and his side of the council were serious about this. They'd have to get into every territory, though. They couldn't count on the alphas' word that they didn't have a carrier hidden somewhere.

"It's the law," he said, crossing his arms over his chest.

Jacqueline pointed her finger at him. "This is all your fault. *You* wanted to pass that law. *You* wanted to ruin our traditions."

"Damn right, I wanted to. If the traditions you're talking about mean that people, *human beings*, are being hurt, then they have no place in the forest."

"You can't do this."

"The laws we passed yesterday say otherwise. The majority of the council agreed to build a team that would enter the various territories and make sure no one is being hurt, and that's exactly what we did last night. And if you weren't aware of it, we *did* find a carrier chained to the ground in a shed. He didn't have windows or any food and water in the shed. You should be glad we managed to save him, but of course, since I suspect you have at least one carrier if not more in your territory in the same state, I understand why you're not."

Jacqueline made a strangled sound and rushed toward Calder. Calder didn't want to hit her, because he knew she wouldn't be able to hurt him beyond scratches and bruises, but to his surprise, Abel stepped between them, and when Jacqueline didn't slow down, he slapped her so hard that the sound was enough to get the other council members in the room to stop yelling.

Jacqueline stumbled away with one hand raised to her reddened cheek. Her eyes were wide as she stared at Abel. "You slapped me."

"And you were having a tantrum. Stop this. We're council members. We were elected for a reason, and it wasn't to fight with each other because we didn't get what we wanted. You passed that stupid law that all unmarried carriers had to be handed over to the council when you had the majority, and not one of us tried to attack you, even though that law was cruel and gave abusers the permission they needed to continue doing what they were doing. You're an adult. Act like it."

Calder had always known Abel had a spine of steel, and he was grateful to see it now. The fate of the carriers was important to him, especially now that Philip was in his life.

Someone cleared their throat. "You understand why the alphas are angry, though, don't you?"

Calder turned to Kennedy, the skunk council member. "I do. We just took away a carrier from your alpha. I don't know if you were aware of Turner's presence in that shed, but if I find out you were, I'll do everything I can to get you kicked out of the council."

"You have no right to do anything like that. The council has always only been a cushion between the humans and the shifters in the forest. That's all. You can't go into the territories and do what you want."

"The only reason we want to enter the territories is to save people, and that's all the law allows. You don't have to worry about anything if you don't have carriers stashed somewhere." Calder looked around. "You said the alphas are unhappy? Who was contacted by their alpha?"

A few hands rose, and Gwen, the fox council member, said, "A few of them are here. The skunk and the rodent."

Good. Calder hadn't expected that, but he hoped he'd be able to sneak out and go to the team when they headed to rodent territory, or at least let them know Alpha Gruber was here and wouldn't try to stop them. With the alpha at the council meeting, they'd have a better chance to get into the territory and out without anyone fighting them.

Kari had known things would be more complicated today. Calder wasn't with them, and his presence had carried a lot of weight the night before. It had kept the surfeit in control. They hadn't wanted to do anything against a council member, but the same wouldn't go for the rodents. Calder was at the council building, and the team was on its own.

Kari didn't mind. They'd have to be on their own eventually, so the sooner they started, the better it would be. He just hoped it wouldn't get Burnell hurt.

"What can you tell us about the mischief?" Terrence asked.

Kari looked at the entrance of mischief territory. "For one, they shouldn't have Burnell."

"Right. Because he's a weasel."

"A mink. But minks and weasels are cousins, if you will. That's why I think Burnell used to live with the gang. I don't know how he ended up in rodent hands, but he shouldn't have." The gang that had been supposed to be Kari's home was made up of several animals—weasels, of course, but also minks, otters, and ermines. Burnell should have been a gang member, but instead, he'd been sold to the rodents. Kari was only mildly surprised. The rodents had a bad reputation in the forest, right along with the coyotes.

"He's probably been sold."

"I agree. Either by the old alpha, or by the beta who took his place when he died."

"Not the new alpha?"

"I don't think so. He's young, and he hasn't been alpha long enough to do this kind of thing." And even though Kari would never admit it out loud, he hoped his half-brother was nothing like their father. He needed to trust that the gang would be okay, even though none of them had tried to help his dad.

He'd seen enough in the forest to know how an alpha could keep control over his people. Alphas used fear to make everyone do what they wanted, and it was always best for people and their families to stay away. He hoped Milton would change things, but he wouldn't be sure of that until he gave Milton a chance. He was terrified to do that, and he wanted to focus on helping Burnell and any other carrier who was still being abused, but eventually, Kari would have to face the fact that he had a half-brother, and he probably should talk to him.

"It would be easier for us to deal with the gang," Terrence murmured.

"I agree. From what I know, the new weasel alpha is a good man. The rodent, not so much."

"The entire mischief should be eradicated," someone grumbled behind Kari.

He agreed. He knew that Seamus, the husband of the next badger alpha, was a rodent and that his early life hadn't been easy. He'd been abused, then rescued by the badgers. The man who had abused him had been killed, but his son had taken his place, and things hadn't changed. Even though the new alpha had tried to show that he was a better man than his father, everyone in the forest knew the truth.

The mischief needed to be eradicated because rodents were evil. Kari was sure that some of them were decent people, but so far, he hadn't seen any evidence of that, except in Seamus.

"I suppose we should head to the alpha's house and try to convince the people there to give up Burnell," Terrence said.

Kari snorted. "You don't think it's going to be that easy, do you?"

"Of course not. The council wouldn't need our team if things were easy."

Kari gestured toward the road that would lead them to the alpha's house. "Lead the way, boss."

Terrence glared at him, but he stepped forward. The rest of the team followed him, all of them tense and aware of the fact that they might be about to walk into a fight.

They managed to get to the alpha's house before anyone stopped them. Kari wasn't surprised that security in the mischief wasn't great. He'd been able to come and go as he wished in his weasel form, and he'd discovered Burnell was there.

"Where is he?" Terrence asked in a murmur as they watched a man come out of the alpha's house and face them on the porch.

"In this house. He's kept in the back. His room is a little better than the shed Turner was in, but not by much."

"He's tied up?"

"He wasn't the last time I was here, but I wouldn't put it past them if they know what happened yesterday."

Terrence nodded and straightened, facing the man on the porch. "We're here on orders of the council," he said.

The man—Kari was pretty sure it was the beta, although he'd never spent enough time in mischief territory to make sure of it—crossed his arms over his chest and glared. "I don't care why you're here. You're not taking one step further."

"The council passed new laws yesterday. We have the right to be here and to search the territory to make sure no one is getting hurt."

"You have the right to turn around and leave. We won't hesitate to shoot otherwise."

The sound of several guns being cocked reached Kari's ears. He groaned. He should have known about this. It was kind of obvious. Rodents were tiny in their shifted forms, so they didn't often face other shifters that way. They preferred to rely on guns and whatever arsenal they had in their territory.

This wouldn't end well for the team if they pushed.

Terrence raised his hands. "It would be better for everyone here to do this the right way. The council won't be happy if you don't allow us to come in."

"Like I said, you're not going anywhere except back home. Walk away before we start shooting."

This was only their second mission, and nothing like anything they'd faced before. Terrence looked at the team, and while a few members nodded, Kari knew he wouldn't push them into danger, not when they could avoid it and when they were at a disadvantage in front of guns.

Terrence gestured. "Let's go to the trucks," he said.

"You take those trucks and leave," the beta yelled.

"We'll be back," Terrence said.

"And we'll be waiting for you."

Kari followed the rest of the team back towards the trucks. He listened to them talk for a while, but none of them could come up with an idea to get into mischief territory and take away Burnell.

"We can't barge in," Terrence said. "They'll shoot, and there's nothing we can do about that, not even in our shifted forms. I might be able to take a few bullets without too much damage, but I'm not looking forward to it, and I doubt that would be enough for us to get to Burnell."

"What do we do, then? We can't leave Burnell here," Miranda said. She was a deer shifter, but she was a strong and brave as the rest of the team, even though the deer were known in the forest to be the soft kind.

Kari thought that was bullshit, and Miranda was a perfect example of that.

Kari had had enough. He stepped away from the team, knowing they wouldn't even notice he was gone. They were trying to do the right thing while also protecting each other, and while Kari understood that, he also knew they couldn't wait to get to Burnell.

He hid between the trees and quickly took his brand-new uniform off. He left it on some branches and shifted, heading toward the alpha's house. He knew where he needed to go. He'd already been there lots of times, to make sure Burnell was okay and had enough food and water to go on.

Burnell was still in his bedroom — or rather, his cell. He had his back pressed against the wall under the window, which was why he didn't notice Kari was there right away. There were bars at the window, but Burnell could still open it from the inside, and he did so as soon as Kari started scratching at the glass.

"Kari? Is that you?"

Kari wiggled between two of the bars. It was a tight fit, but as long as he could get in and out, things would be okay. He dropped to the floor and shifted. "Hey, Burnell."

Burnell grinned. He was underfed, unlike Turner had been, but just as dirty. Kari hadn't come around in a while because he didn't want to raise suspicions, not when Burnell's freedom was so close, and while he felt guilty, he hoped that Burnell's thinness would help him sneak between the bars. "I wasn't sure it was you. Haven't been around in a while."

Kari gestured toward the window. "I'm here to take you away."

Burnell's eyes widened. "Away?"

He'd asked Kari to do it several times, and Kari had explained to him that he didn't have a safe place for him to stay or enough support to do it.

But now, he did.

"Come on. We have to be quick. The team the council put together just confronted the beta, and I'm sure the guy is going to come around to check on you since we asked about you. We need to be out of here as soon as possible." Kari wished he could give Burnell some time to think, but they couldn't afford it.

Luckily, Burnell didn't ask questions. He stripped and shifted, then looked at Kari. Kari gently took him in his hands and held him to the bars. Burnell's coat was entirely brown, unlike Kari's, which was brown and white. Except for that, they could have been twins, even though they weren't the same species, and Kari hated that Burnell had to go through what he'd gone through.

Burnell scrambled to get out, and Kari quickly shifted and followed him. He had more experience in this, so he took the lead, turning around a few times to make sure Burnell was still running beside him.

He was. He had to be exhausted, but he was moving, and that was the important thing.

The team was still talking when Kari got there, and Kari didn't waste time to stop and take his uniform from the tree. He rushed to one of the trucks, shifted, and opened the door, ignoring the questions and yelps that rang around him in favor of picking up the still mink Burnell and throwing him into the truck.

"I left my uniform in a tree. We need to go before they realize Burnell isn't there anymore."

Just then, they heard someone yelling, "He's gone!"

Calder knew the moment the team managed to get Burnell out of rodent territory. Alpha Gruber, who'd been yelling right along with the skunk alpha, got a phone call. Everyone in the room, including the council members who were on the alpha's side, seemed to hold their breath.

"What do you mean, he's gone?" Alpha Gruber snapped.

Calder had no idea how the team had managed to get Burnell, but how didn't matter. As long as Burnell was out of rodent territory, everything was good.

Calder looked at the skunk alpha. The man was pissed, but there was nothing he could do to get Turner back. He hadn't given the council a good reason why Turner had been chained to the ground in the shed behind his house, and he wouldn't be able to. Turner had been abused, and the alpha would never get his hands on the poor man again.

Calder wasn't sure what to think of the alpha's son, though. He wanted to keep an eye on Jasper, who'd come with his father but hadn't yet said anything. Calder wanted to think that Jasper would eventually be a better alpha than his father, but of course, he had no way to be sure of that. Jasper's presence might mean he was on his father's side, or it might mean that his father wanted to show him how to be an alpha. It was anyone's guess, and Calder made a mental note to keep an eye on Jasper as time passed. Hopefully, Jasper would realize it was wrong to keep people chained. And if he didn't, if he became like his father, the council would have to do something.

Maybe one day they'd be able to pass a law to make sure that no one in the forest was abused, not just carriers. In theory, it was already that way, but with the council not having a say in how the various groups were led, it was next to impossible to make sure everyone was safe.

Alpha Gruber was still yelling into his phone, while Jasper, the son of the skunk alpha, was shuffling around as if unsure what to do. Calder caught his eye and arched a brow, curious to see what Jasper's reaction would be. To his surprise, Jasper gave him a quick grin. Maybe he wasn't on his father's side after all.

Alpha Gruber hung up and turned toward Calder and Abel, who were sitting together at the table. He pointed a finger at them. "This is all your fault. How dare you do this?"

Calder rose from his chair, pressing his hands on the table and leaning forward. "No, how dare *you*? You locked up a man who'd done nothing wrong. He didn't even have a blanket or water." Calder couldn't be sure, since he hadn't heard from the team yet, but he was ready to bet that was the case.

"He's mine."

"And that's where you're wrong. This council passed a new set of laws yesterday. We created a team that is authorized to go into any territory in the forest to make sure no one is being abused, especially carriers. They're allowed to take away the carriers who are. It's the law. And let's not talk about the fact that you *bought* Burnell. He's not a rodent. He's a weasel, and that means he belongs with the weasel gang, not with your mischief."

"The vote was a trap. I know my council member didn't vote for this."

"Maybe not, but we had the majority, and that's all that matters when it comes to new laws, as I'm sure you know. No matter what you think of it, it is the law, and it should be respected. And just so you know, the law includes punishment for those who buy human beings, including carriers. We won't allow you to do anything like this ever again."

"You have no right to stick your nose into mischief business. It has always been this way, and nothing will change that."

He was right, in a way. The new laws only said that carriers had to be treated like every other shifter and that the council team was allowed to enter the various territories to make sure the carriers there were okay and take them away otherwise. Of course, Calder had made sure the law was clear on the fact that carriers couldn't be bought and sold, but everyone knew it would be nearly impossible to make sure they weren't. Even with the team, the forest was vast, and every alpha had more than enough space to hide people they didn't want to be found.

But that wouldn't stop the council. It wouldn't stop Calder.

"I don't care what you think. The council was created to protect the forest against humans, and that includes behavior that might put us on the humans' radar. Do you really think they'll ignore the human trafficking that's happening in here?" Calder was pretty sure they would. As long as it didn't hurt humans, they didn't care.

But it was a risk none of them was ready to take, and that included Alpha Gruber. The council might not be able to get rid of him, but the humans could. They had the power to eradicate the entire forest and its inhabitants if they wanted to. No one here wanted to risk that.

Calder swallowed. "Every single shifter in the forest has agreed to follow council rules. You didn't protest when the council passed a law that said that all unmarried carriers had to be handed over to them. Why is that? Might it be because your council member knew about Burnell and that you weren't about to give him up? Or because your council member promised you not to say anything and to keep her eyes shut to whatever you were doing to the poor man?"

"You have no right," Alpha Gruber said from between gritted teeth.

"I have all the right. I'm a council member, and these new laws are official. Either follow them, or you'll be dealt with, and I doubt you'll find that pleasurable."

Calder gestured at two guards who'd come in to stand by the council members when the yelling had started. "Can you please show the two alphas to the exit? We're done here."

"You can't dismiss us this way," the skunk alpha protested.

"I can, and I'm doing it. No matter how much you protest, this is the law, and have to follow it just like you followed all the others."

The guards moved closer to the two alphas, and Calder noticed Jasper talking to the bear council member, Marjory. He had no idea what was being said, but she didn't look distressed. If anything, she looked confused but pleased.

Jasper left with his father and Alpha Gruber. Calder waited until they were out the door to flop back in his chair and rub the bridge of his nose. He could have done without the yelling first thing in the morning, but at least he knew Burnell was safe now. He wanted to call Kari and ask him what had happened, but most of all, to check on him and make sure he was okay, but he didn't.

Kari was learning to work with the team. He'd never had that before, and Calder didn't want the other team members to resent him for sleeping with a council member. He didn't even know if Kari wanted that fact to be known, although since they'd had sex in his car, maybe he did.

"Well, that was something," Abel said.

They still had to deal with the council members who'd voted against the new laws, but Calder wasn't sure he could take more yelling today. He yearned to go home and check on Kari, and he wondered if he could find a way to leave early. Maybe, if the only thing the council members could do was yell. They didn't have a way to change the new law, not with the minority. They could try convincing one of the council members who'd voted in favor to change their mind, of course, but Calder knew none of them would. There was too much at stake for too many people.

They'd won the battle. Hopefully, they'd also win the war.

"What the fuck were you thinking?"

Kari sighed. He'd known this was coming, but he'd hoped Terrence would wait until they left the Bishop house behind. Instead, they'd only just stepped out of the house. They were still on the porch, for fuck's sake.

Kari turned to face Terrence and crossed his arms over his chest. "I was thinking that we were wasting time. You know what would have happened if I hadn't gone in there."

"I didn't give you the order to do it."

"You didn't give me any order, period. You were hanging around with the rest of the team, and you didn't know what to do."

Terrence's cheeks flushed. "Be it as it may, I am still your team leader, and you only move when I order you to."

"So what? Should I have left Burnell where he was? What do you think would have happened to him once the beta went back inside? He would have moved Burnell, *that's* what would have happened. He would have moved him, and we might never have been able to find him again. Is that what you wanted? To lose Burnell?"

Terrence raked a hand through his hair. "Of course not."

Something flickered at the corner of Kari's vision, and he turned to find Burnell staring at him and Terrence from the window of the living room. He sighed. He didn't want Burnell to have to listen to this.

He walked back inside, wondering if Burnell needed something.

"Where are you going? I wasn't done talking to you." Terrence yelled.

Burnell rushed to Kari in the entrance. "Are you okay? Why is he yelling at you?"

"Don't mind him. He's just pissed that he doesn't have as much authority over me as he thought he had. Is something wrong?"

Burnell shook his head. "Not really. It's just, you know, a lot of people."

Kari understood. He might not have been a prisoner like Burnell, but he'd spent his life alone. He still wasn't used to being around all these people, including the team. "Have you had something to eat?"

"I need to talk to Burnell," Terrence said. His voice was softer, and Kari knew he was trying not to scare Burnell.

Terrence wasn't a bad man. He might have been out of his depth when it came to Kari, but that didn't mean he'd change what had happened if he could. He was as happy as Kari was to have freed Burnell, even though he'd been yelling at Kari for it only seconds before.

Kari turned to Terrence. "Why don't you talk to him over lunch? I'm sure he's hungry, and he can talk while eating."

To Kari's relief, Terrence nodded. "Of course."

The three of them settled in the kitchen. Kari's father was there, and he busied himself making sandwiches for Burnell. Burnell was nervous, bouncing his knee and looking around the room as if he expected someone to burst out of the fridge and attack him. Kari didn't blame him. It would take him some time to trust these new people, no matter how many times they told him he was safe now.

"I'd like for you to tell me how you ended up in rodent territory," Terrence said.

Burnell looked at him. "Why? Will you do something to the man who sold me to them?"

"Unfortunately, there's nothing we can do. New laws were passed, but they're not enough, and they're not retroactive. What happened to you wasn't a crime until now."

Kari dug his fingernails into his palms. He hated that nothing would happen to the two alphas who'd hurt Turner and Burnell. Terrence was right—what Gruber and Rhodes had done hadn't been a crime when they'd done it. Nothing would be done to them, even though they'd abused Turner and Burnell.

Or at least, nothing *official* could be done to them.

"Then what does it matter?" Burnell asked.

"It matters because we're going to keep an eye on everyone who was involved in this. We might not be able to arrest them for what they did, but they *can* be arrested for other things, and if they try to hurt you or anyone else now that the law has passed, they will. I know it's not enough, but it's all I can do."

Burnell sighed. "It was my alpha. Well, I guess the beta. He acts like the alpha, but he's not, not really. He's the acting alpha until the alpha's son is old enough to take his place. That didn't stop him from selling me to the rodents, though."

"Do you know when it happened?"

"I was fifteen."

God, Kari was going to kill those two men. The beta and Alpha Gruber were on his shortlist of people who didn't deserve to breathe. He'd never promised not to kill anyone else once he became part of the council team. He was glad he hadn't now.

"And how old are you now?" Terrence asked. His voice was calm, but Kari thought he could hear the restrained fury in it.

"I'm not sure how long ago it was, but I think eighteen."

"All right. I'll inform the council about this. Thank you for talking to me."

Terrence got up and looked at Kari. "Are you coming back to the council building with us? We have to report to the council."

"I'll come later. I want to have some time with my father." Hearing Burnell's story made Kari want to make sure his dad was okay, even though Julian was standing right in the kitchen with him.

Kari's father had been in a situation that was different yet similar. He'd been abused when he was little more than a kid, and while he'd freed himself at seventeen, the rest of his life had been hard, up until now. Kari didn't want Burnell to have to go through that, and he was glad he'd disobeyed Terrence's orders, even though Terrence hadn't exactly told him he couldn't act on his own. But it had been implied, and they both knew it.

Kari didn't regret it. He'd do it again if he had to. It might make him a wildcard, but he didn't care, as long as he saved carriers.

"All right. I'll tell the council that you're making sure Burnell is settling down, since he recognized you from before. You're going to have to talk to them eventually, though."

"I will. I'm not an idiot. I know I have to work as a team member if I want to be a part of it."

Terrence rolled his eyes. "Could have fooled me today." To Kari's surprise, he patted Kari's shoulder on his way out. "But you did well. You need to learn to listen to orders and to ask permission to do things before you do them, but I'm aware that we might never have found Burnell if you hadn't acted. Just, you know, talk to me first next time."

It had never occurred to Kari that Terrence might have told him to go ahead if he'd told him what he was planning. He was so used to working on his own—having no one to answer to—that he hadn't stopped to think twice. He was going to next time, though. He wanted to be part of the team, and he'd get kicked out if he didn't follow its rules.

Kari's father dragged him out of the kitchen as soon as the plate with the sandwiches he'd made for Burnell hit the table in front of the poor man. Kari should have known his dad would realize he was planning something. They knew each other well enough that Kari's father could read him easily.

Julian waited until they were in his bedroom to turn on Kari. He put his hands on his hips and glared at him. "What are you planning?"

"Why do you think I'm planning something?" Kari asked even though he knew he wouldn't get out of this conversation.

"I know you. I pushed you out of my—"

Kari raised his hands. "I don't need any details, thank you. And yes, you're right. I *am* planning something."

His father sighed. "Of course you are. What is it?"

"I'm going to kill Gruber and Rhodes."

His father briefly closed his eyes. "Kari, you can't be the judge and jury. It's not your job, nor is it your role. You can't make that kind of decision."

"Maybe not, but you heard Terrence. Nothing can be done

about them. The council isn't going to be able to stop them if they want to continue buying and abusing carriers."

"As far as you know, all the carriers are here now."

"As far as I know, yes. But there might be others out there. Carriers have been sold and bought for decades. Alphas hid them to make sure they weren't discovered. The only reason I knew about Turner and Burnell was that they were kept close to the alpha's house. But if one of the alphas is keeping his carriers somewhere else, maybe deeper in his territories, I have no way to know about them."

"And what is killing those two men going to solve? How is it going to help?"

"It's going to make me feel better. I told you, someone has to do it, and since the council won't, I will." And Kari didn't care what anyone thought about it. Since the council couldn't do anything to stop them, *he* would.

CHAPTER SEVEN

This was easy, easier than Kari had expected. You'd think that when someone had already managed to sneak into your territory that same day, you'd beef up security, but Alpha Gruber hadn't. He probably didn't know how Burnell had escaped, since only Kari's team knew, but still. Gruber had lost Burnell. How was he not panicking?

Kari hated how confident and cocky the man sounded. He could hear him talking with his beta in his office, and he moved closer. He wanted to hear what was being said. He had to wait until the beta left the room to do what he'd come to do anyway. He wanted to kill the beta, too, but that would have to wait. His main target was Gruber, and the man would never leave his office alive again.

"How did they do it?" Gruber asked.

"I don't know. I saw them leave. There's no way they could have snuck into the house, not with me here."

"Well, they found a way, and you need to know how they did it. I'm not going to risk the other two."

Kari's heart felt like it stopped beating. The other two? Did that mean they had another two carriers in their territory?

"They won't find them. You were right when you decided to separate them from Burnell."

"How did they find out about Burnell anyway?"

"I don't know."

There was a slam as if Gruber had hit his desk. "You don't seem to know anything. Why the fuck are you my beta if you can't answer a few simple questions?"

"It's not easy. The guards never told me about anyone sneaking into our territory, so I don't understand how they knew. Maybe the man who sold him to you told them?"

"I doubt it. He'd be in trouble if he had. Did you make sure the other two are safe and where they should be?"

"As soon as I hung up with you. They're there."

"Good. Make sure they *stay* there. I'm not going to be as forgiving as I was today if something happens to them, especially the pregnant one."

Shit. Kari was here to kill Gruber, and he would, but he needed to find out where those two carriers were. He couldn't take them home with him, since he'd come on foot, but he could help them hide and contact his team to have them retrieved. There was no way anyone pregnant could walk to safety. Kari didn't know how far along the man was, but he wouldn't risk it. If he managed to get them out soon, the team could come right away. The carriers would be safe at the Bishop house before the night was over.

"Go make the rounds," Gruber snapped.

Kari resisted the urge to follow the beta and slit his throat before he could leave the house. He waited about half an hour, long enough to be sure that the place was empty except for Gruber. He didn't want to be interrupted, especially since things couldn't be as fast as he'd thought they would be. He needed to get the position of the two carriers from Gruber, and he knew the man wouldn't talk easily.

He snuck in through the open window. Gruber's back was to him, and he didn't make a sound when he hurried under the desk. He waited for a bit to make sure Gruber didn't suspect he was there, and then he moved behind Gruber again.

He shifted, his focus going to the letter opener on the desk. It looked like a knife, and it would do the job. He reached past Gruber, who was watching porn on his computer, and grabbed the letter opener. Gruber noticed him, of course, but by the time he reacted, Kari already had the knife pressed against his throat. He felt Gruber swallow, the movement of his throat making the knife rise and lower again.

"What do you want? Who are you?" Gruber asked.

"I'm your worst nightmare," Kari said. It sounded a bit trite, but it was true. Gruber just didn't know it yet.

"You won't tell me. I get it. Can you at least tell me what you want from me?" Gruber's voice shook, but he sounded surprisingly calm.

"The two carriers you were talking about with your beta. Where are they?"

"You can't take them. They're mine."

Kari pressed the letter opener harder against Gruber's neck. Gruber sucked in a breath and tried to move back, but Kari didn't let him. "Tell me, or this isn't going to end well for you." It wouldn't either way, but if Kari wanted Gruber to tell him what he wanted to know, he needed the man to trust he wouldn't kill him if he did.

"They're at the back of my territory, towards the end of the forest."

"I need you to draw me a map."

"Of course." Gruber grabbed a piece of paper and a pen from his desk. He probably thought Kari wouldn't be able to leave the house before he called the guards, and he would have been right if Kari had been planning on keeping him alive.

Gruber quickly drew the map, and Kari made sure he knew exactly where to look, since he wouldn't be able to ask Gruber about it once he'd slit the man's throat. "They're both there?" he asked.

"They are."

"You said one of them is pregnant. Are you the other father?"

"Yes."

"You raped him?" Kari didn't have to ask to know he had, but he wanted to see if Gruber would admit it.

"It took . . . a bit of convincing."

"In other words, yes, you raped him."

"He was mine to do whatever I wanted with. I bought him, and I paid a lot of money to have him. You won't get away with this, whoever you are. I'll find you, and I—"

Kari was quick, sliding the knife to the side, pressing hard enough that he was sure Gruber wouldn't survive. This wasn't the first time he'd killed a man, and he didn't have an ounce of regret as blood spurted all over Gruber's desk. He let go of Gruber, and the body slumped forward, still moving as Gruber tried to keep the blood from leaving his body. It didn't last long, and Kari didn't move until Gruber was dead. The porn was still playing on the computer, and Kari raised the volume so no one would think of entering before he had the time to hide the carriers.

He cleaned his bloodied hands on Gruber's shirt and shifted again. Sneaking out the window was as easy and simple as sneaking in had been. No one tried to stop Kari because no one was aware of his presence. He'd memorized the map, which was a good thing, since the sheet had been under Gruber's body and was now covered with blood. It wouldn't take him long to run there, but he still pushed himself. He hoped no one would find Gruber's body until the next morning, since the man lived alone, but he couldn't be sure. There was always a certain amount of risk when he did this, but this time, he wasn't the only one in danger.

The cabin was where Gruber had said it was. It was small, and the first thing Kari noticed was the lock on the door. There were windows, but like in Burnell's case, bars blocked them. Gruber hadn't made escape easy for the carriers, which was no doubt one of the reasons they were still there.

But Kari had experience in this, too.

He walked around the house to make sure no one else was there. He would have been surprised to find the place devoid of guards if he hadn't heard the conversation between Gruber and his beta, but Gruber had sounded so smug that he'd been able to hide the two carriers. He didn't think anyone knew about them, and Kari wouldn't have found out if he hadn't been listening in.

He shifted to his human form and broke one of the windows. He was grateful Gruber hadn't put guards there even after what had happened today. He heard voices inside, two people moving, and he called out, "My name is Kari. I'm a weasel shifter, and I'm a carrier, like you. I'm here to get you out."

Kari waited a moment, and sure enough, a face appeared at the window. The man was young, although not as young as Kari had feared. "You're a carrier?" the man asked.

Kari nodded. "I can't get you to safety on my own because I don't have a vehicle, but I want to help you hide and call my team. They'll come to get you, and you'll be safe by the end of the night."

"How can we trust you?"

"I know you don't. I don't need you to. I just need you to follow me out of this cabin. What will you risk? You're already prisoners, and I know Gruber raped at least one of you. What are you going to lose if you leave this place?"

"He's going to come after us if he doesn't find us here when he comes."

"He won't. He's dead." Kari raised his hands, which were still dirty with blood. "I killed him."

The man's eyes widened. "Good. I hope you made him suffer. I'm Gallagher, and I'm a weasel shifter, too."

"Are you the pregnant one?"

"No. That's Misha. He's a porcupine."

"How far along is he?"

"About five months."

That meant he'd probably move easily enough. "Can you both shift?"

"Of course. Wait here. I'll have him shift and hand him off to you."

Getting Gallagher and Misha out of the cabin was relatively straightforward—a bit more complicated in Misha's case, but doable. Kari suspected the main reasons they hadn't left was that they didn't have a place to go once they were out, and they were alone. They didn't know who to trust. It had been safer for them to stay where they were, but it wasn't anymore.

Kari cradled both of them to his chest, ignoring the prickle of Misha's quills on his skin. "I need you two to stay in your shifted form. I'll find a tree with a hole that's easy to find with directions. I'll walk to badger territory. I'll put you down once we're there, but I think it would be better for both of you to wait without me. I'll be faster in my weasel form. I'll go to the badger alpha and tell him what's happening. He'll send people to take care of you."

There was nothing the two could do but nod, and Kari started walking. He'd have to make an anonymous call to Terrence, but thankfully, the cabin where Gallagher and Misha had been was close to the edge of badger territory, since rodent territory was narrow.

They were safe, and Kari hoped they were the last two carriers in danger in the forest.

Calder was exhausted. He'd thought the hard part of his day was over after the meeting—if it could even be called that, because there had been way too much yelling for it to be a professional meeting—but he'd been wrong. Even finding out that Kari had acted on his own hadn't been the worst part.

Calder had expected that.

But he hadn't expected Kari to kill a man.

There were no doubts in Calder's mind that Kari was the one behind the murder of Alpha Gruber. He couldn't say he regretted the man was dead, but he was angry. Neither he nor Abel had told Kari that he needed to stop killing if he wanted to be part of the council team, but Calder had thought it was obvious. If Kari wanted to work with the council, he needed to do things the right way, and killing people just because he felt like it *wasn't* the right way.

Calder flopped onto his bed and rubbed his eyes. He didn't even have the energy to take a shower, even though he desperately needed one.

He'd been on his way home when he'd gotten a phone call from Terrence. Terrence had told him that someone who wished to stay anonymous had called about two carriers just inside badger territory. The man hadn't given Terrence any other details, and neither had the two carriers, once he and the team had found them. Terrence and Calder hadn't missed the way they kept looking at Kari, who'd gone with them since the carriers were in badger territory.

Calder hadn't been sure what to tell Terrence, especially not once they'd found the body. Terrence had to know Kari was the killer, but to Calder's relief, he hadn't said anything — yet. There had been too much to do, between taking the carriers to the Bishop house and having the healer check on them, then going to rodent territory even though the rodent beta hadn't wanted them there.

He hadn't been able to stop them, though. He hadn't known something had happened to his alpha, and in the beginning, he hadn't believed them. But Calder and Terrence had insisted, and when he'd finally led them to Alpha Gruber, they'd found his body together. The beta had kicked them out once he'd realized what was happening, but it was enough.

Calder had contacted the rest of the council members to let them know Alpha Gruber was dead, but there was nothing else he could do. It wasn't his place.

But it *was* his place to confront Kari, since he was almost a hundred percent sure Kari was behind this. Calder had looked for him at the Bishop house, but he'd been nowhere to be seen, and Julian had looked worried. That had been enough for Calder to know he was on the right track.

Not that he'd had any doubt. Kari was probably the only one in the entire forest who'd have the balls to do something like this.

Calder sighed and rolled to his feet. He needed a shower, because he didn't want to wake himself up with his stench. He'd probably have to do more damage control tomorrow, and that meant he needed a good night's sleep.

He was already back in bed when he noticed the window slowly opening. He was only wearing pajama pants, so he wasn't equipped to defend himself, but he suspected he wouldn't have to. The only person who snuck in and out of his house was Kari, and sure enough, it was him who climbed into the bedroom and just as slowly, closed the window behind himself. He probably thought Calder was asleep since the room was dark and Calder was in bed, and while Calder might have faked it in any other situation, now wasn't the time to do that.

He sat up. "What the fuck were you thinking?" he snapped.

Kari startled, but Calder's tone wasn't enough to cow him. He crossed his arms over his chest and looked at Calder, and Calder knew he was glaring even without being able to see it. "What are you talking about?"

Calder pushed the blanket away and got up. "You *know* what I'm talking about. You killed Alpha Gruber, didn't you?"

"Do you have any proof of that?"

"Of course not, and you know that, too. You didn't leave any proof behind. But I can't believe you were this stupid."

"I'm not stupid. I did something the council should have done. You weren't going to arrest the asshole, and no one else was going to do anything about it."

"And you decided that killing him was a good idea?"

"Yes, I did. And stop being a hypocrite. I know you wanted it, too. You might even have done it if you weren't a council member. That man abused and raped carriers. Your Seamus was in the rodents' hands before he came here. You found the pregnant carrier. Do you think the boy became pregnant because he wanted to?"

Calder rubbed his hand over his face. He was tired, and he didn't want to fight with Kari, especially not when he understood where Kari was coming from. "Be that as it may, you had no right to make yourself judge and executioner. You can't do that anymore, not now that you're a part of the council team. You have to act the right way if you don't want to be kicked out. You're lucky Terrence didn't say anything tonight, and I'm not sure he won't tomorrow."

"You and Abel decided I could be on the team."

"Maybe, but Terrence is the one in charge of it, and he'll decide if you can't be on it anymore."

"It's not fair."

"What's not fair is that you killed a man."

Kari stepped forward as if he might hit Calder.

Calder didn't move, because he knew Kari wouldn't. He might be a cold-blooded killer, but he only killed when he had a very good reason. Both Oscar and Alpha Gruber had been men who didn't deserve to live. Calder couldn't deny that. And yes, maybe he wished he could have done what Kari had done.

"He deserved to die. The forest is a better place with him

gone," Kari spat out.

He didn't understand, did he? Calder *was* angry about what Kari had decided to do on his own, but mostly, he'd been terrified when he'd realized what had happened. Kari could have been hurt, and Calder wouldn't have known about it for hours, possibly longer.

He pointed at Kari. "You'll never do that again. I need to be sure of that. If you find other carriers, or if you suspect people of doing what Alpha Gruber did, come to me. Come to the council, or at the very least, talk to Terrence."

Kari slapped Calder's hand away. "Who do you think you are for telling me what to do? I might have had sex with you, but—"

"Having sex with you has nothing to do with this."

Kari arched a brow. "No? Then why are you hard right now? Is it because of me, or because of the power you think you have over me?"

Dammit. Calder had hoped Kari wouldn't notice. He *was* hard, but it wasn't because he had any kind of power over Kari. He didn't. But as a council member, he was so used to people bowing to him and doing what he wanted that Kari's stubbornness and free spirit was a pleasant change. "I'm hard because you're gorgeous and infuriating and stubborn, and I want you in my bed, all the time. I was terrified something had happened to you, and even though we've only been having sex for a short time, I—"

Kari launched himself at Calder. Calder had just enough time to grab him before they toppled to the bed, Calder spread on his back with Kari straddling him. He was only there for a few seconds, though. Then he scrambled of Calder and pulled at Calder's pajama pants to get them off.

Calder had no idea why Kari was this frantic, but he didn't mind. He knew Kari was okay, but he still needed to reassure himself. He had no idea why, and he wasn't about to analyze his emotions right now, not when he was about to get laid.

Kari managed to get Calder naked, then focused on his own clothes. Calder scrambled to get closer to the nightstand to get a condom, and possibly lube, but Kari was already back on him, and Calder had to calm him down. "Lube," he breathed out.

Kari nodded once and grabbed the bottle. "You do the condom. I'd take care of this."

Since he knew better than Calder how much lube and stretching he needed, Calder wasn't about to protest. Instead, he did as Kari had said and focused on the condom. He tried to rip the packet open, but his fingers were slippery.

"Are you done?" Kari asked, already climbing on top of Calder again.

Calder shook his head. "Can't open it."

Kari snatched the condom from Calder's fingers, tucked one corner of the packet between his teeth, and ripped it open. He made quick work of rolling it on Calder's cock, and finally, he was sitting on Calder's lap, taking Calder inside of him.

Calder clutched at Kari's hips and let him do all the work since it looked like that was what he wanted. Kari needed to be in control right now, and Calder was more than happy to give him that.

Calder focused on giving Kari as much pleasure as Kari was giving him right now. He held Kari with one hand while rubbing the fingers of the other around Kari's cock and jacking him off on the same rhythm as Kari was moving—frantic and deep, as if he wanted to become one with Calder. He shuddered when he came, painting Calder's chest with his cum. Calder let go of Kari's cock as soon as Kari was spent and focused on himself, grabbing both of Kari's hips and thrusting into him hard and fast until the pleasure building in his groin exploded and he had to close his eyes.

Kari flopped on top of him, and Calder could feel him

breathe in and out. He took a risk, wrapping his arms around Kari and holding him close until Kari had enough.

Kari knew he needed to move. He'd allowed himself to stay with Calder that first night, but only until Calder had fallen asleep. He was tired, though, and he knew that if he stayed, he'd fall asleep, too, and he couldn't do that. He needed to get to his father, but more importantly, he couldn't allow himself to do this. He'd already been more intimate with Calder than he should have. Things could only end badly if he stayed, and he didn't want that.

He pushed away from Calder. He was relieved when he felt Calder reach between them to hold the condom down, and as soon as he knew Calder had it in control, he climbed off him and rolled out of bed.

He felt something trickle between his thighs as soon as he was an upright position, but he didn't have time to clean the lube of himself. He wasn't surprised he'd used too much of it in his haste, though. He should have taken a bit more time to stretch himself, but he'd wanted Calder inside him.

He reached for his clothes, putting his t-shirt on, but before he could get to his pants, Calder's voice stopped him. "You can use the bathroom to clean up, you know."

Kari slowly turned to face Calder. Calder was still stretched on his back, his cock limp and resting against his thigh. He hadn't taken the condom off yet, and he looked debauched. Kari felt smug at the thought that he'd been the one to put that lazy smile on Calder's face. "Thank you. I will."

"I'd also like you to stay."

Kari wanted to say yes.

Calder chuckled. "Or if that's too much for you, you could stay until I fell asleep like last time."

Kari could do that. He dropped his jeans and nodded, then

gestured to the bathroom. "I'm going to clean up."

"You do that. I'll make do with what I have here."

This was too much intimacy for Kari, so he slipped into the bathroom. He closed the door and leaned against it, closing his eyes and breathing in and out.

He could do this. He might not be used to it, but people had sex every day, and that didn't mean they were in relationships. Calder had never said anything about a relationship. He probably wouldn't want one, not with Kari anyway. Kari wasn't a relationship kind of guy. He'd lived most of his life alone with his father in the forest. He knew how to read and write, but that was about it. Calder, on the other hand, was a council member. He was in charge of so many people's safety and lives. Just the thought terrified Kari.

Kari pushed away from the door and flipped the light on. He was still wearing his t-shirt, but he was naked under it. He washed his face, then grabbed the washcloth and took care of his thighs and ass.

He noticed the smell when he was about to rinse the washcloth. It smelled of lube, but not just of that. Kari had never had sex without a condom, but he'd jacked off often enough to know what semen smelled like.

His stomach churned. The chance of him getting pregnant was slim. Even though carriers were more fertile than women, it didn't mean one time would get him pregnant. Still, he felt like throwing up by the time he had to leave the bathroom before Calder got worried and came to look for him.

Calder was sitting in bed, the light on his nightstand turned on now. He looked up when Kari came in and rubbed the back of his neck. "I guess you realized the condom broke?" he asked.

Kari laughed, but it wasn't a happy sound.

Calder clearly knew it. He winced and gestured at Kari to sit on the bed. "Look, I know this wasn't smart, but I promise you, things will be okay. I get tested at least once a year, and I haven't had sex with a lot of people since the last time I did. When I did, I used protection. There's no way I have anything I can pass on to you, but if it makes you feel better, I can go to get tested tomorrow morning."

Of course Calder was only worried about disease. He didn't know Kari was a carrier. Kari hadn't told him.

And now Kari might be pregnant, and he would have to face this on his own.

Kari sighed. He knew he should tell Calder why he was so freaked out, but he couldn't bring himself to do it. He didn't want Calder to look at him differently, to worry that he wasn't strong enough to be part of the team. He didn't want Calder to obsess over the fact that he might be pregnant.

"Are you still staying with me tonight?" Calder asked. His voice was quiet, and he was obviously ready to take no for an answer.

It was endearing. Kari might not be looking for a relationship, but if he were, he'd wanted to be with Calder.

He climbed into bed and snuggled against Calder's side, avoiding looking at him. He didn't think he could, not right now.

Calder kissed the top of his head. "Everything will be okay, I promise. I'm healthy, and I'm sure you are, too. It was an accident."

Kari hoped he was right. He didn't know what he'd do if he got pregnant. He wished carriers could have birth control they could swallow like women did, but none of those pills worked on them. The only thing that did was condoms, and while Kari had never had a problem with them, obviously, once was more than enough.

He waited until he was sure Calder was asleep to slip out of bed. No matter how hard he tried, he knew he wouldn't be able to rest. His mind was twirling with possibilities, with what might happen, and he needed his father. They'd been there for each other, with no one else in their lives, ever since Kari had been born. He knew he should let go now that his dad had a chance at a new and normal life, but he was finding it hard. His dad would let him in if he needed to stay with him for a bit, though, so Kari quickly dressed and left Calder's house the same way he'd come in.

He went inside the Bishop house through the window. He knew which room was his father's, and he didn't want to have to explain to the guards why he was there.

His dad was asleep, but he woke up as soon as Kari made some noise. He sat up and looked around in the darkness. "Kari?" he asked.

Kari was the only one who would come into his bedroom at night this way. They'd been sharing a bed since Julian had moved into the Bishop house, and he'd probably been expecting Kari.

"It's me, Dad." Kari took his jeans off and sat on the edge of the mattress. "Something happened."

"You mean, something more than you killing a man tonight?"

Kari closed his eyes. "You know why I did it. He had another two carriers."

"I know. They came in earlier. I might not be happy or agree with what you did, but I understand why you did it, and why it had to be done. I wish I could make you promise you won't go into a situation like this one alone ever again, but I know better than to ask that of you."

Kari shook his head. If he was pregnant, he wasn't going to be doing anything like that for a while. "That's not—" he didn't know how to finish that sentence.

His father's hand on his arm made Kari sob. Then his dad was there, wrapping his arms around him and pulling him against his chest. Maybe Kari should feel bad because he wasn't a child anymore, but he clung to his dad. He wasn't crying, but he needed to be close.

"Do you want to talk about what happened?" Julian asked.

"I had sex with Calder."

Kari's father made a strangled noise. "It wasn't the first time, was it?"

"No, but it was the first time the condom broke."

"I see. Does he know you're a carrier?"

"I didn't tell him. I couldn't."

Kari's father rubbed his back. "I know how scared you are right now, but obsessing over this won't help. You'll have to wait at least a few weeks before you take a pregnancy test. Try not to think about it. Nothing you can do or say right now is going to change the outcome."

Kari knew that, but he couldn't help but wish he wasn't losing control of his life.

CHAPTER EIGHT

K ari turned to one side, then the other. He poked at his stomach, but from what he could see in the mirror, it still appeared the same it had two weeks ago.

When he might have gotten pregnant.

There were no external signs it had happened, but Kari knew it would be too soon for that even if a baby was growing in him. Two weeks were barely enough to have a positive pregnancy test, let alone start to see a bump. There was no way for him to understand if he was pregnant by staring at his reflection, but for some reason, he had done this almost every day, several times a day.

He couldn't stop thinking about how he might look with his stomach distended and full. He didn't care about ruining his figure, or whatever. He didn't care if he had stretch marks. His body was a tool, just like a gun might be. But he did care about the fact that he still had no idea what he'd do if he *was* pregnant.

Kari's first instinct was to refuse the baby. He'd had plans, and they didn't include getting pregnant and becoming a father at twenty-five. People would start looking at him like he was weaker and not as able to be a part of the team as he was. Hell, they might not even keep him on the team once they found out he was a carrier. The team members and everyone working with them were good people, so Kari knew they wouldn't do it because they thought he wasn't good enough, but rather because he needed to be protected.

He hated the way people thought carriers were fragile and

delicate just because they could get pregnant. He *wasn't* fragile and delicate. He'd killed more people than most of the team members he worked with.

He supposed he was lucky Terrence hadn't kicked his ass off the team once he'd realized that Kari was the one to kill Alpha Gruber. They hadn't talked about it, and Kari suspected Terrence was going to behave as if he didn't know anything. That was perfectly okay with him, because he didn't want to have to explain why he'd done what he did again. The fight with Calder had been bad enough, and it had led to him staring at his stomach in the mirror.

And he still didn't know whether he was pregnant or not.

The point was that once he started showing, he wouldn't be able to continue working with the team. He might even be taken off the team permanently, and that wasn't something he wanted to have happen. That meant getting an abortion was the most logical way to go about this, and Kari knew he should take a test and go through with it.

But for some reason, he couldn't. He couldn't stop thinking about what the future might be like if he kept the baby.

Calder didn't know Kari was a carrier. He'd probably be shocked if Kari told him, but Kari wasn't sure he'd do that. He hadn't talked to Calder or snuck into his bed since that night, and he wasn't planning to do either of those anytime soon. Of course, it would be hard to hide his status if he kept the baby, but that wasn't something Kari had to think about now.

He did have to think about what he wanted to do, though. If he decided on an abortion, he needed to do it as soon as possible. But if he wanted to keep the baby, then he had no idea where to start. He'd never thought of himself as a father. He'd never thought he'd have a family. He wasn't made to be a father.

Yet he needed to deal with the fact that he might become

one.

What would Calder do if he found out about this? Would he want to have a family with Kari? Kari knew that what they'd been doing was nothing more than sex, even though they'd been exclusive. That had mostly happened because he didn't have the time to look for other people to fuck, although he had to admit he wouldn't have looked for anyone else even if he hadn't been busy. He liked Calder. There was no denying that. Calder was a good man, and Kari could have done worse if he was pregnant.

Knowing didn't help much.

He suspected that if Calder found out he was a carrier and that he was pregnant with his baby, he'd try to get Kari to stop working, maybe to move in with him. He'd want to keep Kari safe for the sake of the baby. He'd try to clip Kari's wings, and that wasn't something Kari wanted to deal with. He'd fought hard for his freedom. He wouldn't let anyone take it away from him, not even the other father of his baby.

Kari huffed and dropped the seam of his t-shirt to cover his stomach again. Staring at himself in the mirror wouldn't help. He couldn't keep thinking about what-ifs. He couldn't keep thinking about *this*. Obsessing wouldn't help, and neither would continue staring at himself in the mirror.

He didn't have to go to work today, though, and he wasn't quite sure what to do with himself. He'd been living with his father at the Bishop house, and even though everyone there was aware of it, no one had said anything. Calder's main reason for Kari not to stay at the house had been that he wasn't a carrier and that he might scare the carriers who lived there, especially the abused ones. No one but his dad knew that Kari might be pregnant or that he was a carrier, but everyone seemed to have no problem accepting his presence. No one had tried to get him to leave, which was good, because he had no intention of abandoning his father, even though he was with people they could trust.

Kari would have to make a decision sooner rather than later, but he wasn't ready yet. He had no idea how to do this. He had no idea how to be a father, how to have a relationship with Calder, or if that was something Calder would want. Hell, Kari didn't know if *he* wanted it. But keeping the baby would mean Kari and Calder would be connected for the rest of their lives, and it was something Kari needed to think about.

He left his father's bedroom to go look for him. He felt like a child who needed his dad to feel better, but he and his father had only had each other for so long that it was hard to let him go.

Kari wasn't surprised to find his dad on the couch with Kaspar. The two had been spending a lot of time together ever since Kari's dad had moved into the Bishop house, and it was good to see his father making friends.

They both looked up when they heard Kari come in, and to Kari's surprise, they both smiled. He groaned and climbed onto the couch, half on top of his dad, and snuggled against his father's chest. His father wrapped his arms around Kari and held him, and Kari finally relaxed.

"What's wrong?" Kari's father asked.

"You know what's wrong," Kari whined. He didn't want to say the word in front of Kaspar, although if he really was pregnant and if he kept the baby, Kaspar would find out soon enough. The morning sickness hadn't started yet, but it would eventually, and there was no way Kari would be able to hide it from a house full of carriers, including at least one pregnant one.

Julian rubbed Kari's back. "You know there's an easy way to find out what's going on," he said.

"But I don't want to know for sure."

"You're going to have to eventually. The sooner you do,

the more time you'll have to make a decision."

"But how can I make a decision? I've been thinking about this for the past two weeks, and I still don't know what I want to do. Knowing for sure won't change that."

"Maybe not, but at least you'll know you have a limited amount of time to decide. I remember how this was. It's terrifying, but not knowing makes it worse. Just go to my bathroom. I made sure to put one of the things you need in there."

"Will you come with me? Wait outside the door?"

Julian kissed the top of Kari's head. "Of course. You don't even have to ask."

Calder was worried. He hadn't seen Kari in two weeks, not since the night Kari had killed Gruber. The only reason Calder wasn't tearing through the forest to find Kari and make sure he was okay was that he already knew Kari was. Terrence talked to the council regularly, and Calder had made a point of asking him about Kari. Kari went to work every day. He was integrating well with the team. The only one he seemed to be avoiding was Calder, and Calder couldn't help but wonder why.

He and Kari hadn't made any promises to each other. They hadn't even talked about what they were doing. The sex had been great, but Calder wanted more. He'd realized that *asking* for more would have sent Kari running, though, which was why he hadn't. Now he wished he'd at least brought it up. Maybe he would know why Kari had ghosted him. He couldn't ask Kari about it, since Kari had been avoiding him. Calder didn't even have a clue where to find him or where Kari was spending his nights. He was tempted to go back to the cabin Kari had shared with his father, but he knew better than to confront Kari there.

"Are you even listening to what we're saying?" Thomas

asked. He sounded amused rather than offended by Calder's distraction.

Calder sighed and leaned back in his chair in front of Thomas' desk. "I'm sorry. My head isn't into this."

"We noticed," Abel said. "It's not like you, though. You were one of the people who pushed the most for the team. You should be happy now that they're functioning and visiting the territories to check for carriers."

They had been. They'd started with the people allied with the cete so they could be sure they wouldn't get problems entering their territory. So far, they hadn't found other carriers, but they hadn't expected to. The carriers in those territories had already been brought to the Bishop house. They were safe and as happy as possible considering the circumstances. But they had to start somewhere, and they already knew they'd have a fight on their hands once they went to the territories of people like Karl.

"I am," Calder said. "This is what we've been working on for weeks."

"What is it, then?" Thomas asked.

Calder knew Kari wouldn't be happy if he told the two men what they'd been doing, but they were Calder's best friends, and he needed advice. He didn't want to lose Kari, even though he still wasn't sure what they'd had. He wanted to continue seeing Kari and to find out how things between them could change and if they could become more than the sex Kari had tried so hard to keep the focus on.

Calder looked at Abel, then at Thomas. "This has nothing to do with work."

Thomas rolled his eyes. "Since when do we only talk about work? We grew up together, asshole."

Thomas was older than Calder, but he was right. They'd grown up together, just like they'd grown up with the rest of the cete. There weren't a lot of them left, and that meant they were close to each other.

Calder raised his hands. "Of course. It has to do with Kari."

Neither men looked surprised.

"I haven't seen him around a lot lately," Abel said.

"Neither have I. Actually, I haven't seen him in two weeks. I know he's okay, because Terrence mentioned how nicely Kari is working out with the rest of the team, but if it weren't for him, I'd be tearing through the forest trying to find Kari and making sure nothing had happened to him."

"I didn't know you two were close."

He hadn't because Kari hadn't told anyone, and Calder hadn't known if Kari would be okay if he did. "We had sex. More than once."

Abel wrinkled his nose. "Aren't you afraid he's going to, I don't know, kill you in your sleep?"

Calder snorted. "He'd have to actually sleep with me for that to happen. So far, he's snuck out the window as soon as I fall asleep."

"Besides, Kari isn't a bad guy," Thomas said.

"I never said he was a bad guy," Abel answered. "Just that he's scary, and we all know he killed at least two men. They deserved it, but still. I don't know if I'd be able to fall asleep with him in my bed."

Calder had never had that problem. He wasn't afraid of Kari even though he knew what Kari could do. Kari wouldn't hurt him because he wasn't the kind of man Kari hurt. "I'm okay with falling asleep with him. I wish I could do a lot more than falling asleep with him."

Thomas narrowed his eyes. "You like him. It wasn't only sex, was it?"

"Not on my side. But we never talked about it, and I have no idea why he's been avoiding me in the past two weeks."

"What happened the last time you were together?"

"I yelled at him. It was right after Alpha Gruber died, and

we found those other two carriers. We all know Kari is the one who killed Gruber, and I wasn't happy about it. I told him he was taking unnecessary risks, and that he couldn't be judge and executioner because it wasn't his place."

Abel grimaced. "I bet that didn't go down well."

"It didn't. He yelled back that I was trying to control him or something." Calder didn't remember the exact words, but he'd been able to understand that Kari was terrified Calder was going to try to get him to stop being who he was.

"Then he left?"

Calder looked down at his hands in his lap. "No. Then we had sex. We got into bed after that, and I fell asleep. He was gone when I woke up the next morning, which wasn't surprising, but I expected to see him again just like I had the other times."

"But you didn't."

"You're right, I didn't. I have no idea what happened. We did fight, but since he stayed after that, I don't think things were that bad. Now I feel like I should apologize, but I have no idea how to do that since he won't even come near me."

Thomas tapped his fingertips on top of his desk. "What do you want from him? Is it only that you miss the casual sex?"

Calder had had enough time to think about it, so he knew the answer to this. "I want more. It was never casual for me, except maybe the first time. But I could tell Kari was special even then."

"So you want a relationship with him?"

"I do." Calder had a hard time imagining how that would be, but he knew he wanted Kari in his life. Life would never be boring with him and it, that was for sure.

"Then you probably should talk to his father."

Calder had thought about it. He knew Julian would know where his son was, but also that he had no reason to tell Calder. Calder had no idea if Kari had told anyone what they'd been doing. If he had, though, he'd have told his father. The thought of facing the father of the man he'd been fucking was intimidating, especially since Calder wanted to stay in Kari's life. "That was my next step."

"But you have to be sure what you want from Kari. He might not be a bad man, but we both know he hasn't had an easy life, and he's wary as fuck. He'd rather run from you than talk to you, as I'm sure is obvious to you by now. There's also the fact that he has to stop taking justice into his own hands. The council and the alphas are here for reason, and it's not right."

Calder knew that was going to be a problem. Kari wanted to save all the carriers in the forest so they didn't have to go through what his dad had been through. It was a noble goal, but he wasn't going at it the right way. Even if Alpha Gruber had deserved to die, it wasn't right that Kari had been the one to kill him. Gruber should have had to stand in front of the council to explain his actions. Not all the council members would have been okay with killing him, but it would have been justice, unlike what Kari had done.

That wasn't something Calder was looking forward to talking to Kari about, but it also wasn't the main thing Calder was worried about. Kari's ways were set because of the life he'd had, but they could change. Kari was only trying to protect his father, and now, he wasn't the only one working toward that goal anymore. He needed to understand he could relax and take a step back, that he could protect people even working with the council team rather than going out on his own.

Calder wanted to help him accept his new reality, but that would be impossible if Kari didn't give him a chance.

It was positive. Of course it was. Kari had expected it, and he'd known it was a fifty-fifty possibility. He wasn't sure what he'd hoped for, but there was no denying the two lines on the plastic thingy in front of him.

"Kari? Is everything okay in there?" Kari's father asked from the bedroom.

Kari wished his dad had come into the bathroom with him, but he was too old to go to the bathroom with his dad. He should have opened the door as soon as he was done instead of waiting for the result of the test, though. Right now, he wasn't sure he could walk to the door and open it.

He was sitting on the floor, staring at the test on the counter. He wasn't sure he could remember how to breathe, and his chest felt tight. He tried to tell his dad that, but the only thing that came out of the mouth was a croak.

"Kari? You're worrying me."

Kari's dad was right to be worried.

"All right. That's it. I'm coming in. I hope you didn't lock the door, because if you did, I'm getting Kaspar, and we're kicking it down," Kari's father said.

Good thing Kari hadn't locked the door. He knew his father was serious. He always was when it came to Kari's safety. "It's open," Kari managed to say.

"Good." The door creaked as Kari's father's head appeared. "Can I come in?"

"Of course."

Instead of looking at the test on the counter, Kari's father sat next to Kari on the floor. "I take it it's positive?"

"Yeah. It's positive." And even though Kari had known it was a possibility, he had no idea how to deal with this. He didn't know what he'd do. He didn't want this baby, yet at the same time, he did.

"I'm not sure if I should tell you I'm sorry or not," Kari's dad said. He wrapped his arm around Kari's shoulders and kissed his temple. "I remember how finding out I was pregnant felt. It wasn't the same situation, but I'm pretty sure the dread and fear are the same. I didn't know what to do, either. I felt alone, but you're not. You have me, and I'm pretty sure you also have Calder, even though you've been avoiding him for the past two weeks."

Kari tugged on a strand of his hair. "I can't be pregnant. I have too much work to do. You know how the team and Calder are going to act once they find out I'm pregnant. They'll put me on the sidelines, and I don't want that to happen. I've worked too hard to be part of this team." And it didn't matter that by work, he meant that he'd killed. Oscar's death was the reason he was here, but he didn't regret it. Oscar's death was also the reason the council had been able to put new laws in place that would benefit all carriers.

"Things are changing, Kari. It's probably true that Calder and the others will try to protect you, and I know you feel like you don't *need* protecting, but they won't think you're weak just because you're a carrier."

"Maybe not, but you know they'll try to protect me anyway. They won't allow me to go out with the team again."

"I know you don't like the thought of that, but maybe it's not a bad thing. You've been fighting for years. Things are finally changing, and I want you to be able to enjoy this moment. You don't have to keep fighting, not all the time."

"Things might be changing, but it doesn't mean everyone is safe. I'm pretty sure the coyotes have other carriers."

Kari's father paled. "You're sure?"

"Not yet. I'd have to sneak into band territory to make sure of it, but Calder and everyone else wouldn't want me to if they knew I was pregnant, and to be honest, I'm not sure I want to, either. I don't want to put my baby in danger. I don't want to be selfish, but I also don't want to stop, not when I know there are people in danger." Kari hated it, but tears prickled his eyes, and since the only person he'd ever allowed himself to cry in front of was his dad, he didn't resist.

His father pulled him closer, rubbing his back and making soothing sounds that brought Kari back to his childhood.

Neither of them had had an easy life, but Kari knew his father's life had been even harder than his. Kari had always been protected, whatever happened. His dad made sure of that.

And Kari wanted to do the same for his baby.

He was terrified at how much having a baby would change his life. He felt like keeping the baby would make all his work worthless, even though he knew it wasn't true. No one could change what he'd already done. Even if he did nothing else, he was still the reason the council had passed those new laws, and the carriers would be protected and safe. It might not happen anytime soon, but it would. Kari was sure of that.

And he might not be allowed to be part of the council team while he was pregnant, but that didn't mean he couldn't go back after he'd had the baby. He wasn't the baby's only father. He wouldn't be the only one taking care of him.

Except he and Calder had never talked about this. Calder didn't even know Kari was a carrier. He was probably worried about Kari's disappearance, but he couldn't suspect the reason behind it. What if he didn't want to have a baby with Kari? What if what he and Kari had had was only physical? What if Kari had to raise his baby on his own, or worse, what if Calder tried to take it away from Kari?

He'd have good reasons to. Kari was a killer, even though he thought he'd been right to kill. No one would defend Kari because he was no one, while Calder was a council member and the best friend of the badger alpha. Kari didn't have a chance against him.

But he knew Calder wasn't like that. Calder was a good man, and while he might be shocked at Kari's pregnancy, Kari knew he'd do the right thing. He wouldn't try to take Kari's baby away from him. Beyond that, Kari had no idea what would happen.

"I think you should talk with Calder," Kari's father said once Kari was done crying.

"I know. He needs to know about the baby."

"He does, but that's not exactly what I meant. You have to tell him about the pregnancy, of course, but I think you should also talk to him about your feelings. Even though you're pregnant, it doesn't mean you have to come off the team right away. You won't start to show for a while, and the baby is more protected than you think in your belly. I think that as long as you don't run straight into danger, your position on the team shouldn't be in danger. But of course, I don't have a say in it. That's why you have to talk to Calder."

"You're right." Kari straightened and rubbed his face to get rid of any traces of tears. "I need to talk to him, and I won't back down. I want to stay on the team, at least until I have no choice but to stop."

"Go to him, then."

Kari would do more than that. Calder was this baby's other father, and there was no changing that. Even if nothing else happened between Kari and Calder, Calder deserved to be with the baby and to be present during the pregnancy. "I think I'm going to move in with him."

Kari's father blinked at him, then laughed. "Of course you're already thinking that far. I hope things work out for the two of you. But if they don't, you know you'll always be welcome here. The others in the house won't care if you stay here with me."

"I know." Kari hadn't realized he had more of a family them he thought. He had his father, of course, but over the past few weeks, he'd gotten to know the carriers in the Bishop house. He knew something was happening between his dad and Kaspar, and that no one there, not even the guards, would try kicking him out.

He packed quickly. He didn't have a lot of things to begin with, and he hadn't allowed himself to unpack in his father's room. It looked like he'd been right not to, although not for the reason he'd expected.

Calder wasn't expecting anyone to knock on his door, but he certainly wasn't expecting Kari to be on the other side of it when he opened it. After avoiding him for two weeks, it looked like Kari was over it.

Kari pushed past Calder, barging into the house as he if he belonged there. He was carrying a backpack, and he dumped it at the bottom of the stairs. He looked around, then at Calder. "Are you alone?" he asked.

"Of course. What are you doing here, Kari? Not that I'm not happy to see you, but I was starting to think you were avoiding me."

"I was." Kari faced Calder.

Even though Calder suspected he was doing his best to appear calm, Calder didn't miss the small signs that he wasn't.

"I'm moving in."

Calder blinked. "I'm sorry?"

"I said I'm moving in. I've been staying with my father, but I'm pretty sure something's going on between him and Kaspar, and I don't want to cramp his style."

This was a bit complicated to process. Calder didn't care who Kari's father was sleeping with, and actually, he'd rather not find out. But his brain was stuck on the first part of Kari's declaration, and he wasn't sure what to do about it. "So that's the only reason you want to move in with me? Because you think your father needs his bed to have sex?"

Kari wrinkled his nose. "Please. I don't want to think about my father having sex. And it's not the only reason I want to move in with you."

Calder was relieved. He was surprised that Kari was here right now and that he wanted to move in, but he wasn't opposed to it. It was sudden and quick, there was no denying that, but it didn't mean it would end badly. "Why else?" Calder had to know.

"You're not going to say no?"

"I'm not." Calder was amused. Kari had never been shy about taking what he wanted, be it becoming a member of the council team or having sex with Calder. That was exactly how Calder liked him. He didn't want Kari to change just because they were having sex, or hopefully, because they were a couple.

"Oh. Okay, so you want to know why I want to move in. Well, I like you, which is a good thing, since I'm pregnant with your baby."

Calder blinked. He swallowed. He blinked again. "I'm sorry?" he croaked.

Kari pressed a hand against his stomach. "I know I should have told you I was a carrier before we started having sex, but I thought we'd be safe using condoms. I didn't want you to start thinking differently of me or to try to keep me away from the team. But now the condom broke, and I'm pregnant. I swear it was you. I haven't slept with anyone else in months."

Calder raised a hand. "I never said I didn't believe you." Calder was having a hard time thinking. In his wildest dreams, he couldn't have imagined this was why Kari was here. He hadn't even known Kari was a carrier, for fuck's sake. "I think I need to sit down," he moaned.

He was too far away from the living room to be able to get to the couch, so he pressed a hand against the wall and slid to the floor. He couldn't breathe, and he had to close his eyes for a second.

He felt Kari sit beside him, but he didn't move away. Kari awkwardly patted Calder's knee. "I know this isn't what you were expecting, and I'm sorry. I should have told you before. I never thought you'd get me pregnant, though."

Calder shook his head. Even though Kari hadn't told him he was a carrier, his pregnancy wasn't his fault. It wasn't like he'd been trying to get pregnant. The condom had broken, and neither of them was at fault. They'd been in a rush, and they hadn't stopped to think for long enough.

And now they had to deal with the consequences.

Calder swallowed and opened his eyes. "I understand why you didn't trust me with the knowledge that you're a carrier."

"I didn't say I didn't trust you."

"But you thought me and the team would treat you differently. And you're not wrong. You know we view carriers as treasures, and you've been fighting so hard that I probably would have obsessed over your safety. I'll be honest. I don't like the thought of you sneaking into people's offices to slit their throat. That has nothing to do with you being a carrier or pregnant, though."

"What does it have to do with, then?"

"Kari, you have to realize that things didn't stay physical for me when we started having sex. I like you. I like how fiercely independent you are. I like that you're not afraid to take what you want when you want it. You were unapologetic about wanting to have sex with me, and you didn't let anything stop you. The same goes with protecting your father and the other carriers in the forest. I never thought carriers were weak. You guys have to go through some of the hardest things imaginable. You're incredibly strong, but I also think that sometimes, you need to be able to rely on other people and stop being strong. The same goes for you." And Calder hoped he'd be the one Kari could rely on. He was afraid to push too much, though.

"Maybe. But you know what my life was like before and why I'm not sure I can do it."

It was too soon. Calder knew that. "And that's okay. You don't have to do anything. You don't have to move in here if you don't want to. I don't know if you're doing it for the baby or because you think you owe me anything, because you don't."

Kari pressed a hand against his stomach again. "It's your baby, too."

"But it's inside *you*. That means you make all the decisions. When did you find out you were pregnant?" Had he hidden this for the two weeks he'd been away? No. That wasn't possible. They'd had sex two weeks ago, and that was when the condom broke. He probably had only found out recently.

"About fifteen minutes ago, I think? But I knew it was a possibility. I had two weeks to get used to the idea."

"So you *have* thought about it."

"Yes. I'll be honest. I'm not thrilled about this. I don't want to get kicked off the team, and I think there are other carriers still being abused in the forest. I'm pretty sure the coyotes have at least one, probably more. They're the only territory I wasn't able to sneak into yet. I don't want being pregnant to be an obstacle to saving other people."

"Does that mean you don't want the baby?" Calder hated the thought of abortion, but like he'd told Kari, it wasn't his body. He wouldn't be the one carrying this baby for nine months. The only thing he could do was tell Kari he'd be there for him, that he'd support him whatever he decided, because that was what he'd do. He might be the other father, but until the baby was born, he didn't really have a say in it.

Kari sighed. "Honestly? I don't know. I never thought I'd be a father. I thought I'd hide my carrier status forever because I don't want people to think I'm weak. I don't know how to be a father, or even how to be a boyfriend to you. Boyfriends and babies aren't my life. I sneak into territories, find carriers, and kill people. That has nothing to do with fatherhood."

"It doesn't mean you can't be a father. You care, a lot. It's obvious in the way you treat your father, and I know that most of what you did was for him. You'll love our baby just as much as you love your father. But it's your decision to make. Just know that if you decide to keep the baby, I'll be there with you every step of the way, both with the pregnancy and the baby's life. We don't have to be a couple for that to happen, although I won't deny that I like you and I want more than sex with you."

"What if I decide to have an abortion?"

Calder swallowed. "Then I'll hold your hand during the procedure. I'll take you home and settle you on the couch and make sure you're okay. You're welcome to move here, even if you never have the baby. I told you, I want more than sex with you, baby or not."

Kari peered up at Calder. "What do *you* want? And don't say it doesn't matter because I'm the one carrying the baby. I already know that."

Calder smiled. "This is what I like about you. You're not afraid to speak your mind. And yes, I wish you'd keep the baby. I hadn't thought about being a father because I haven't had a boyfriend in too long, but I'm not against it. I've always wanted kids, even though the concept was nebulous at best. And I can't imagine a better man to have a baby with."

Kari leaned his head against Calder's shoulder. "I'm not too sure about that, but I guess we're about to find out."

CHAPTER NINE

K ari had known this would happen. He'd been sure of it, and he'd been right.

He wasn't allowed to go into coyote territory with the rest of the team.

He glared at Calder, even though it wasn't Calder's fault. Terrence had made the decision, and no amount of glaring at him would change his mind. Kari didn't want to go to Calder and ask him to be put back on the team. They might be trying to figure things out together, but Kari was his own man, and he didn't need anyone to help him.

If only Terrence hadn't caught him throwing up in the bathroom.

Kari had wanted to find the carriers he was sure were in coyote territory right away, but Terrence had put a stop to it. He'd wanted to be sure they needed to expose Kari to danger by sneaking into coyote territory, but as far as Kari knew, no one had proof that the coyotes had carriers.

Kari didn't think it possible they didn't, though. He knew the alpha well enough to be sure of that. Hell, the old alpha had kept his own son miserable because Josiah was a carrier — but he'd kept him around because he'd known having a carrier could be useful. It was a small miracle that he hadn't sold his son.

So Kari knew there were carriers to be saved, but he couldn't go. Terrence didn't know Kari was a carrier or that he was pregnant. He thought Kari was sick, and Kari was more than happy to let him think that for the moment. What he wasn't happy about was that he wouldn't be able to go with the team to save the carriers in coyote territory.

He'd still been forced to come to the meeting, though. He spent the entire time glaring at Terrence, who ignored him as if he wasn't even there. And now he had to watch the team leave the room and go to work while he was stuck in the alpha's house.

He hated Calder. He hated being pregnant.

Terrence paused on his way out and patted Kari's shoulder. "You'll see, it's probably just stomach flu or something like that. You'll be back on the team as soon as you feel better."

That didn't make Kari feel better. He knew it wasn't stomach flu, just like he knew he wouldn't be back on the team soon. He would have to tell Terrence that he was pregnant eventually, and the longer he waited, the more Terrence would be pissed when he did. Kari wouldn't have cared normally, but he wanted Terrence to trust him. That wouldn't happen if he lied to him. He already had done that when he hadn't told him he was a carrier. Terrence wouldn't take Kari hiding his pregnancy well — and Calder wouldn't, either, not in the long run.

Kari sighed. "I know." How could he be angry at Terrence when it was obvious that Terrence was doing the right thing, even though he wasn't aware of the entire situation?

"Besides, you're part of the team. That won't change because you're not working this mission with us."

That made Kari feel better, although only marginally. He supposed he should feel grateful that he still had a job, although he wasn't sure that would continue once he told Terrence about the baby. Carriers weren't supposed to be warriors. That was one of the reasons most of them were hidden in the Bishop house.

But Kari wasn't only a carrier. He was a man, a fighter, and he knew how to kill and how to defend himself. He knew how to shoot. He'd earned his spot on the team, and he wouldn't let anyone take it away from him.

Calder stepped closer to Kari as they watched the door of Thomas' office close behind the team. "I'm sorry you couldn't go with them," he said.

Kari snorted. "No, you're not. At least be honest about it."

Calder shook his head, but Kari wasn't in the mood to listen to him. He didn't want to be told that he had to think about the baby now. He knew he had to do that. He wasn't an idiot. He was pregnant, and that changed things, no matter how much he hated it. He hadn't expected to be thrown into the middle of a fight, but he also hadn't expected to be kept at home. He was only a few weeks pregnant, for fuck's sake.

Kari left Calder in Thomas' office and stomped his way back to Calder's house. At least this was going well. He and Calder had taken to living together as if they always had, which was weird, considering the only person Kari had ever been close to was his dad.

Kari was relieved Calder didn't follow him home, but his absence gave him too much time to think. What if something happened to the team because Kari wasn't there? *Dammit.* Terrence knew Kari could shoot. Why hadn't he asked him to keep an eye on the situation from far away? Kari was a decent sniper, even though Terrence had yet to see that.

Kari's gaze trailed toward the stairs. Calder had offered him a guest room, and Kari was using it to store his stuff, including his guns. He'd shared Calder's bed since he'd moved in, and he didn't want that to change. He liked having an extra space for his things, though.

His things that included a gun he could use to keep the team safe if one of the coyotes tried to attack them.

Dammit. Kari didn't like knowing he was about to disobey a direct order, but that wasn't going to stop him. He knew he had to start learning to play by the rules, but this was a stupid rule. He was okay, as Terrence would realize if he knew Kari was pregnant. Sitting in a tree with a gun wouldn't hurt Kari or the baby.

Kari rushed to the spare bedroom. He quickly changed out of the uniform the team was supposed to use and into darker clothes, then grabbed his rifle.

He'd explored coyote territory a bit, but he'd stuck close to the alpha's house. He hadn't had the time to go deeper, and this alpha didn't keep his carriers close by. That was why Kari hadn't found them. He doubted the alpha would allow the team in, and that meant they wouldn't go far from the house. Kari knew exactly where he could go to keep an eye on the situation and intervene if he needed to.

Kari had honed moving through the forest in his weasel form while dragging a huge-ass gun down to an art form. He'd done it hundreds of times, and he knew how to move, how fast he could go, and what paths would be more accessible to him. Luckily for him, coyote territory wasn't far from the cete. He only had to cross into bobcat territory to get there. Maybe he should start leaving his guns around in the forest for when he might need them, but he didn't trust the people he shared the forest with not to touch them.

He arrived before the team. He wasn't surprised — Terrence would have wanted them to stop before entering coyote territory to have one last briefing about what was about to happen. He'd want to warn the team that the coyotes wouldn't be happy to see them, even though everyone already knew that.

Kari had no reason to stop. He settled into a tree on the side of the alpha's house and put his gun together. It wasn't comfortable, but he was used to this. This had been his life before he'd moved in with Calder, and he realized he missed it. He knew he'd have to step back once he started showing, but that moment hadn't arrived yet. Calder would be pissed once he found out about this, and Terrence might kick Kari's ass off the team, but Kari wouldn't forgive himself if something happened and he could have stopped it.

It took the team another five minutes to arrive. Kari couldn't hear what was being said from a distance, but he had a good idea. The alpha wasn't happy to have the team there, and he was making it known. He clearly wouldn't allow them in, but Terrence wasn't backing down.

That was when one of the alpha's men attacked. Kari had no idea why the man thought it was a good idea, and he didn't care. The coyote attacked from behind, like a coward. He didn't know Kari was there, and he fell with a neat tiny red circle on his forehead. There was a moment during which no one moved, then Terrence looked from the fallen man to the trees were Kari was hiding. Kari knew he would get his ass chewed out when they were back, but he didn't care, and Terrence didn't have the time to think about that right now because the alpha's people attacked.

It was a mess. Kari helped as much as he could, but it was hard because everyone was on top of everyone now. He took out the coyotes who'd shifted because he was sure they weren't part of the team, but he limited himself to that. He didn't want to shoot a team member by mistake.

It didn't take long for the team to win. Kari wasn't sure why the alpha didn't have more people with him at the house, but he was glad for it. They got a good ass-kicking, and when the team finally left after several hissed conversations and sticking their noses around band territory, they took the three carriers the coyotes had been hiding with them.

Kari might not have been in the middle of the fight like he wished he had, but he'd helped. He'd helped, and he hadn't put himself or the baby in danger by doing it. Surely that would be enough for Calder and Terrence to see that he could continue doing this for a while.

"He did *what*?" Calder asked. He had to make a real effort not to yell. This wasn't Terrence's fault, and really, Calder should have seen it coming.

"He was there. I can't be a hundred percent sure, of course, but I doubt anyone else would have had a reason to be there in the trees and to shoot at the guy who attacked me."

Calder closed his eyes. "He didn't fight with you?"

"If you're asking if he came out of his tree to kick ass, he didn't. He stayed where he was, and he took down the coyotes from there. He was a big help, but we'd have managed without him."

"Of course you would have. You're professionals." And Calder was starting to doubt Kari was.

He *wasn't* a professional. He'd learned how to fight and how to shoot by himself. He was self-reliant because he'd had to be. He didn't have anyone but his father, or at least, he hadn't had until now. It would take more than a few weeks for Kari to change, but that didn't mean Calder had to like it.

"I know you're angry," Terrence started.

"Damn right I am. He put himself in danger."

"But he does that every time he goes out with us."

Calder knew Terrence couldn't understand why Calder was freaking out—he didn't even know Calder and Kari were a thing. They weren't hiding it, but it wasn't like they were screaming it from rooftops, either. "I know, but you gave him a direct order, and he disregarded it."

"I'll make sure to let him know what I think about that. I half expected him to, though. I knew he wasn't happy about staying home, but I didn't want to risk it since he's sick."

Kari needed to tell Terrence about the baby, dammit. Calder understood why he didn't want to, but he was pregnant, and it wasn't something he could ignore. "Thank you for calling me. You're taking the carriers to the Bishop house?"

"We are. I already contacted the healer, so she'll be there when we arrive."

"Let me know how things go." Calder didn't want to freak out the two new carriers, and there was no way for him to know if they'd be afraid of him. He'd go eventually, but he could give them a few hours to start relaxing. He'd need answers after that, though. The coyotes weren't happy about having their carriers taken away, and Calder suspected they wouldn't just stand back and let this happen.

Terrence was lucky he'd already hung up when Calder heard the front door open. He'd rushed home as soon as Terrence called him because he knew that was where Kari would come back to.

Kari was cautious when he came in and closed the door behind himself, but there would be no sneaking around Calder. Calder leaned his shoulder against the doorframe of the living room door and crossed his arms over his chest as he watched Kari take his boots off. How had he managed to drag the black clothes he was wearing and his gun all the way to coyote territory and back without looking like he was about to die from exhaustion? Calder had no idea, even though he knew how resilient Kari was.

"You can stop sneaking around," he snapped.

Kari startled. "Are you trying to give me a heart attack?"

"I could ask the same from you. What were you thinking?"

Kari grimaced. "I take it Terrence called you?"

"Of course he called me. He's your boss. He told you to stay put, and you disobeyed his order. What was he supposed to do?"

Kari crossed his arms over his chest, mirroring Calder's position. "I helped them. The only reason he wanted me to stay home was that he thought I was sick. You know I'm not."

"You're right, you're not sick, but you *are* pregnant. You can't continue ignoring that."

Kari's eyes narrowed. "So that's why you're so angry. You were worried about the baby."

"Yes, I was worried about the baby."

"You shouldn't have been," Kari snapped. "The baby's fine. No one even realized I was there until I started shooting, and once I did, everyone was too busy to mind me. Your precious baby is okay."

Calder blinked. He could tell something was up with Kari, and he quickly thought about what he and Kari had just said and about the fears he knew were seated deep in Kari.

Kari was afraid to be seen as only a carrier, a man who could have babies. That was why he'd never told anyone but his father until he got in pregnant.

Calder was an idiot. "I was worried about *you*."

Kari snorted. "Of course you were. That's why you asked about the baby."

"I didn't. I told you you would have to accept the fact that you're pregnant, and that's because you're going to have to. You can't do things as if you weren't."

"I'm just as capable as I was before. The fact that I have a baby growing inside me doesn't change that."

"I know. But you can't deny the pregnancy is influencing you. You're not sleeping well, and you're exhausted most of the time. I know you want to feel useful, but you shouldn't push and put yourself in danger the way you did. What if someone had realized where you were? What if they'd come to you and had dragged you out of the tree?"

"I just told you your baby is fine. You can stop worrying."

"Dammit, Kari." How was Calder supposed to make Kari see he cared for him? "Look, I'm not saying I wasn't worried about the baby because I was. But most of all, I was worried about *you*."

"Because your baby won't survive without me, not yet anyway."

"No, idiot. Because I like you."

Kari blinked. "What?"

Calder shook his head and pushed away from the doorframe. "I like you, Kari. Sometimes, I don't understand how you can be so smart yet so blind. Why do you think I wanted you to move in with me?"

"To keep an eye on me and the pregnancy."

"No. I wanted you to move in because I like you, just like I told you." And he hadn't believed him, obviously. "Sex with you is fantastic, but that's not the main reason I want to be with you."

"The baby is?" Kari asked. He didn't sound as sure as he had before, though.

"No. I want to be with you because I like you. It was sex in the beginning, but it hasn't been just that since the first time we slept together. I thought you'd realized that, but it's obvious you're not as good with feelings as you are with guns. I was falling in love with you even before you told me you were pregnant. I've been wondering if we could have something that's more than sex for weeks."

Kari shook his head. "I don't understand why, though."

"Love doesn't have reasons."

"Love?" Kari didn't sound convinced.

Calder hadn't intended to have this conversation now because he thought it was too soon. He expected Kari to run away because he wasn't used to dealing with this kind of talk, but he was still there, and from what had just happened, they needed to talk now. "Yes, love. How could I not be falling in love with you?"

Kari shrugged. "No one has before."

"That's because you didn't let anyone close enough to you for them to. But how could I not fall in love with you? You're so strong. You put everyone else before yourself and your needs. You've been taking care of the carriers who were being abused even when no one else knew about them. You made their lives acceptable even while they were abused and raped. You did everything you could to help them, and you did so without expecting anyone to thank you. You don't want people to see you only as a carrier, but Kari, I don't think anyone does."

"Because they don't know I'm one."

"Maybe. But they've gotten to know you as Kari, the fighter and the man who's been protecting people for years without help. They know you for the man who killed Oscar and made all of this possible. Some of them might look down on you once they find out you're a carrier, I'm not going to lie to you about that. But most people, including your team and me, aren't going to change what we think of you. You're still the same Kari, even with that baby inside you, and I want you in my life."

"Even if I decide to get an abortion?"

Calder briefly closed his eyes. "Even then. It would hurt. I never realized how much I wanted to be a father before you told me you were pregnant. But like I told you when you informed me of the baby, it's your body and your decision. I'll be here for you, whatever you decide. I want you to keep the baby, but if you don't want to, it's your choice. Maybe we can talk in a few years and see if the time is more right than it is now."

Kari hadn't expected that. He probably should have, since he knew Calder was different from the other men he'd had sex with. He should have realized this was where things were headed, but he hadn't, or maybe, he hadn't let himself recognize it.

Kari didn't do love. Most of the time, he didn't do sex either, because as his current situation showed, it was too risky. He didn't know how to behave in this situation, what to tell Calder, and more importantly, what *not* to tell him. Calder was waiting for an answer, though, and Kari had to give him one.

He cleared his throat. "I didn't expect that," he admitted. Truth was probably his best bet right now.

Calder's smile was soft. "I know you didn't. I was going to wait before telling you this because I didn't want to scare you away, but I think you needed to hear it now. From the way you were talking, it was obvious you thought I cared only for the baby and what could have happened to him."

That *was* what Kari had been thinking. He'd known Calder liked him, of course. Calder wasn't the kind of man who had sex with someone he didn't like. They'd shared a bed since Kari had moved in with Calder, and again, that wasn't something Calder would do with someone he couldn't stand.

But falling in love with Kari? *That* was something Kari hadn't expected.

"I can tell you're freaking out," Calder said.

Kari shook his head, but he thought Calder might be right.

"Like I told you, I'll be here for you whatever you decide, and that isn't only about the baby. You can stay here even if you decide you don't want to be with me. I know we've been sharing a bed since you moved in, but there's a reason I gave you a guest room. You can move in there, and I won't mind. I don't expect anything from you, neither for staying here nor for the baby. We can raise him together without being a couple."

Kari knew Calder was being honest. He didn't expect Kari to share his bed. If Kari wanted to, he could move to the guest room and continue living with Calder even if they were never more than friends or co-parents.

It was strange, but it felt good.

Men usually wanted only one thing from Kari—sex. If one of them found out Kari was a carrier, then he might want to get Kari pregnant. But that was it.

Calder was different. He wasn't lying when he said to Kari that all the choices in this situation were his. He wouldn't force Kari into anything Kari didn't want. He wanted the baby, and he wanted a relationship with Kari, but he'd accept it if Kari wanted neither of those things.

Kari didn't know what he wanted. He was pretty sure he would keep the baby, and he felt something for Calder, but did that mean he wanted to *marry* Calder? That was where things would eventually go if they stayed together, and Kari didn't want to ignore the possibility. He'd never let himself imagine a future in which he had a husband and children. He'd allowed himself to think about his father having a better life, but he'd always thought he'd continue fighting and hiding.

He had a chance at more. He knew it wouldn't be easy to balance his old life and his new one—what he wanted and what he could have, and what Calder wanted. He'd never had to do something like this, but he'd also never backed down from a challenge. He was already halfway through this one. He was pregnant with Calder's child, and they were living together.

But could he trust Calder the way he wanted to trust him?

Kari didn't do trust. He never had. His father had trusted his alpha, and the man had raped him and impregnated him with Kari. The alpha should have been the one person to protect Julian, and he'd done exactly the opposite.

He wanted to trust Calder, and if he was honest with himself, nothing he'd seen from Calder's behavior or his life pointed at Calder not being a trustworthy person. Calder was the cete alpha's best friend. He'd been chosen as a council member because Thomas thought he could trust him. He'd fought to help carriers and make their lives better, to make them equal to everyone else in the forest. He was still working on that, and he wouldn't stop until he got equality.

But that was different, wasn't it? Kari had to trust Calder on the personal level, and the only person he'd ever done that with was his father. There had never been any questions about trusting him, though. Kari had grown up with that trust.

It was different with Calder. Kari was going to have to let go of the constant distrust and fear that he was doing the wrong thing.

"You don't have to make any kind of decision right now," Calder said softly. "I know this is overwhelming for you. You can stay here for as long as you want, I promise. I don't expect anything from you."

But that wasn't fair, either. Calder was putting a lot into this. He wanted Kari to be his boyfriend. He wanted them to have the baby and be a family. It would be cruel for Kari to let him hope, then possibly take everything away from him. Kari might not feel up to giving Calder a definitive answer, but he could tell him how he felt. Calder would understand.

"I want everything you just said," he admitted. "But I'm not sure how to do this. You know I've never had a relationship, and I certainly never had a baby. I didn't expect all of this to happen."

"We can figure things out together. I'm not going anywhere."

Kari reached out. He was pretty sure this was the first time he'd initiated any affectionate touching. Sex, he didn't have a problem with, but this was different.

He took Calder's hand and linked their fingers together. Calder was bigger than Kari, and his skin was warm.

Calder looked down at their hands, then back up at Kari,

and he was smiling as if this was everything he could have hoped for.

Kari swallowed. "I'm not saying no to a relationship. I think I want that, too. But I don't know how to do this. It's just like what happened today. I should have talked to you and told you what I wanted to do, but I thought you were going to try to stop me. Being in a relationship means compromising, and I don't know if I can do that. I'll try, but that's all I can promise."

"It's been a while for me too, and I don't think I was ever as serious as I am now. I don't expect you to want to marry me tomorrow, Kari. We can never get married if that's what you feel more comfortable with. But I do want to see if we can have a future together, if not for us, for the baby. I don't want us to be the kind of parents who hate each other."

Kari shook his head. That could never happen. He could never hate Calder. "I don't want that either. But I do want to keep the baby."

Calder's lips curled into a smile. "You do?"

Kari nodded. "I've been thinking about it ever since I realized it might be a possibility. I'm terrified. I have no idea what I'm doing. I always thought that having a baby would be the worst thing that could happen to me because it will expose me as being weak. I know people will look at me differently once they find out I'm a carrier, and I've been fighting against this for most of my life. But I trust you. I *want* to trust you. I know you don't think I'm weak because I can get pregnant. Because I *am* pregnant."

"Of course not. Carrying a baby doesn't change who you are."

And that was why Kari wanted to try. "You really were worried for me? Not for the baby?"

Calder pulled Kari against him and wrapped his arms around him. He kissed the top of Kari's head, and for the first time, Kari allowed himself to relax against someone who wasn't his father. "I won't lie. I *was* worried about the baby and what might happen to him. But mostly, I was worried about you. I know it's not realistic, but I never want you to get hurt. I wish you wouldn't put yourself at risk, which is kind of stupid since you're a part of the team. It's something I'm going to have to learn to deal with, just like you'll have to learn how to be part of a couple. This is new for both of us, but we can do it if we both want it."

And Kari wanted it. He could admit it now.

He wanted what Calder was offering, and he would take it.

CHAPTER TEN

K ari didn't want Calder to realize he felt like he might puke any second. Calder had worked hard to cook their dinner, and after the afternoon they'd had talking heart-to-heart, Kari wanted things to go smoothly.

Throwing up on his plate *wasn't* the right way.

He knew it wasn't his fault. He was pregnant, and he was starting to feel it, even though he wasn't showing. He'd never really thought about what pregnancy entailed. His father had explained it, of course, and Kari had known to be careful, but he'd never realized how *hard* being pregnant could be.

His stomach ached. Calder had suggested calling the healer, but Kari thought she was more needed by the carriers who'd been rescued today than by him. He'd called his father to ask him if he knew what was going on and if it might be dangerous. He'd been terrified that he'd put the baby in danger by following the team to coyote territory. His dad had reassured him, though. Kari's body was changing to accommodate the baby, and a few aches and pains were normal. Calder had still insisted that Kari should see the healer soon, and Kari agreed.

"You don't like it?" Calder asked. "I can cook something else, something different. Do you have cravings?"

These were the moments in which Kari didn't understand why he was still wary of being with Calder. It was so obvious that Calder cared. "This is fine," Kari said.

"Are you sure? It's not a bother."

"It's not the food. I'm just a bit nauseous," Kari admitted.

144

He hated feeling vulnerable, but he was starting to realize that he could be if it was in front of Calder. Calder wouldn't use Kari's weaknesses to hurt him. If anything, he looked like he wanted to take down the moon and put it at Kari's feet.

"I think I have some ginger tea somewhere. I need to remember to buy you some the next time I go grocery shopping. Actually, why don't you come with me when I go? I don't know if you already have cravings, or if you'll ever have them, but I'm sure there are things you want to eat that I don't usually buy."

How was Kari supposed to resist this man? Calder was adorable. "Just let me know when you go."

Calder's smile was a reward in itself. He looked more relaxed now that they'd talked as if Kari finally admitting he wanted a relationship with him allowed him to let go of the tension. Kari hadn't even realized this was a thing. He hadn't realized how much the way he behaved had impacted Calder.

Kari reached for Calder's hand on the table and gave it a quick squeeze before turning back to his dinner. He still felt awkward showing Calder how he felt about him, but he knew that if he forced himself through it, it would become easier in time.

A knock on the front door interrupted them. They looked at each other because that didn't sound like an ordinary knock. "Are you expecting someone?" Kari asked.

"No. You?"

Kari snorted. "The only person who could visit me is my dad. I doubt he wants to leave the Bishop house anytime soon, though. Besides, he knows he can call me anytime he wants."

Calder got up, and Kari followed him. If something had happened, he wanted to know it. He hoped Calder would tell him if that was the case, but he wasn't going to risk it, not yet.

Kari didn't recognize the man standing on Calder's porch, but since he didn't yet know everyone in the cete, it wasn't surprising. Calder knew him, though, and he frowned. "What's wrong?" he asked.

"Thomas sent me. There's a group of coyotes at the edge of cete territory. They're coming in."

"They're here to take back their carriers," Kari said.

The man looked at Kari. "I don't know. I'm just here to pass on the message."

"What does Thomas need me to do?" Calder asked.

"He's waiting for you at his house."

Calder nodded, and the man left. Calder and Kari looked at each other. Kari knew Calder's first instinct was to ask him to stay home so he'd be safe, but he also knew that Calder was aware of the fact that his answer wouldn't be yes.

"I want you to stick with me," Calder said.

At least he wasn't ordering Kari to stay home. He already knew better than to do that. "As long as I'm not needed anywhere else. I'm still part of the team."

Calder grimaced, but he nodded. "I know you're used to sneaking around, and you're a great shot, especially from a distance. If you're needed, I hope it will be as a sniper and not a fighter." He hesitated. "I know you can decide, and that you will if you need to. I also know you'll be careful and that you'll keep the baby safe as much as possible. But if you have a choice, please, do what you did earlier today and shoot the coyotes down from a distance."

Part of Kari bristled at Calder's requests, but he nodded. Calder was right. Kari didn't just have himself to think of anymore, and he would be safer at a distance. Being there wouldn't mean he wasn't part of this, that he wasn't doing what he could to keep the cete safe. "I'll try to stay away. I can't make any promises, not if I see I'm needed, but you're right. My talent as a shooter will be more useful than my fists."

Calder nodded. "Thank you. I know how hard this

concession is for you to make."

Kari shook his head. He hooked a hand around Calder's neck and pulled him down. He pressed their lips together, wishing there was more he could do, that he had more time. "Compromises, right?" he said.

Calder smiled at him. "Compromises. We can both make them."

Kari grinned. "Look at us being all coupley and everything."

As much as Kari was enjoying this and wanted to continue, he and Calder needed to move. He kissed Calder one last time and rushed upstairs to change and grab his gun. Adrenaline had apparently stopped his nausea, and he hoped that would continue until he was back home. He wouldn't mind puking everything he'd eaten today if his body waited until it was safe for him to do it.

He and Calder headed toward Thomas' house. They weren't the only ones on their way. Kari noticed guards gathering, taking orders, and moving to protect the cete. Thomas was right in the middle of things, standing on his porch and giving orders. Terrence was there, too, and he glared at Kari when he saw him. Still, he didn't try to send Kari away, which Kari took as a win. He needed to talk to Terrence once this was over. Terrence deserved Kari's honesty.

Thomas looked up when Calder waved at him. Kari followed Calder up the porch steps, and they crowded together. "What's going on?" Calder asked.

"A group of coyotes. Karl is one of them. We haven't talked to them yet, but I suspect they're here to take the carriers back."

"Do you think they have a chance to break through and get to the Bishop house?"

"I doubt they know it exists. I've already called the bobcats, and they're sending people, just in case. But along with the bears, I think we have enough people to make sure we kick the coyotes back to their territory without too many problems." Thomas looked at Kari. "You'll help?"

Kari didn't know if Calder had told anyone about the baby. He wouldn't be surprised if Thomas knew, since Thomas was Calder's best friend, or at least one of them, Abel being the second one.

Kari nodded. "Calder suggested I stay at a distance like I did earlier today. I can take the coyotes down, as long as I'm sure of their identity." If they were smart, they wouldn't shift, but Kari wouldn't count on that.

Thomas nodded. "You're the expert here, so I'm giving you free rein. Talk with Terrence if you need to, then get into position. From what the guards told me, we have ten minutes max before the coyotes are here."

Kari nodded and turned to leave. He already knew which tree he'd climb into. Calder caught his arm before he could go, though, and Kari turned to look at him, wondering if Calder had changed his mind. Was he about to order Kari to stick around?

Instead of doing that, Calder shook his head and kissed Kari's forehead. "Be careful. Please."

Kari nodded. "You, too."

He hoped they'd both make it out of this in one piece.

He *needed* them to.

Calder knew Kari was watching them, and it made him feel better. He knew enough of Kari's ability with a gun to be sure that Kari would take down anyone who stepped too close to him. Kari's position had more than one advantage as far as Calder was concerned. It kept him safe, and it gave him a chance to keep everyone else safe, too, which was important to Kari.

It was hard for Calder to let him be when he knew Kari wanted to put himself in danger, but Calder would need to get used to it. This didn't have anything to do with him. He might be in love with Kari, but that didn't mean he could control Kari's life. He didn't *want* to control Kari. Kari wouldn't be Kari if he wasn't the free spirit he was.

"I don't like this," Thomas murmured.

He and Calder were standing in the middle of the road, waiting for Karl and his men. They hadn't tried to sneak in as much as they'd barged in and waited for Thomas' guards to find them. They hadn't been apprehended yet, but they had to know the guards were there alongside them as they headed toward Thomas' house. Calder wasn't sure how Karl intended to do this, to be honest. He didn't have the manpower to take over the cete, especially not with the bears backing the badgers.

What was he thinking?

Well, that was probably easy to understand. Karl had never struck Calder as a particularly smart man. Cruel, yes. Bad-tempered, yes, but not smart.

The coyotes finally appeared on the road, and Thomas and Calder straightened. They were surrounded by guards, some of them bears. Morris hadn't come by because this was Thomas' territory, but he wasn't far, and with him were more bear shifters. He'd have Thomas' back.

"You encroached in my territory," Thomas said when Karl was close enough to hear him.

"You did first."

Thomas crossed his arms over his chest. He looked entirely at ease, and Calder knew he was. All the cete members who weren't fighters were safe. The Bishop house and the carriers who lived there were safe, too. The only people around were fighters except for Calder, and he had enough faith in Kari's abilities to be sure nothing would happen to him. Karl might be trying to scare them, but it wasn't working.

"I did nothing of the sort," Thomas said.

"You took my carriers."

"Again, I had nothing to do with that. From what I know, the council sent its team to make sure you weren't abusing carriers. If they took anyone away from your band, then it probably means that you weren't treating them the way they ought to be treated."

Karl looked like he wanted to throw himself at Thomas. Calder was pretty sure he did. "I paid for those carriers. They're mine."

Calder cleared his throat. He wasn't looking forward to having Karl's attention on him, but he was a council member, and he represented the council in this situation. "I'm sure you're aware of the fact that the new laws were passed. The council has every right to send its team into the various territories to make sure no one is getting hurt. In this case, the carriers that were found in your territory were underfed, dirty, and sported obvious signs of abuse such as bruises and wounds. The team did what it was created for and took the carriers away."

"I don't care about the team. I don't give a fuck about the council. I paid for those bitches, and you better hand them over to me before I come in and take them."

Yep. This was going exactly the way Calder had expected it to go. "I'm sorry, but that won't be possible." Even though everyone there knew how this would end, Calder had to try to keep things calm and to find an arrangement that would make everyone happy. He doubted anything could make *Karl* happy, though, except maybe being able to hurt one of those poor men who had been found in his territory.

"You had no right to come into my territory. *I* am the law for the band, not the council. It's always been like that, and I won't allow it to change."

Of course he wouldn't. He was one of those men who felt powerful when they were able to hurt other people. He was cruel, and he should never have been put in charge of anyone, let alone an entire coyote band. Of course, he'd inherited the charge from his father when the man had died. No one had protested, because it was Karl's right, even though it was a fucking stupid idea.

The council needed to do something about that. Calder understood why the council had been created the way it had in the beginning. Shifters had just been out away in the forest. They'd lost the freedom they'd had before humans had found them and decided they needed to be contained. The council had helped divide the various territories, but they'd agreed to stay out of what happened in them. The council's first and earliest task had been to make good with the humans so they wouldn't change their minds about giving the Allegheny forest to the shifters. They needed to keep an eye on both humans and what was happening in their world and what happened in the forest. The less the humans noticed the shifters here, the better it would be for everyone there.

But as the years and decades passed, things should have evolved. There were a lot more shifters in the forest now, and they needed to follow a set of laws that weren't in place. The council had always kept away from that role, but maybe it was time to step up instead. People like Karl shouldn't be allowed to have as much power as he did over human beings. He shouldn't be allowed to abuse people, to hurt them, whatever they were.

The carrier thing was only an excuse. It was easy for Karl to abuse those men because everyone had always told them they were inferior and weak, that they deserved to be treated this way, and that it was their duty to accept it without resisting. They'd been trafficked, and no one had tried to stop it. Calder didn't even know they existed before they'd been retrieved. It wasn't fair, and Calder wanted to work on that.

He'd have to make it out of this in one piece first, though.

Kari hated not being able to hear what was going on. It had never been a problem before, but this was Calder he was watching—the father of his child and the man he was falling in love with. Kari needed to keep him safe, and that would be easier if he could hear what the fuck Karl was saying.

Karl was angry. That much was obvious. He'd been yelling at Thomas and Calder ever since he'd arrived, and Kari commended their patience. If it was up to him, he'd already have punched Karl right on his smug nose.

But it wasn't, and Calder and Thomas were trying to keep things calm. Kari doubted it would work, but at least they wouldn't be on the wrong side of this.

Karl stepped even closer. Whatever Calder had just told him, he didn't like it, and when he reached for Calder, Kari shot at his feet. He made sure not to hit him, no matter how much he wanted to, because he knew Calder wouldn't be happy with him if he did. This was a warning shot, and the next one wouldn't be to the ground. Kari hoped Karl realized that.

Actually, he hoped Karl didn't. He wanted nothing more than to put a bullet into Karl's head.

Karl jumped back and looked around. Kari was ready to shoot again if he touched Calder, but he didn't.

Kari wasn't used to being so afraid for anyone who wasn't his father. His worry for his dad had always been there, for as long as Kari could remember. He'd realized how strange their lives were when he was very young, and he'd made sure to always protect his dad.

But this was different. This was Calder. This was a man Kari felt strongly for even though they weren't related. He had no idea how to deal with that.

What he *did* know was that he would keep Calder safe.

And if that meant shooting Karl, then Kari was all for it.

Karl was yelling now. Kari could hear him from where he was, even though it was hard to understand separate words. Karl was angry, but then anyone who'd been shot at probably would be. Kari hadn't thought one bullet would be enough to get Karl to step back, and he was right. Karl was right there in Calder and Thomas' faces, still yelling, but everyone knew there wasn't much he could do right now.

From what Kari could see, Karl had acted on instinct. He hadn't thought the way an alpha should. He probably had barely taken five minutes to think about what he was doing before gathering the half-dozen people who were with him. Even though there weren't a lot of badgers, they wouldn't have a problem taking on Karl's group. Seven against at least fifteen would be a walk in the park, and Karl had to be aware of that.

He'd had a gut reaction, and he'd lost. He'd be back, though. He might have lost this fight before it even began, but it didn't mean he would back off from the war. He thought it wasn't right. He wanted those carriers back, whatever that entailed. If he could take Thomas' ass as he did so, he'd be more than happy to do it.

But not tonight.

Kari watched, satisfied, as Karl finally moved away. Calder was safe for the night, and Kari allowed himself to relax. The badger and bear guards followed Karl in his group until they disappeared at a distance, and only then did Kari put his gun down.

It wasn't over, but for now, they could take a breath.

He rushed back to Calder. He'd left his gun and the case it was contained in at the tree, unwilling to waste time when he wanted nothing more than to check in on Calder and make sure he was okay.

He barged through the tree line, not slowing down until he reached Calder, who was talking with Thomas. The two men looked up, and Calder opened his arms. Kari threw himself between them. He wrapped himself around Calder's body and closed his eyes, breathing his scent in.

"Are you okay?" Calder asked.

Kari snorted and looked up. "I should be the one asking you that."

Calder smiled. "Of course I am. You had my back."

The weight lifted from Kari's chest. "I did." He felt slightly embarrassed knowing how vulnerable he was making himself in front of Thomas, but he knew it was something he needed to work on.

Calder wasn't going to want to hide their relationship. Kari was starting to understand it had nothing to do with the baby. Calder wanted to be with Kari, and Kari wanted the same thing. Hiding would only complicate things, and for once, Kari wanted to be happy.

Thomas cleared his throat. "We need to have a meeting. This isn't over."

Kari agreed. "I want in." He hoped he'd be allowed in, but he had no way to know what Thomas knew. Would Kari's relationship with Calder be enough for Thomas to keep him out of this? Or maybe Kari's pregnancy? Kari didn't know if Thomas was aware of it, but it was a possibility.

Thomas nodded. "Of course. I think you're the best shooter we have."

Kari had never been so grateful for all the time he'd spent shooting in the forest. That was how he'd learned to be a sniper. He'd had a lot of free time when he'd been growing up, and working on his abilities was paying off. He might be a carrier, and he might be pregnant, but he was contributing. He was helping to keep the cete safe, and that was all he'd ever wanted.

They gathered in Thomas' office. Kari stayed close to the wall, out of sight. He watched as Thomas, Calder, Terrence, and Morris—who'd just arrived—sat around Thomas' desk. There were other people there, of course, like Alex and Dimitri and Levi, but Thomas would be the one making decisions. It was good to see that he was ready to listen to everyone, though. He might be the alpha, but he knew he couldn't do this on his own. He'd do everything he could to protect the cete, not himself. The cete was the more important thing here, not him. Kari wished all alphas were like him.

"We need allies," Alex said.

"We already have allies," his father pointed out. "But you're right. We need them to take a step forward and show Karl they support us. We need to show him and the council members who are against us that we're not weak and that we won't back off just because they want us to."

"Are they going to back us, though?"

That was the main question, wasn't it? The cete's allies were in this because Thomas had offered their carriers a safe place to stay. He hadn't asked anything from them in exchange, which was precisely the kind of man he was. The most honorable thing would be to come to his rescue now that he was asking for help, but Kari wasn't sure there were a lot of honorable men left in the forest.

All the alphas wanted to keep their territory safe. Most of them wouldn't want to put their people in danger by helping Thomas, even though they knew Karl was in the wrong.

"We need to contact them," Calder said. "It's no use to start wondering if they'll help us. We need to be sure who will send people and how many if they do. Once we have numbers, we can start planning. We don't have a lot of time. Karl might have acted on instinct tonight, but he won't tomorrow. He's probably already plotting against us, and we need to do the same thing."

Kari agreed. "I think we should let him come to us," he said. He was relieved when no one asked who he was or what he was doing there.

"It might put the cete in danger, though," Levi said.

"Or we could use it to our advantage," Kari continued. "Karl is rash. He might be plotting right now, but even if he does come up with a plan, he probably won't follow it, and he definitely won't allow anyone to help him. He thinks he's the strongest and smartest guy around. He won't let anyone else in his band have a say in this. He won't listen to the more experienced fighters he has. He'll rush into this without thinking about how we might meet him. We need to be ready for that. We can make sure the people on our side are hidden in the forest and will be able to act in seconds if they need to, but they don't necessarily have to be in sight. It would be better if we kept them hidden and Karl only saw the badgers, and maybe a few bears. I'll make sure to keep everyone as safe as possible. Karl probably won't realize it's a trap until too late. But we need the numbers to do that. We need allies."

Planning was the best Kari could do, even though he yearned to be in the middle of the fight.

But he couldn't only think of himself anymore. He had Calder to think about, and of course, their baby.

He wasn't alone anymore, no matter how strange that was. He had a family, and he needed to keep everyone in it safe, including himself.

CHAPTER ELEVEN

K ari already had enough of meetings, even though he'd never been in one until recently. But they'd had one last night, and now they were in yet another one, and everyone was on the phone.

The same people who'd been there last night were here today. They were all talking to other alphas, trying to convince them to show their support for the cete against Karl. Kari didn't think Karl would care who supported the cete unless there were fighters involved, and so far, no one had volunteered any.

Kari could understand that. If his father's life had been in danger, he would have turned down Thomas' request for help. But Thomas had opened the cete to every carrier in the forest. All those alphas hesitating and saying no to helping him had people in the Bishop house. How could they not see their carriers would be safer if Karl got kicked back into his territory?

Kari didn't understand them. Thomas had been there for them when they'd needed him. He'd given their carriers a safe place to stay. And now that they could help him in return, all of them were scurrying back to their territory. Hell, Kari had heard at least a few who wanted to pick up their carriers.

Now that the laws had changed, the carriers would be safe in their territories. They didn't have to hide anymore, even though, as Karl was showing, they might need to. What would stop him from attacking another territory once he was done with the cete?

Not that Kari thought Karl would win. There was no way that would happen. Even if everyone else kept their distance, the bears weren't going anywhere. Two of Thomas' sons were married to bear shifters. That made the bears and the badgers a family, and while the badgers' numbers were on the smaller side, the bears' weren't.

But Kari was still angry. Even if the bears were enough to help with the badgers against the coyotes, he hated how everyone else was betraying Thomas. They should be right there with him, helping him and thanking him for what he'd done, and instead, they were running away with their tail between their legs.

Calder hung up his phone and sighed. He rubbed his forehead, and Kari knew his conversation hadn't gone the way he'd wanted to go. He reached out and massaged Calder's neck, and Calder rolled his head and leaned into the contact.

"How bad is it?" Kari asked.

Calder looked at him. "I'm sure we'll be able to get through this with only the bears."

That was what Kari had feared. People were ungrateful assholes, and this was one more proof of that. "It's not fair. Thomas helped them, and now they won't help him?"

Calder pressed his palm against Kari's hand on his neck, keeping it there. "I know it's unfair, but that's life. You know that better than anyone else. Most of the people I talked to want to help, but they don't dare to. They're afraid their people are going to get hurt, and you have to admit it's a good reason to stay out of it."

Kari did understand, but it didn't make things easier to accept. "What can I do?"

Calder shook his head. "I don't know. Nothing, I think. A few of the alphas will come later today to take their carriers home. They don't want them around when Karl arrives."

"And you're going to let them?"

"Of course we are. We always knew the carriers would eventually go home. They're not prisoners."

They weren't, and that meant they might be able to do something. What if they refused to leave? What would the alphas do then? Would they drag their carriers away kicking and screaming? Or would they be forced to stay and help? There was no way they'd abandon the carriers when they were in danger, and that meant they'd have to do something to help.

Kari straightened in his chair. Calder narrowed his eyes at him and cocked his head. "You have something on your mind," he said.

"I do."

"Do I want to know what it is?"

Kari smiled at him and kissed his cheek. "Probably not. I'm going to go visit my father, since it's obvious I'm of no use here."

Calder blinked, but he didn't protest, even though he had to know Kari was planning something. "Of course. I'll let you know how the rest of the meeting goes."

Kari suspected he already knew, but he wasn't going to let that get him down. He had a plan now, and he needed to implement it.

He would show the alphas and the rest of the forest that the carriers weren't weak, that they didn't have to obey orders they didn't agree with. They weren't soldiers, and even though they owed their alphas respect, that didn't mean the alphas should rule over them and let someone else decide their life for them.

Kari doubted anyone realized he'd left except Calder. That was more than okay with him. He wasn't going to do anything illegal, and he doubted anyone in the room would try to stop him if they knew what he was planning, but he didn't want to risk it. He still wasn't sure who was aware of the fact that he was a carrier, or that he was pregnant. He didn't want anyone to tell him he needed to take a step back, because he wasn't going to.

He ran almost all the way to the Bishop house, urgency pushing him. He was out of breath when he got there, but he also felt good. He was doing something, something that mattered and that hopefully would save lives. He hoped that if Karl realized how much support the cete had, he'd back down. He couldn't be sure of it, but he didn't think the man was suicidal. This might not be the final solution to the problem Karl represented, but it was a step in that direction, and they'd have more time to deal with things once Karl retreated in his territory.

Kari rushed into the Bishop house, startling one of the carriers who was coming down the stairs. Calum pressed a hand over his chest, and Kari barely managed not to roll his eyes at the dramatic gesture. "Do you know where my father is?" he asked.

Calum glared at him. "I'm not your secretary, or your father's."

"I never said you were. I just asked you if you knew where he was. You can say yes and tell me where, or you can say no, and I'll go away." That wasn't hard, was it?

"Behind the house. He and Kaspar went for a walk."

Kari would need to ask his dad what was going on between him and Kaspar, but that had to wait. He left Calum behind and headed to the kitchen. He was lucky to find is dad and Kaspar coming in, and the rest of the room filled with carriers. A few of them were cooking while the others were setting the table and talking. They looked like a family, and they were close. Kari hoped that meant they'd want to help. Even if only a few of them did, things would be better for the cete.

"I need to talk to everyone," he said.

He had to repeat himself a few times before he got

everyone's attention. Once he did, he turned to look at Chris. Chris was the next in line for the bobcat alpha position. Once his father stepped down, he'd become the alpha, even though he was a carrier. That gave him leverage that none of the other carriers had. "You know what happened last night?" he asked.

Chris nodded. "Karl."

"Yes, him. Thomas and the others are trying to get alphas to back them, but none of them want to. They're grateful Thomas took the lot of you in, but they won't help him. Some of them are coming to pick you up so you won't be in the middle of the fight if that's what ends up happening."

Chris frowned. "But that's not fair. Thomas and the cete gave us a safe place to stay. They give us a home and a family. They protected us. We have to help them."

That was what Kari had hoped to hear. "You can."

Chris blinked. "How so?"

"Refuse to go home. If you stay here, then your alphas won't have a choice. They'll have to provide Thomas with guards and fighters to protect you against Karl. They won't want to risk you. That's why you're here in the Bishop house. You won't be able to fight, but this, you can do."

Kari didn't want to put any of them in danger, and he knew most of them wouldn't be able to fight their way out of a wet paper bag. They'd been sheltered, hidden away because they were carriers. But this was their time to shine. They might not be able to assist in a physical fight, but they could do this. They could help, and they would show the world that carriers weren't weak.

Calder hoped Kari had managed to do what he'd been planning, because the alphas were starting to arrive.

The deer had agreed to help, but that was it. While they

weren't fighters, Calder was grateful for any kind of help. Hopefully, Karl would see their numbers and decide he was better off going home and leaving them alone. Calder had hoped for more, if anything because Thomas had always been ready to help anyone who needed him, but they'd have to deal with this as it was.

Or maybe not. Everything depended on Kari and what he'd done. Calder had no idea what he'd been planning, but he suspected he would find out soon enough.

Calder had volunteered to go with the alphas to the Bishop house so they could pick up their carriers. It would give him a chance to see Kari. Things had been frantic today, and Calder felt like he'd barely had any opportunity to spend some time with his boyfriend.

His boyfriend. It had been a while since he'd had someone in his life, and he knew Kari was it for him. He would be it even without the baby, but the pregnancy was making things as perfect as they could be. Calder had never thought much about becoming a father because he'd never been with a man or woman for long enough to start talking about it. He hadn't been with Kari long, of course, but the way he felt for him was so different from how he felt for his exes that he knew it would work. It would take a lot of work, especially considering Kari's issues, but they could do it.

Calder was convinced of that.

"I'm sorry about this," Dan said.

"Don't worry. We understand." And Calder did. Dan had his clowder to think about, and even more importantly, his twin sons. Chris would be alpha one day, and Dan needed to keep him and his brother safe. It was more important to him than to any of the other alphas concerned.

"I wish things were different, but Chris is—"

"Don't worry about it. You know Thomas won't hold this against you. We do wish we had more help, but we do understand why you and the others can't do anything." Even though Thomas wouldn't have hesitated if Dan had asked him what he was asking of Dan.

Luckily, they'd reached the house. Calder might understand why the alphas were holding back, but it didn't mean he was happy about it, and he certainly didn't want to discuss it any longer than he already had. He didn't need explanations or apologies. He needed fighters, and he didn't have them.

He didn't knock as he led the alphas inside. The lower floor of the house was open to anyone allowed there, and Calder and the alphas were. Calder was surprised at the level of noise coming from the living room. Even with so many men and women living in the house, they were usually pretty quiet, and they seldom gathered the way they had today.

They stepped into the living room, and all hell broke loose.

Calder was glad he wasn't one of the alphas, but especially Dan. His twin sons made a beeline for him, and they weren't happy. Calder suspected it had to do with Kari, who was leaning against the wall with his arms crossed over his chest looking like the cat that ate the cream.

"How can you not be willing to help the cete?" Chris asked. He seemed to be the spokesman of the group, which wasn't surprising.

Dan blinked at him. "How do you know?"

"How I know doesn't matter. None of us is going anywhere. We talked about it, and we decided we were going to stay in the Bishop house."

"Chris, you'll obey me—"

"Not when you're doing the wrong thing. I'm sorry, Dad. I know you're doing what you think is the right thing, but I don't agree with you, and I'm old enough to make this decision. We all are. We won't fight, but if staying here means you and the other alphas will help the cete, then we're not going anywhere."

Calder was so damn proud of Kari. He couldn't be in the fight, but he was doing what he could to make sure the cete won. He'd managed to convince Nico and the other carriers to be on his side, and that was more than Calder had expected.

His phone rang while the alphas were still fighting with the carriers, so he took it outside. Kari followed him, but he didn't say anything as Calder answered. "Hello?" Calder said.

"Cal. You're still at the Bishop house?" Thomas asked.

"Yes. Do you need anything from here? Or from me?"

"I'm still in the middle of things here, but I was just told that the new weasel alpha is waiting to meet one of us."

"Did you tell him I would get back to him as soon as possible?"

"By waiting, I mean here. He's at the edge of cete territory. I'd go myself, but I'm still busy here."

Calder groaned. He had no idea what the weasel alpha wanted, and with Kari being a weasel and his past, he wasn't sure he wanted to talk to the man. He knew the alpha was Kari's half-brother and that he'd taken his father's place only recently, and that meant no one knew which side he was on. "Did he say why he was here?"

"I think he heard that some of the carriers we recently found are weasels."

Calder wasn't surprised the news was already spreading. The team had taken the carriers straight to the Bishop house every time, but people had noticed. Rumors were running rampant, and more than one alpha had asked Calder about the carriers. He hadn't given them an answer because he didn't know whether the carriers would be okay with it. "I'll talk to him. Get someone to walk him to the house if you can. I'd rather not spend too much time at the edge of our territory until we know what Karl is planning." Maybe the man would be on their side.

Calder would take every and any help at the moment.

He hung up and looked at Kari. "You know what's happening?"

"Someone wants to talk to you?"

"The weasel alpha. I'm not sure why he's here, but he's doing things the right way. He asked to see Thomas. Thomas can't talk to him right now, though. He wants me to do it." Calder hesitated. "Do you want to come with me?" He realized how heavy this question and choice where. He wouldn't push Kari either way, even though he thought that Kari should try to talk to his brother.

Milton was new. He was only twenty, and as far as Calder had been able to find, he was trying to do the right thing and correct the mistakes his father and the former beta had made. Only the future would tell if he was a better alpha than them, although Calder doubted it would be hard.

Kari bit his lower lip. "Do you *want* me to come with you?"

"I always want you to come with me. But I know how you feel about the weasel gang. I know you've never talked to your brother and how much you hate his father." Calder was careful not to say that the old alpha was Kari's father. Biologically, he was, but he knew Kari didn't consider him anything more than a sperm donor.

"I don't know. I want to talk to him, but how am I supposed to be sure he's not like his father?"

"Even if he is, you don't have to go with him. You're a part of the cete now, and I won't let anyone take you away from us. Your place is here, with me, unless *you* decide otherwise. But I won't deny that having another ally in the forest would be a good thing, especially now. It's up to you, though."

Kari leaned against Calder. "I want to say yes."

"Then do it. Does he know who you are?"

"I don't think so. I told you, I've never talked to him, and I don't think his father even knew my dad was pregnant when he ran away."

"Then you don't have to tell him who you are. Come with me and meet him. Talk to him. If you feel comfortable enough with him that you want to admit you're brothers, then do so, but otherwise, you don't owe him anything. You don't owe anyone anything."

"I'll come," Kari said with a nod. "But thank you for giving me the option to say no."

Calder kissed the top of his head. "Always. I know it's going to take you a while to believe me, but I have no intention of controlling you in any way. I want you to be happy, and only you know how to make that happen." But hopefully, Calder would find out how to do it, too.

He wanted nothing more in life than to make Kari happy.

Kari went to find his dad before he and Calder left to talk to Milton. Julian had suggested Kari reach out a few times after Milton had stepped up as the alpha, but Kari hadn't. He'd been perfectly fine with only his dad in his life, and he was terrified at the thought that Milton could be like their father. Nothing he found out about him made him think he was, but that fear wasn't rational.

Kari wasn't surprised to find his dad and Kaspar together. Kaspar hadn't needed to put his foot down to have his alpha help the cete since he was a bear shifter, so both of them had stayed out of the conversation. Kari had noticed his father watching him while he spoke to the carriers, but they hadn't had the occasion to talk about it yet. He wanted to do that now, but he and Calder needed to go. Still, he wanted his dad to know what was happening.

Julian got up from the couch when he noticed Kari. He smiled and opened his arms.

Kari rushed into them. He should probably feel bad

because he wasn't a child anymore, but he missed his father.

"That was a nice speech," Kari's dad told him.

"I wanted to help the cete as much as they're helping you."

"I'm proud of you."

Kari nodded and stepped away from his father. "I have to go. The weasel alpha is here to see Calder. He wants to talk about the carriers we found in coyote and rodent territory."

Kari's father looked at him, his eyes narrow. "You mean your brother?"

Kari shook his head, but Milton *was* his brother, even though his first instinct was to deny that because he was afraid to remind his father how he'd been brought into his world.

Julian's expression softened. "We already talked about this. I want you to have a relationship with your brother. You both deserve it."

"I know."

"Do you? I know you're afraid of reminding me of what happened. It's not something I'm happy to think about, and I didn't deserve to go through that, but I did, and it brought me you. That's the one thing I'll never regret. You're my son, and I love you, and I think you and your brother deserve to have a relationship. You can't help who your father is or how you were brought into this world. I won't punish you or Milton because of something he had no control over. If Milton is a good man, then I want both of you to have this."

He reached for Kari again, and Kari took his hand. His father squeezed and kissed Kari's forehead "You've helped me create a new life. You took me away from the cabin and showed me I could have more. You've been helping so many people in the forest, even though they don't know it. It's time for you to stop focusing only on others and think about your own life. You're in love and building a family. I think that family should include Milton."

Kari wanted it to. He'd never had a brother. He'd only ever had his dad, and Julian was right. Their lives were changing, and they weren't alone anymore. Kari should probably start to act like it, no matter how hard it was. This was a new opportunity for both him and his dad, and they needed to take full advantage of it. "I'll meet with him. I won't tell him who I am in the beginning because I want to talk to him and see what kind of man he is."

"I thought everything you found out about him pointed to the fact that he's a good guy."

"It does. He's been trying hard to fix things with the gang. He has a lot of things to work on, and he doesn't have a lot of experience, but he's trying. I mean, he's here for the carriers. I think he cares about them and is horrified that his father and the beta sold weasel shifters, but the way he's going to go about this will tell me a lot about him."

If Milton insisted that the weasels go home, then Kari would have to put his foot down and tell him to fuck off. If he agreed to what Gallagher and Abbott wanted, then Kari would be more inclined to tell him they were related.

"You'll do the right thing. You always do."

Kari didn't know if he deserved his father's unrelenting faith, but he was glad for it. Between his dad and Calder, Kari was starting to believe he could have a normal life, and that he wouldn't have to watch from afar anymore.

He left Julian and Kaspar behind. Calder was waiting for him in the entrance, and he smiled when he saw him. "All done?" he asked.

"All done," Kari confirmed.

"You told him about the weasel alpha?"

Kari opened the door and stepped out. The sooner they did this, the sooner he could see if Milton really was a good man and if they could be brothers. "I did. He's been telling me to try to talk to him for the past few years, since Milton became the alpha, but I haven't yet."

"You weren't sure you could trust him."

Kari loved that Calder understood him without him having to explain himself. It was probably obvious, but no one else but Kari's father would have realized it. Now Calder did, too, and that meant he could read Kari and that he understood him more than most people. Kari had let him get close, and he hoped he wouldn't regret it.

Kari waited until they were in the car — Calder had driven to the house, the alphas following him in their own vehicles — to explain. "I don't want you to tell Milton we're brothers."

Calder didn't even bat a lash. "I won't. That's yours to explain."

Kari shouldn't have worried about it. "Thank you. I want to be sure he's the kind of man I think he is before I tell him. I don't know if he'll want to meet my dad, or if he's going to try to convince us to go back to the gang, and I don't want him to have more leverage against me."

"I already told you, you and your father aren't going anywhere unless you want to. The cete is your home now. I know it's probably hard to get used to, especially with your dad living at the Bishop house with all the other carriers instead of in his own house, but once this is over and we're sure you guys are safe, you can have your pick of houses in cete territory." Calder pause. "Or in sleuth territory, I'm pretty sure."

Kari couldn't help but smile. "You noticed that, didn't you?"

"I think pretty much everyone in the house noticed that. You're not angry?"

Kari blinked. "About my father possibly having a boyfriend? Why should I be angry?"

Calder shrugged. "You've had your father to yourself all your life. It wouldn't have been surprising if you'd been possessive of him."

Kari understood where Calder was coming from, but that wasn't him. "I'm happy he has this chance for a new life. He deserves to be happy, and if Kaspar is part of that happiness, I don't have anything to say about it."

"But you'll kick Kaspar's ass if he hurts your dad."

Kari wanted to say yes, and his first instinct *would* be to kick Kaspar's ass like Calder had said, but it wasn't his business. "My dad is an adult. He can defend himself, and he can stand up for himself. I'm not going to stick my nose into his relationship with Kaspar. I hope Kaspar won't hurt him, but as far as I know, it's a possibility in all relationships. No one is perfect, not even my dad."

"I know it's probably not my place, but I'm proud of you."

Kari looked away. What was it with people telling him they were proud of him today? He didn't understand it, and he didn't want to talk about it. He was glad when Calder parked in front of Thomas' house and he could rush out as fast as he could. He ignored Calder's chuckle and waited for him on top of the porch, unwilling to go inside on his own if he was about to stumble onto Milton.

The door opened just as Calder got there. Thomas waved them in. "Milton is here. I kicked everyone else out because I'm too curious about this. It's not like the phone calls were having a lot of luck anyway, not until Kari did what he did at the Bishop house, and they weren't necessary once that happened."

Kari wasn't sorry. Actually, it was the opposite. He was satisfied and smug that the carriers were standing up for themselves and the cete. He grinned at Thomas, who smiled back. "It was the right thing to do," Kari said.

"I don't know about that, but I'm glad you did. Good job, Kari." He gestured toward his office. "He's waiting for us. I didn't tell him about you, of course, and I haven't asked him exactly what he's doing here yet. I thought you'd want to be here for that."

"I do."

"Let's go, then. The sooner this is over, the sooner we can go back to the preparations against the coyotes."

Calder could see the resemblance. Milton's hair was longer than Kari's, but it was the same color, and it curled the same way. Their eyes, too, were the same—a beautiful hazel that looked dark with emotions. Milton didn't know who Kari was, but this was a big step for him anyway. He'd taken over the gang from a horrible man, and he was making amends for something he hadn't had a hand in. He had no way to know how the other alphas in the forest would react to him, and he was understandably worried.

Calder hoped for Kari and Milton's sake that Milton was a good man and that they'd eventually be a family. Calder would be more than happy to welcome Milton in his life. He didn't have a family, not a blood one, and even though blood didn't matter, he wanted Kari to have that. He'd already had so much taken away from him. He deserved all he could have, and Calder wanted to give him the moon.

Since that wouldn't be possible, he'd settle for a brother.

Milton rose from the chair he'd been sitting in when they walked in, but Thomas gestured at him to sit back down. "We have no need for ceremony here. You might be young, but you're an alpha, just like me."

Milton still looked nervous, but Thomas had a way about him that put people at ease. Milton smiled. "It's not ceremony. It's basic respect."

Thomas' smile widened. "If things continue this way, I think I'm going to like you."

"Good. I need allies." Milton set back into the chair. "Taking my father's beta's place hasn't been easy." His gaze strayed to Calder and Kari. He didn't ask who they were, but he had to wonder.

"This is Calder. He's the badger council member," Thomas said. "And his boyfriend, Kari. Kari is a weasel shifter."

Milton blinked, but to Calder's surprise, he didn't ask why a weasel shifter lived with a badger cete.

"Now that everyone knows who everyone is, why don't you tell us why you're here?" Thomas asked.

To Calder's surprise, Kari sat in the chair next to Milton. Kari usually tended to stay on the outside of meetings, hovering close to the walls, and Calder had expected him to do the same today. The situation had to be even more stressful for him than the other meetings had been, yet there he was, forging ahead and putting himself in the spotlight.

Milton linked his fingers together in his lap. "As I'm sure you know, my father died about ten years ago. I was ten at the time, too young to take his place. His beta stepped up and became the honorary alpha. It was only supposed to be until I was eighteen, of course, and my mother made sure I learned everything I needed to know to lead the gang. I never knew what my father and his beta did, not until I became the alpha."

"I doubt your beta stepped down willingly, even though he was only an honorary alpha," Thomas said.

"You're right. He didn't. But he underestimated how much tradition means. Most of the gang members expected me to take my father's place, and when the beta started creating problems for me when I turned eighteen, they made it known." Milton swallowed. "They came to talk to me, and they told me what had been going on ever since I was a child."

"And that would be?"

"I never loved my father very much. He was a hard man, and he treated my mother and me coldly. I don't know if he ever loved us, and I'm not going to speculate. I was kept away from him when I was a child, but I can't say I was entirely surprised when I found out he was an abuser and a human trafficker. I hate what he did and what his beta continued to do when he died. I want to fix things, but I'm not sure where to start. I found out from the beta that he and my father sold at least two weasel shifters." His gaze moved to Kari.

Kari's eyes widened, and he shook his head. "I'm not one of them. Trust me. I wouldn't have gone willingly if I had been. I didn't grow up with the gang."

Milton frowned, but thankfully, Thomas stepped in again before he could start asking questions Kari might not be ready to answer. "And you're here to see the weasel shifters?"

"I am. I know they were brought here, and I know they might not want to talk to me, which is fine. I just wanted to make sure they were okay, and to apologize for what was done to them. I realize that an apology is going to be nowhere close to good enough, but it's all I can offer them for now. And of course, they're welcome to come back to the gang if they want to."

"Will you demand they do? They're carriers, and you're their alpha. They're precious."

Milton jerked back. "They're as precious as any human being is. Their ability, what their bodies can do, doesn't matter, not to me. My mother raised me to see all human beings as equal. But I can't deny my life is easier than theirs. I want to do everything I can to help them heal. If they want to come back to the gang, they're welcome to, of course. I can guarantee no one in the gang will try to hurt them, not again. But I won't force them to come back if they don't want to. I realize they probably associate bad memories with the gang and the territory. If you don't mind keeping them here, I won't push for them to leave."

"You just want to check in on them?" Kari asked.

Milton nodded. "I do. I have no authority over them. I don't expect anything from them. But I want them to know that if they need a place to be, they can come to the gang. It was their home once, and it can be again, or at least, I hope so. I won't lie and say things are perfect, but I'm working toward making the gang a safer and better place for everyone who lives there. I'm not like my father. I still don't know every-thing he did, but I'm going to find out, and I'll do what I can to make sure his victims are compensated."

Words could be deceiving, and Milton might be lying, but Calder didn't think so. The man was young, and he'd only been an alpha for a year or so. He was eager to do things, and to do them the right way. He wanted to heal the wounds his father and the beta had inflicted on the gang and on the carri-ers who'd called it home. He didn't seem to have learned yet to control his tone and his expression, to hide what he was thinking and feeling, and Calder thought he was telling the truth.

That might not be enough for Kari to decide he wanted to tell Milton they were brothers, but as far as Calder was con-cerned, he didn't think Milton was a danger to Gallagher and Abbott. If the two shifters agreed to meet with him, Calder wouldn't try to stop it.

Thomas nodded. "I'll reach out to them and ask them what they want to do. I can't promise anything, of course, but I'll make sure to contact you if they agree to talk to you. I won't force them, though."

"I don't want you to. Like I said, I don't expect anything from them. I just wanted to make sure they were okay. I can only imagine what they went through, and how traumatized they are. I hate myself for not doing more and sooner."

"You've only been the alpha for a year, if even that. You couldn't have done anything. You were only ten when your father died. I understand feeling responsible, but you shouldn't hang on to that, not when it's obvious you weren't. You're doing the right thing by reaching out to them and giving them a choice. I think you'll be a good alpha."

Milton's cheeks pinked. "Thank you. That means a lot to me. I had no one but my mother to teach me how to behave and how to do the right thing. It's a bit of a shot in the dark, but I wasn't going to let the beta continue to hurt the gang, not when I could stop him."

Thomas looked at Kari. He arched a brow, silently asking him what he wanted to do. Calder had seen that expression enough times to be able to read Thomas.

Kari cleared his throat. "You know what your father did."

"I know he trafficked carriers. He sold them to people who abused them."

"He also abused them himself."

"You talk about that as if you have information I don't."

"That's because I do. Your father was an abuser. He was a rapist."

Milton jerked back. "I knew he was cruel, but—"

"But you didn't know about that? You didn't suspect?"

"I was only ten when he died. I had no idea what he did. My mother told me a lot, but not everything." He hesitated. "A rapist?"

"Yes. He raped my father. My dad was only seventeen, and when he realized he was pregnant, he ran away. He lived in the forest ever since and had me on his own."

Milton's eyes widened. "You mean—"

"I mean we're brothers."

CHAPTER TWELVE

Kari held his breath after said the words. He didn't know how Milton would react to the news that they were brothers. He couldn't have expected it when he'd requested to meet Thomas. No one would have. He had to be shocked, and there was no way for Kari to tell which way his reaction would go.

Kari could imagine it, though. Milton was probably horrified at what his father had done. It seemed he was the kind of man who would be, and Kari was glad. He wouldn't have told Milton the truth otherwise.

It had taken Kari years to wrap his mind around the fact that his father had been raped and that he was a result of that traumatic experience. Milton might not want to get to know Kari because he'd always be a reminder of what his father had done. Kari would understand that. He thought he'd done the right thing by telling Milton who they were to each other and how it had happened, but he might have been wrong.

Nothing would change if Milton hated him. Kari would be sorry he didn't have a shot at having a relationship with his brother, but he'd live without it. He had until now.

Milton swallowed loudly. "My brother?" he asked with a croak.

"Half-brother, if you want to be precise. But yes. We have the same father."

Milton narrowed his eyes. "You older than me."

Kari wasn't sure where he was going with that. "I am. I'm twenty-five."

Milton slowly nodded. "That means you should be in my place."

Kari blinked. "I'm sorry?"

"You should be the alpha. You could have taken over years ago."

Kari jerked back. He'd never thought about that. He didn't *want* to think about it.

Thomas cleared his throat. "Calder and I are going to go to the kitchen to get coffee and leave you two to talk. If that's okay with both of you, of course."

Kari knew Calder would stay if he asked, but this was something he felt he needed to do on his own. Milton wouldn't attack him. Even if he did, Kari was more than able to defend himself. He could kick Milton's ass and not break a sweat.

But that was physical. Kari didn't know what was about to happen, and it might be hard for him emotionally. It probably would be, even if Milton decided they were family, but Kari doubted it would be that easy. Calder wouldn't be far, though, and Kari could go straight to him as soon as the conversation with Milton was over. Calder would take him home, and they'd snuggle into bed and talk—or not talk, if Kari didn't feel like it.

He looked at Calder and nodded, silently telling him he'd be okay. Calder squeezed Kari's shoulder on his way out, his just as silent answer that he'd be there for him if he needed him. Kari already knew that, but it was nice to have a reminder. It was too easy for him to forget that he could rely on someone other than his dad now. He still wasn't used to it, and it would take him a while to get to that point.

Milton and Kari waited until the door closed behind Calder and Thomas to look at each other again. Kari wasn't sure how to answer Milton's accusation. He licked his lips. "I don't want to be an alpha."

Milton snorted. "You're the eldest son. You don't have a choice."

"I do. I'm a carrier, and I'm pregnant. You can understand the gang wouldn't be pleased if I tried to take your place."

Milton's eyes widened, and his gaze fell to Kari's lap. Kari touched his stomach, but he wasn't showing yet, so there was nothing to see.

"The council member is the other father?" Milton asked.

"He is."

Milton hesitated. "But you weren't sold to him, right? He didn't buy you."

This wasn't what Kari had expected, although he should probably have seen it coming. "I chose him. Like I told you, my father ran away as soon as he realized he was pregnant with your father's child. He lived in the forest until a few weeks ago, right along with me. It was a good life, but it was lonely, and I'm glad the cete welcomed him. He won't have to work as hard as he did since I was born to make it. He doesn't have to worry about food or shelter anymore."

Milton raked a hand through his hair. "I'm sorry. If I'd known—"

"You wouldn't have been able to do anything. I don't think anyone knew about my father's pregnancy. He made sure not to tell anyone because he knew what your father would do to him if he found out. I was lucky he ran away, because your father would have probably sold me once he realized I was a carrier."

"I'm starting to see that he was much worse than I thought. I'm sorry this happened to you and your father, Kari. I don't know how to make things up to you."

Kari had thought about it for years. He'd alternated between feeling petty and wanting his father to be compensated for what had happened to him. He was over that now, though. "I don't want you to make things up to me, and I don't think my father does, either. We had a hard life, but we were happy. We were safe, even though we had to hide to make sure of that. He moved out of the cabin we had at the edge of the territories. He lives with the other carriers now."

"Do you think he'll want to come back to the gang?"

"I have no idea. I don't even know if he'll want to talk to you, although he encouraged me to tell you we're related. But he's finally making friends, and he has a home that's more comfortable than anything he's had for the past twenty-five years. There's also the fact that I live in cete territory, and I'm not going anywhere. I don't know if he'll want to be close to my baby and me, or if he'll want to go back to the cabin."

"Of course. I understand. But would you let him know he's welcome in gang territory? He can go back to his cabin if that's what he wants, and I'll make sure nothing happens to it."

"I'll talk to him. I'd be more comfortable if he stayed here until this mess is over, though. I'm sure you know what's going on with Karl and the other alphas, and even though I think I can trust you, I'd rather have my father close."

"I know I didn't tell this to Alpha Steele, but I want both of you to know the gang is behind you. We'll support you any way we can against the coyotes and anyone else who attacks you. I would have told him that even if I hadn't found out about you, but I didn't have the time. You shocked me."

Kari chuckled. "I think I shocked myself. I didn't know I was going to tell you about it when I walked into this meeting. I've been watching you from afar, and I know you've been trying to fix the things your father and his beta broke, but I don't know you. I hope you're one of the good guys, and it looks like you are, but I'm sure you understand why trusting people is hard for me. I lived with my father for twenty-five years, and I didn't have anyone else. We couldn't afford to put ourselves in danger that way. But the cete welcomed us, and I'm starting a family with one of its members. It made me think that maybe you and I could talk and maybe become the brothers we are through blood."

"I want to say yes."

"But looking at me reminds you of what your father did." Kari had expected it, so it shouldn't hurt as much as it did.

Milton shook his head. "You had nothing to do with that. It wasn't your fault, and I won't hold it against you. I already knew my father wasn't a good man. I'm surprised at how bad he was, but I won't ignore it, and like I said, I won't hold you responsible for it. You had no choice in what happened, and neither did your father."

"What's the problem, then?"

Milton sighed. "I might not have lived isolated in the woods, but it doesn't mean my life was good. I had my mother, and while everyone else treated me with respect since I'm my father's son, his beta made sure my life was hell. He never intended to give over his power to me, and I had to confront him and kill him. I know it was the right thing to do, but I'm afraid it makes me more similar to our father than I wish to be. I don't want you to be afraid of me or to think badly of me. And I'm not sure where to start when it comes to being a brother or even a friend."

Milton was as frightened of this as Kari was. Kari hadn't thought about that, but it made sense, and he found himself reaching for Milton. "I don't think you're like our father. You might have killed his beta, but you did it for the right reason, and you're still behaving the right way. You want carriers to be free and safe. You're ready to help the cete to make that happen. That's all I'm asking for right now. Being brothers isn't going to come naturally to us, and it's not going to be easy, but I'm stubborn. If I want something, I get it, and that includes having a relationship with you."

Milton smiled. "Good. I think that as long as we're honest

with each other, this can work."

Kari hoped it would. He wanted a family, even though he'd never allowed himself to think about it.

It looked like he might be about to get it.

"Who do we have on our side now that the carriers have stood their ground?" Calder asked. He needed to distract himself from what was happening in Thomas' office.

He wanted to barge in and make sure Milton wasn't hurting Kari, either physically or mentally, or emotionally. He knew Kari would kick Milton's ass if he looked at him the wrong way, but his feelings were different. It would only take a few words to hurt him, and Calder didn't want that to happen.

Thomas checked his phone. "The bobcats, the fox, the opossum, the raccoons, and of course, the deer."

"The bats?"

Thomas shook his head. "They can't afford to, or at least that's what their alpha said. I told him it was okay and that we weren't expecting anyone to help, even though we were grateful for anyone who could stand by us."

Calder was irritated, since the bat alpha had trusted Thomas with his carrier, but he understood where the man was coming from. Bat territory was small, and the colony didn't have a lot of members. They were somewhat isolated, and they'd always been, which was one of the reasons Calder had been surprised when Ralph had brought Calum to the Bishop house. As long as the bats were on the right side and wouldn't fight *against* Thomas and the others, things would be okay. Neither Calder nor Thomas would hold the bats' absence against Ralph and his colony. They were still trusting the cete with Calum, and that was an indication they wanted the same thing.

"We have enough allies as it is anyway," Thomas pointed out.

"Only because Kari stuck his nose into this."

Thomas laughed. "You're right. We probably wouldn't be where we are now if it weren't for him. You're going to have your hands full with him, but I think you're up for the task. You fit well together."

Calder hesitated. He and Kari hadn't talked about who to tell Kari was a carrier and pregnant, so Calder had kept it to himself. He wanted to tell Thomas about it, though. Thomas was his best friend, and Kari would no doubt understand that Calder needed someone to talk to. Calder hoped Kari wouldn't get angry, and he didn't think he would, but Kari was always hard to read. Like Thomas had said, he was a handful, and Calder was still learning him and the way he thought.

"Being a carrier runs in families," he began.

Thomas blinked. "I already know that. I have two carrier sons, remember?"

Calder rubbed the back of his head. "I know. I'm trying to tell you something, so shut up and let me work myself up to it."

Thomas raised his hands. "Go ahead."

"There's something you need to know about Kari. He's a carrier, like his father."

Thomas cocked his head. "I can't say I expected that, but knowing him, I'm not surprised he kept it a secret. He's very keen on making sure everyone knows he's strong enough to be on the council team."

"That's not the only thing."

"Oh?"

"He's pregnant. We weren't planning on it, but it happened, and we're keeping the baby."

Thomas' smile widened. "Again, it's not something I

expected to hear, but I'm happy for you. Or shouldn't I be? You never really talked about having children."

Calder shook his head. "It's fine. We're still working things out because neither of us expected this to happen, but I *am* happy, and I think Kari is, too. Of course, all the stuff happening in the forest right now isn't making things easy on us, but once Karl has been dealt with, I think things will slow down." Or at least, he hoped so.

"Well, you know that whatever you need, you can come to me. I'm happy you found someone to share your life with, and I think that Kari will be good for you. And you'll be good for him, I suspect."

Calder prayed his friend was right. Most days, he still had no idea where he stood with Kari, even though they were officially a couple.

They heard the office door open, and Calder's back went ramrod straight. He didn't know what to expect when Kari stepped into the kitchen, but he was relieved to see the smile on his boyfriend's lips. Milton was right behind, and while they both looked a bit shocked, Calder thought things had gone well.

"Everything okay?" Thomas asked.

Milton nodded. "Perfect, Alpha Steele."

"Call me Thomas. Most alphas in the forest are on a first-name basis with each other. Besides, you're family now."

Milton straightened. "That's right. We are." It wasn't by blood, but no one in the room cared about that. Milton certainly didn't seem to.

"I'm happy everything went well," Thomas said.

"About that. I know the coyotes have been creating problems. How much support do you need from the gang?"

Thomas hesitated. The gang was still a bit of a mess from the decades of bad guidance. Milton probably had more than enough on his plate without having to add a fight with the coyotes on it. "We have six alphas on our side, seven with you. It should be enough to face the coyotes, especially since I doubt Karl expects it. I don't want to ask too much from the gang, but I realize you probably want everyone to know you're supporting us."

"You're right. I would have done this even if I hadn't found out Kari is my brother, but as things are, I want the weasels and the badgers to be close. I know you and the bears have an understanding and that you're pretty much a huge family. The gang might be a mess after what my father and his beta did, but I won't back down. I want to help."

Knowing that Thomas and Milton needed to talk, Calder took Kari's hand and gently pulled him out of the kitchen to give the two men the space they needed for their discussion. Kari and Calder had nothing to do with it, since neither of them was an alpha, and they didn't make the kind of decisions alphas had to deal with. They didn't go far, stopping in the hallway, and Calder crowded Kari against the wall, cupping his face with both hands. "How are you feeling?"

Kari smiled up at Calder. "How do you mean? Mentally, or physically?"

"Both. The meeting went well, but I know it couldn't have been easy for you."

"You're right. It wasn't. Facing what happened to my father again was hard, especially since I didn't know how Milton would react to it, but everything went well. He agreed he wants to try to have a relationship with me. We both do."

"That's good." Calder had expected it, but he was relieved. It was obvious Kari was happy, and Kari deserved that and so much more.

"It is. I know the gang probably won't be able to help much against Karl, but you said six alphas agreed to help?"

"They did, thanks to you. We should have enough people even without the weasels, although I'm sure Milton will send at least a few guards. He wants to be part of this, and Thomas won't deny him that."

"Good. Milton is trying hard to do the right thing for the gang, but he's alone. I don't even think he has a beta yet. He has no idea how to deal with most of this stuff, and the only reason he's been doing the right thing is that he's a good man. He'll need help. Do you think Thomas would want to do that?"

"I know he will. It will be like between the badgers and the bears. We became a family when Levi and Dimitri got married, and the same will happen between the badgers and the weasels."

Kari's smile turned into a smirk. "Is that a sneaky way of you asking me to marry you?"

Calder's brain froze. He couldn't think beyond the word *marry*. He opened his mouth, then closed it again.

Kari chuckled. "I was teasing you."

Calder's brain kicked back into gear. "Is that something you might want one day?"

Kari blinked. "Maybe? I never thought about getting married or having kids. It seemed too outlandish, like it wasn't something I could have."

"But now you can."

"One day, sure. With everything that's already happening, I can't even begin to think about marriage. Besides, we don't know each other. What if you decide you don't want to be with me once the baby is born?"

Calder doubted that would happen, but he understood why Kari was hesitant. "I'll ask you in a few years, then."

He knew he and Kari would still be together by then. He wasn't going anywhere, and he didn't think Kari was, either. They were in this together, for the long run. Putting a ring on Kari's finger would be nice, but Calder could live without it, as long as he had Kari — and he did.

Kari wasn't sure going home was a good idea, even though they were almost a hundred percent sure that Karl wouldn't attack tonight. Thomas had sent a few of his guards into coyote territory to check in on Karl and what he was up to, and they hadn't been surprised to find the territory was a mess. Karl was trying to gather as many fighters as he could, but they weren't eager to work for him. He hadn't treated them right, and now they didn't want to fight, especially not *this* fight. He could order them to do his bidding, and he could yell at them, but even though they'd probably be with him when he attacked the cete, it didn't mean they were eager to participate.

Things could still go wrong, but Kari was positive the cete would make it out of this easily.

They might not have if Kari hadn't managed to talk the carriers into resisting being taken away. Almost all the alphas who had a carrier with the cete, except of course the rodents since they were without an alpha for now, and the porcupines, who were still getting used to having a new alpha, were backing the cete.

Thomas had placed guards along the edge of the territory so they'd know right away if Karl and his men approached. From what Kari knew about the man, he wouldn't want to drag things out for too long. The only reason he wasn't there right now, trying to get back the men he considered as his property, was that he was a terrible alpha, and everyone in his band knew it. They didn't want to lose their lives because of something like this, and Kari didn't blame them.

"You're thinking hard tonight," Calder said.

Kari scowled at him, but he made sure to keep it playful. He didn't want Calder to think he was angry with him. "Are you saying I don't usually think hard?"

Calder chuckled and wrapped his arm around Kari's shoulders. "Of course not. You always think, which is one of the things that is so interesting about you. One would think you were the kind of guy who acts first and thinks later, but that's not the case. Everything you do, you thought about time and time again. You're convinced of it. I might not always approve, but I know it's never a gut reaction."

He was right. Even when Kari had killed Gruber, he'd thought about it. He'd weighed the pros and cons, and he'd decided he didn't mind killing the man if it meant the forest would be safer.

Even though he was afraid Karl would surprise all of them and attack during the night, Kari was relieved when he was finally able to slip into bed. He wasn't very far along in his pregnancy, but it was still kicking his ass. He felt exhausted most of the time, and while his father had reassured him that it was because his body was creating a human being, it didn't help him feel better about it. Kari was used to being entirely in control of himself, and this wasn't something he could control. He could do nothing but wait and see what happened, and while he might not have minded in a normal situation, this was anything but.

He couldn't stop worrying as he settled into bed. If he was honest with himself, it wasn't the fight that bothered him, but the possibility that Calder would be in the middle of it.

Calder wasn't a fighter, not in the physical sense of the term. He fought for the cete and the other shifters in the forest, but that was all talking and arguing. It was his job as a council member. But for the first time, he'd be in a physical fight, and Kari didn't know how to reassure himself that everything would be okay. He'd just found Calder, and maybe that made him selfish, but he didn't want to lose him.

Calder rubbed a hand down Kari's naked side as he stretched out next to him in the bed. "You're worried," he said.

Kari snorted softly. "Aren't you?"

"I'm crazy worried. But I know you'll do everything you can to stay safe, and I have to admit that knowing you'll be away from the fight itself is a relief."

Kari didn't like it, but it was true he'd be more useful as a sniper, at least if Karl attacked during the day. There wasn't enough light for him to do that during the night, although Thomas had said he was working on something to help in that case. "I might not be, if he waits for darkness to attack."

Calder grimaced. "You're right. I would never forbid you to do anything, but I can't deny I hate the thought of you fighting. And before you say it, it has nothing to do with you being a carrier, even though it *does* have to do with the baby. I know you don't like to think about this, but the pregnancy is impacting your abilities and your body. You get tired more easily, and it's perfectly normal."

He *was* worried, wasn't he? He didn't want to offend Kari, and while Kari was grateful, he also knew it was his fault. He'd been touchy about being considered weak and unable to do what others did from the beginning, and now Calder walked on eggshells around those topics.

Kari wanted to fight. They both knew it, and it would be useless to deny it. He wanted to show everyone that being a carrier didn't mean he couldn't fight, and he wanted to contribute, to help.

But he'd already done that. He'd killed Gruber. He'd convinced the carriers to stand up to their alphas. He'd given the cete a better chance of winning against Karl, and he could admit that maybe taking a step back wouldn't be a bad idea. No one would blame him, especially not if they knew he was pregnant. Thomas did now, but even if Kari hadn't been carrying Calder's child, he wouldn't have insisted on Kari fighting — or not fighting. He wasn't that kind of man.

Kari sighed. "How about this? We can compromise. You don't fight, and I don't, either."

Calder blinked. "Are you saying you want to stick with me during the fight instead of being out there kicking ass?"

"I don't want to, no. But I think it's the best thing I can do. If I fight with the others, you'll be worried about me, and I'll be worried about you. I've never been in this situation before, but I want to keep my eyes on you during the fight and make sure nothing happens to you."

"I won't be fighting. I usually don't."

"But you're a council member. That means that taking you out would create an imbalance within the council, and I doubt Karl would back down from that opportunity. I'm not saying he'll come looking for you actively, but if he stumbled onto you, he wouldn't miss his chance to hurt you."

"You want to protect me."

"Just like you want to protect me."

Calder tugged Kari closer, and they wrapped around each other. He kissed Kari's hair, and Kari allowed himself to snuggle against him. This wasn't something he would have done with anyone else because he knew it showed vulnerability. But with Calder, he didn't mind. Calder would never use this against him.

"I don't want you to regret staying back," Calder murmured.

Kari understood where he was coming from. "I don't think I will. The cete has a lot of allies. I made sure of it. They won't be fighting this on their own, and no matter how hard Karl is trying, he won't gather a lot of fighters. He's not seen well in the forest, and most of the alphas are on Thomas' side. Besides, I already helped the cete. I know I did. I don't have to put myself, the baby, and you in danger just because I feel it's my duty."

Calder stroked a hand down Kari's cheek. "You surprise

me every day."

Kari wasn't sure how to answer that. "I didn't do anything."

"A few months ago, hell, a few *weeks* ago, you would have demanded to be in the middle of things. You would have taken it as a personal offense if someone had told you to take a step back. And now, here you are, acknowledging that it might be better for you not to be part of the fight."

He was right. Kari would have thought he was weak if he decided not to fight a few months ago. He would have berated himself for that, but he didn't now. He didn't just have himself to protect anymore. He had to think of Calder and the baby, and while he hadn't realized it before, that was changing him.

"Thomas wants me to go to Bishop house so I'll be as protected as the carriers," Calder said.

"It wouldn't be a bad idea."

"Maybe not, but I'm not going, and it's not because I think I'm better than the carriers. I might need to be protected because of my status as a council member, but I want to show Karl and whatever fighters he manages to put together that I'm not afraid. I won't back down in front of them. What they're doing is wrong, and I want to testify in front of the other council members once this is over. The coyote council member is one of the worst, and she needs to be taken down. Maybe we'll be able to do that, thanks to what Karl is doing."

Kari wasn't convinced of that, but what did he know? He wasn't a council member He barely knew how the council worked. "I want to be by your side, wherever that is."

"I didn't expect anything different from you. We'll both stick to Thomas' house and keep an eye on the fight from there. That way you can do something if you feel you're needed."

And he wouldn't try to stop Kari if Kari thought he had to

fight. Maybe they were both changing and adapting to this relationship.

CHAPTER THIRTEEN

Kari hated this.

He was stuck in Thomas' house, safely away from the fight, and even though he'd agreed to it, he didn't have to like it.

He didn't.

He knew he'd done the right thing. Calder was there with him, and they were both safe. They could see what was happening from the living room windows, and Kari wasn't planning on moving away from them. He knew Calder wouldn't try to stop him if he needed to intervene, and that was a relief. He'd even been the one to suggest they stuck close to the windows.

He'd accepted Kari in a way Kari hadn't thought possible. It made the situation a bit easier to accept.

"Do you see anything?" Calder asked in a whisper.

They were both like little kids, crouching by the window with all the lights off because they didn't want Karl to realize someone was there. Hopefully, he and his coyotes wouldn't get to the house, but they couldn't dismiss that possibility. Karl wanted revenge, and he wanted to hit Thomas as hard as he could. Sneaking into his house, in the place where he lived with his wife and where his children had grown up, would be an achievement. Karl had to realize that the alpha's wife wasn't there, but that didn't mean he wouldn't try. He had nothing to lose.

"Not so far. You know it's early. The guards haven't even seen anyone around."

"Then why are we crouching in the dark? We could sit on the couch until we get the news that Karl is coming."

Kari rolled his eyes — glad Calder couldn't see him. "You're soft."

"Are you saying I'm fat?"

Kari barked out a laugh. "I'd never say anything like that, because you're not. I meant that you're not used to being uncomfortable. I suppose it goes with the council member thing."

"It's not a thing. It's a role. A duty. I do everything I can for the forest and the shifters inside it, and — "

Kari turned and kissed Calder's cheek. "I *know*. I never said you weren't doing a good job, or that your role isn't an important one. I know it is. Not everyone is a physical fighter, and that's okay. We should all do what we are best suited for, which is great because you'd be a mess if you had to fight."

"I should probably be offended, but I'm not. You're right."

Kari sighed and turned to look out the window again. "I know I am."

"You wish you were out there, don't you?"

"Of course I do. I've always been out there. It's hard to stay away."

"Do you wish you weren't pregnant?"

Calder's voice was quiet, and Kari knew he'd accept any answer he'd give. "Right now, yes, but only because I feel I should do more. I don't regret being with you or carrying your baby. I never will. But I'd feel better if I could do something concrete to help."

"You don't like being pregnant."

"Right now, I *hate* being pregnant."

Someone made a strangled sound behind them, and Kari turned to see a group of people standing in the living room door. Since it was dark, he didn't know who they were, but he was angry with himself for not having heard them. Calder was distracting, too much so.

Someone used the torch app on their phone to shine a light. Alex was there, along with Eddie, Dimitri, and Levi. Kari wasn't sure how Levi had convinced his husband to allow him to come, but he was proud to see he wasn't the only carrier here.

"Are you okay?" Levi asked. He sounded hesitant, and Kari wasn't sure why.

Kari rose from his crouch and stretched his back. He didn't know if it was a pregnancy thing, but he was always so fucking uncomfortable. "Of course I am."

Levi stepped forward. "I know we're not friends and that I live in sleuth territory, but you can come to me if you need anything."

Kari frowned. He was even more confused than before. "That's good to know."

"I meant about your pregnancy. I—how—are you okay?"

"I haven't seen the healer yet, but yeah, pretty much."

"Maybe you should see her. If you were . . . if you were raped, there are solutions that don't involve carrying the baby to term."

Kari blinked. "Raped? You think I was raped because I'm a carrier and pregnant?"

Levi rubbed the back of his neck. "I know it's terrible of me to assume, but with everything I've seen during the past few months, I don't want—"

He was *worried*. Kari was slightly offended that Levi thought he'd been raped only because he was a carrier, but he understood where Levi was coming from. Kari knew most people in the cete viewed him as unapproachable, and in the beginning, he'd wanted them to. He didn't know how to deal with people. He didn't know how to make friends. How was Levi supposed to know better if Kari had never allowed him to get close?

Calder sucked in a breath, but Kari shook his head and touched his arm to stop him. "Let me, please." Calder stayed still a moment, then nodded.

Kari turned back to Levi. "I understand why you thought I was raped, but I wasn't. Me being a carrier doesn't make me weak, just like *you* aren't weak."

"Rape has nothing to do with weakness."

"You're right. It doesn't. But you can stop worrying. I *am* pregnant, but I wasn't raped. Calder and I never intended to have a baby this soon in our relationship, but it happened, and we're both happy about it."

Kari couldn't see a lot with the lack of light in the room, but he was pretty sure he'd shocked at least a few people in the small group in front of him. Alex made a weird sound, halfway between a chuckle and sucking in a breath, and Levi almost dropped his phone.

"Calder is the other father?" Levi asked.

"He is. We haven't been screaming it from the rooftops yet because of everything that's been happening, but we're living together, and we're keeping the baby. You don't have to worry about me. I'm fine."

"That's good to know. I'm sorry I assumed and that I was so rude. I should have known better."

Kari shrugged. "It's okay. Like I said, I understand. I've seen enough abused and raped carriers to know you meant well."

Kari was grateful for the phone that rang at that moment. He thought Levi might have kept apologizing over and over again otherwise.

Alex answered, and after his short conversation mostly made up of swear words, he hung up. "They're almost here. I just got told that five or six trucks are headed our way. It won't take them long to get here. We all need to go where we're supposed to be."

Adrenaline kicked him. Kari had to resist the urge to follow them out of the room, but it was easier than he'd thought it would be. It was reassuring to think that Calder needed him, that he needed to stick close to his man to make sure nothing happened to him.

His family's safety was in his hands. Realizing that made him feel better about having to stay behind, and Kari promised himself he'd do anything to make sure Calder didn't get hurt.

He and Calder were starting a life together, and it wasn't something Kari had thought would ever be in the cards for him. He wouldn't allow anyone to take that away from him. He wouldn't raise his baby on his own, not when Calder should be by his side. That was his place. It was where he belonged.

And anyone who tried to hurt Calder would have to pass through Kari first.

This was it. Karl and his fighters were about to arrive, and the fighting would begin.

Calder had no idea how to deal with this. Like Kari had said earlier, he wasn't a fighter. He wasn't even sure he'd be able to protect himself if someone attacked him. It was more probable that he'd curl up into a small ball and yell for help. Kari, on the other hand, looked ready to kill someone if they only looked at him the wrong way. Calder couldn't see much because of the darkness, but Levi's quickly moving phone gave him a hint of how Kari felt.

"You'll be okay?" Alex asked.

Calder nodded, even though Alex probably couldn't see him. "We'll be fine. We went over this already, and we know what we need to do."

"Good. Don't put yourself in danger uselessly." Alex

paused. "Especially now that you're both going to be fathers. Seamus is further along than you are, Kari, but I can too easily understand how terrifying this moment is for you."

Seamus was at the Bishop house with the other carriers. He hadn't been happy about it, and he'd tried to protest, but he was seven or so months pregnant, and no one had been willing to put him in danger. Calder suspected he hadn't wanted to, either, but that he wished he could be with Alex. Calder understood that urge. He felt like if he looked away from Kari even one second, something might happen to him, and he wouldn't be able to do anything to help. It was a terrible feeling, and he was glad he didn't have to hide the way the carriers did.

They disbanded. Calder and Kari stayed in the living room and went to crouch by the window again. Calder peeked outside, but he couldn't see anything yet. That gave him too much time to think, unfortunately.

He couldn't believe Levi had thought Kari had been raped. The thought was enough to make Calder want to hurt someone, even though he understood why Levi had thought that. Not everyone in the cete knew about Calder's relationship with Kari, and Levi didn't live with them anymore. He'd been worried for Kari, and he'd tried to be a friend to him. Calder was grateful for that, but he was even more grateful that Kari had cleared the situation. He didn't want anyone else to think Kari had been hurt. He should have realized that would happen.

"You haven't been telling a lot of people were together," Kari said suddenly. He didn't turn to look at Calder, keeping his focus on the window.

"I told Thomas and Abel."

"Anyone else?"

"No." But they hadn't been hiding. Calder was pretty sure a lot of people in the cete knew about it, even though he hadn't told anyone but his two best friends.

"I hope I didn't overstep by telling Levi about us. I should have asked first."

Calder blinked. It took him a second to understand what Kari was saying, and he could have slapped himself for not realizing before. "You didn't. I want everyone to know. The only reason I haven't been more public about this is that we've had a lot of things to think about and focus on. I hate that our relationship started this way, but unfortunately, there's nothing we can do about it. Until Karl is dealt with, we'll have to focus on him and what he's doing." Even though Calder wanted nothing more than to forget about his job and everyone involved in it until the baby was born, and possibly for the next five years after that.

He wanted to focus on Kari. He knew better than anyone that Kari hadn't had this before. He'd never been in a relationship, and he deserved the world. Calder wanted to give it to him, but he kept being interrupted by assholes who thought they could buy and abuse people.

But it was almost over. No matter how things went tonight, it would be over with the fight. Calder hoped the cete and its allies would win, but he didn't want to think they wouldn't, just in case. Five or six trucks couldn't contain enough people to fight against everyone who had arrived in cete territory, so they had a good chance to make it through this alive.

He wanted to talk to Kari, but now wasn't the moment.

"I understand. I thought that was the case, but I didn't want to assume. I'm glad you don't want to hide our relationship, though."

Calder gave Kari's hand a quick squeeze. "Never. I'm not ashamed of being with you. I'm not ashamed of how we met, how we got together, or how you got pregnant. It might have not been on purpose, but that doesn't mean I'm not blissfully happy about the thought of building a family with you. And

I think we started the right way, at least after you got pregnant. We've been talking, which is what we needed."

"You're right. I know I'm not good at it, but I want to be. I want us to work."

Calder opened his mouth to answer, but headlights caught his gaze.

Karl had arrived.

Calder counted six trucks. They were big, and he couldn't help but notice how many silhouettes jumped off as they stopped. "There have to be at least fifty people here," he said quietly.

"We can deal with that. I know it looks scary because there are so many of them, but you know the cete's numbers. You know it's two against one. We can do this."

"I hope so." Calder didn't want to lose faith, but it was hard when faced with this.

For some reason, he wanted to be out there with Thomas and the others. He knew he'd be useless and that the cete needed him with the council, but he understood why Kari was so angry at being stuck inside the house now. It had to be even harder in Kari's case because he was so used to being in the thick of things.

Calder cleared his throat. "You can go out there if you want to."

Kari jerked. "What are you talking about?"

"I know you want to. I understand why, and you'd be an asset if you were fighting."

"We talked about it. We decided we'd both stay here."

"I know we did, but it was different. We weren't faced with this many people at the time. I didn't fully understand what it would be like." But now he did.

Kari grabbed Calder's hand again and squeezed so hard it hurt. "I'm not going anywhere, and neither are you. Got that? I don't know why you're talking about this right now, but you have to stop."

"All right. Sorry."

"I *do* want to be out there. I feel like it's my duty, and like I'm weak because I'm not. But I know that's not true. I know that this living room is the best place for me to be right now, and it is for you, too. Stop talking bullshit and focus on what's happening outside the windows. I have faith in the cete and our allies, but it doesn't mean they won't need us. We need to be ready if something happens."

Once again, Kari was right.

Calder squeezed his hand and dropped it, turning to focus on the windows like Kari had ordered. He could hear yelling already, and it was hard to resist the urge to go out there and do something.

Kari moved next to him, and Calder wasn't surprised to see a gun in his hands. He'd never seen Kari shoot, not from this point of view, but he knew how good Kari was. "How can you see anything?" he asked.

"I can't, not much. But Thomas told me about the spotlights he had put around the house. He'll turn them on if he feels the need to, and I want to be ready if it happens. It will give me a few seconds to take down as many coyotes as I can, and that will be hard enough because if they're in their human forms, it'll be next to impossible to tell if they're coyotes rather than badgers or bears."

"I think I'll shut up and let you work, then." There was nothing else Calder could do anyway.

Kari kissed Calder's cheek. "Thank you. But you have more than that to do. I'm going to be focused on the window, and that means I might not realize if someone enters the living room. You need to be alert. If you hear anything, let me know. You can't allow us to be surprised. It could be deadly for both of us."

Calder hadn't thought about it, but he was ready to do this.

It was the least he could do, and this way, he'd be doing something to protect the cete—and Kari.

Kari was focused on what was happening outside the window, but he couldn't ignore Calder's presence next to him. It was oddly reassuring, and while Kari knew better than to obsess over that right now, he knew he would do so later. He was so used to being alone in every situation, that every time he'd realized he wasn't, he was in awe.

The spotlights turned on.

Kari had been able to see parts of the fight happening in front of the house, but it was so much easier now. He was ready to take advantage of the light, and the coyotes weren't. They were all blinking and looking around, trying to understand what was happening, and Kari took down four of them before they realized someone was shooting at them. He didn't kill them, even though he wanted to. He knew Calder wouldn't say anything if he did, but Calder didn't like it when he took justice into his own hands, and since he could put the coyotes out of order without killing them, he was going to.

He wanted to be better, for Calder and their baby, and it started now.

Once the coyotes realized Kari was shooting them down, they moved. It was harder when they were fighting with badgers, bears, and the rest of their allies. Some of them had shifted, and Kari was able to see the coyote shifter clearly in those cases, but when they rolled around fighting each other, he couldn't shoot. The last thing he wanted was to hurt someone he shouldn't.

He turned his attention to Thomas. The alpha was in his human form, but Kari knew he'd be lethal in his badger form, too. Badgers were smaller than coyotes, but they were just as aggressive, and their size meant it was easier for them to move. They were faster, like the one jumping on the coyote to Thomas' right showed. The badger closed its jaw on the back of the coyote's neck and pulled. Kari was impressed, and not one bit surprised when the coyote crumbled to the ground.

Then he saw Karl. He was in his human form, which was the only reason Kari recognized him, and he was making a beeline for Thomas. He ducked between people, using them to cover himself, and Kari never had a good shot at him. Kari kept his focus on the man until he got to Thomas.

Kari couldn't hear what was said between the two men, but he had a good idea. Karl was no doubt yelling at Thomas that he'd taken the carriers he owned and that he wanted them back. The man might be an alpha, and he might be evil, but that didn't make him smart. He should have realized bringing only fifty coyotes with him wouldn't be enough. Kari could see their number was dwindling already. The badgers probably wouldn't even need him to continue shooting to win.

But he didn't move. He couldn't risk it.

"Shit," Calder muttered.

"What?" Kari asked without looking at his boyfriend.

"Thomas. I know he's a fighter, but I can't help but be worried about him. Can you shoot Karl from here?"

"I wish I could, but they're too close. I don't want to risk hurting Thomas."

"Dammit."

Kari might not be able to shoot at Karl, but he could shoot at other coyotes. He could help, even though he was stuck in the house.

He noticed three coyotes circling a bear, and decided it was time for him to act. It was easy to shoot down one of the coyotes because they were distracted. They'd already forgotten someone was shooting at them, the idiots.

The bear took care of the other two and looked Kari's way briefly. Kari gave him a small wave even though he wasn't sure the bear could see him. Everyone had been informed of Kari's presence in the house, so they knew not to be startled at the shooting. From what Kari could see, none of the coyotes had brought guns with them, and that was a good thing. It gave the cete an advantage the coyotes didn't have.

Not that they needed it. They were kicking coyote ass, and Kari was enjoying it.

He felt Calder move beside him, but he didn't turn to look at him, not until Calder's presence disappeared entirely. Kari was still keeping an eye on the fight between Thomas and Karl, just in case Thomas needed his help. The two men were both bloody, and Karl was holding one of his arms close to his chest, but Thomas was in pretty bad shape, too. He might get offended if he was rescued by a carrier, but Kari doubted he would, and even then, he wouldn't care. Better to have an alpha who was alive and well than a dead one.

Something soft hit Kari's cheek, and he had to turn around this time. His eyes widened when he realized what was happening behind him. He hadn't heard anything, but a coyote had entered the living room.

Calder *had* noticed it, though.

It looked like the coyote had been in his human form when he walked in because there were shreds of clothes all around the room. Kari recognized some of them as belonging to Calder, but the others had to be the coyote's.

They were fighting. The coyote was bigger than Calder, but he seemed to know as much as Calder about fighting — which was not much at all. Kari didn't know why Karl would bring someone who couldn't fight, but maybe he'd aimed for big numbers more than ability.

Kari wanted to help Calder. He hadn't had the time to teach Calder a few things he should know. He'd thought they'd be safe in the house, even though he'd told Calder to be careful. He was glad he had, but he wanted to do more.

He couldn't shoot. Calder and the coyote were close, circling each other for a few seconds before crashing together, becoming one big ball of fur and hissing sounds.

It was terrifying. Calder was smaller than the coyote almost by half, and even though Kari could see he wasn't defenseless, it wasn't enough. He was petrified at the thought of losing Calder, and he didn't know what to do.

He should be watching the fights outside and taking out more coyotes. He should help the cete.

But he could think of nothing other than Calder and what would happen if he lost this fight.

Calder's jaw clamped on the coyote's shoulder, and he pulled. The coyote screamed, the high-pitched sound going straight to Kari's spine, making it tingle with unease and fear. The coyote tried to catch Calder with his teeth, but he couldn't reach him. He stopped trying and shook himself until Calder had to let go.

Calder rolled toward Kari, but he was back on his feet before he even stopped moving.

His teeth were impressive. Kari should have known better, since he was a weasel, but he'd underestimated badgers. He'd thought they were cute, fluffy animals, and they were—as long as they kept their mouth shut.

Calder's canines were long, and they'd been strong enough to tear out a part of the coyote's shoulder. The coyote was bleeding and limping, but he wasn't stopping, not yet.

He threw himself at Calder, possibly thinking he'd overpower him and pin him to the floor, but Calder reared on his back legs and punched the coyote right on the nose.

Kari blinked. He hadn't expected that, and neither had the coyote.

The coyote jerked back, whining. Calder took that opportunity to launch himself at the coyote again, and even though he was smaller, the coyote was in enough pain and shock to allow himself to be pinned to the floor in the way he'd been trying to do to Calder.

Calder was safe. The coyote would no doubt try to get up, but he was steadily losing blood from his shoulder, and Calder bit him on the throat as soon as he had him in a vulnerable position.

Calder didn't kill him, though. Kari hadn't thought he would, but he held his breath as Calder and the coyote froze.

Then the coyote shifted.

CHAPTER FOURTEEN

Calder hadn't expected the coyote to shift. He'd thought the man would fight to the death, and to protect Kari, Calder had been ready to do just that. It looked like he wouldn't have to, though. The coyote under him shifted, leaving Calder with a mouth full of human skin.

He supposed he should feel lucky he didn't have fur in his mouth anymore.

He hoped the shift meant that the coyote was surrendering. He wasn't surprised. The coyote was painfully young, younger than Kari, and certainly much younger than Calder. He looked like he should have been in school, not in the middle of a fight.

The coyote scrambled toward the wall as soon as Calder released him, his back pressing against it. He looked at Calder with wide eyes as if he expected Calder to throw himself at him and bite him again. His shoulder was a mess of blood and exposed muscle, and Calder's stomach churned at the sight. He'd been the one to do it, but he hated it. The only reason he'd bitten the boy was that he was protecting Kari.

Kari had been so focused on the fight outside the window that he hadn't even noticed someone had joined them in the living room. Calder hadn't expected that, but he'd been there.

The coyote raised both hands. "Please. I'm sorry," he said. Calder blinked. He hadn't expected the coyote to apologize.

He shifted, never looking away from the boy. "What are you sorry for?" Calder asked.

"I shouldn't have attacked. I wasn't going to, but you

threw yourself at me, and — "

"Are you saying it was my fault?

"No. I know this is your home and that I wasn't invited in, but Karl told me he was going to hurt my mom and my sisters if I didn't do what he said."

Calder wasn't surprised. He'd known Karl wouldn't be able to find many fighters, not in such a short time, and not when everyone in the forest knew he was in the wrong. He'd had to force people to fight for him, and the result was the one in front of Calder. Karl was using children to fight his battles for him, and Calder was disgusted. "How old are you?"

"Nineteen. He said I had to fight for him. I'm old enough now."

"You're old enough to go to school, not to fight." The boy looked around, so obviously scared that Calder felt sorry for him. "I'm sorry I hurt you."

The coyote's eyes widened. "You're sorry?"

"I only did it to protect Kari, just like you were fighting for your family. What did Karl ask you to do?"

"I'm not alone. He told us to blow up the house."

Calder blinked. "Blow up the house?"

"Yes. I was supposed to distract you while — shit. We need to get out of here."

Shit was right. If this guy wasn't lying, the house would probably explode within seconds.

Calder reached for the coyote, and the boy cringed and tried to move further away. Calder limited himself to grabbing his good arm and dragged him toward the door. He dumped him there, then turned to Kari, but Kari was already following him. Calder smiled at him, took his hand, and grabbed the coyote again.

Once the coyote realized what Calder was doing, he stopped resisting. He scrambled to his feet, hurrying next to Calder, who wasn't letting go. He had more questions, and he was going to ask them.

They rushed out of the house, half holding each other up. Calder turned, wondering if he should go back and try to find the bomb because it was about to destroy Thomas' house, but Kari tugged on him. Calder turned to tell him what he wanted to do, but it was too late.

It was the loudest thing Calder had ever heard. He acted on instinct, throwing himself on top of Kari, pushing both him and the coyote to the ground as the world went up in a ball of fire around them — and pain. So much pain, more than Calder had ever felt.

Kari protested, but Calder was unable to hear him under the roaring of the explosion. His back burned, and he tucked himself closer to Kari, making sure that as little of Kari's body as possible was exposed.

Calder didn't know how long he stayed there, feeling like he'd never be able to get up. He couldn't hear anything, just a roar, even when he realized the explosion was over and what remained of the house behind him was on fire. His ears buzzed, and every movement hurt.

It took Calder a moment to realize that Kari was trying to push him off his body. He didn't want to move because he didn't want to put Kari in danger, but he thought the explosion was probably over, or at least he hoped so.

"Move!" Kari snapped.

Calder wasn't sure if he could hear him or if he was fooling himself because he was able to tell that was what Kari was saying from the way his lips moved.

Kari pushed him again, gentler this time. "You're hurt," Kari said.

Calder accepted his help and allowed him to manhandle him into a sitting position. His back hurt every time he breathed, and he knew he'd probably sustained wounds from the explosion. Kari, on the other hand, was filthy but unharmed. That was what Calder had been aiming for, so he was relieved, even though Kari looked like he might be about to strangle him.

Kari crouched in front of Calder and reached for him, but he didn't touch him, stopping before his fingers stroked Calder's shoulder. "I'm afraid to hurt you even more than you already are."

Calder shook his head, and that was a bad idea. The world around him tilted, and only Kari's help managed to keep him in a sitting position. Kari grimaced and looked around. "Okay. I need to go find a healer, but I don't want to leave you alone."

"I don't want you to go, either."

Kari rolled his eyes. "You might not want to, but I'm going to." He looked at the coyote. "You," he snapped. "Come here and help him."

The boy looked like he wanted nothing more than to run away, and Calder wouldn't have blamed him if that was what he decided to do. He was in enemy territory, and even though he'd been forced to do this, there was no telling what Thomas would decide to do with him. Thomas wasn't a bad alpha, but he had to show the rest of the forest that no one overstepped and invaded his territory without being punished for it.

Calder was stunned when, instead of running towards the trees, the coyote came to kneel next to him. He gently held onto Calder's arms, and Kari moved behind Calder. Calder could hear a little better now, and he looked around, trying to ignore the pain that made his back feel like it was in pieces—very painful pieces.

The house was gone. What was left of it was on fire, and there would be no salvaging it.

"Okay, you need a healer," Kari said. "Sit tight. I'll be back with her as soon as possible." Kari looked at the coyote. "If you're not here when I come back, I'll hunt you down and slit your throat. And trust me, I'm not lying. I killed the rodent alpha, so killing a random coyote shifter won't be a problem for me."

The coyote nodded frantically. Calder might have laughed if he wasn't in as much pain.

The fights around them were winding down. Karl was losing, as Calder had suspected he would. The only reason he'd blown up Thomas' house was revenge. He'd probably realized he wouldn't win even before he'd arrived, and like a petty child, he'd decided to make Thomas pay.

And now Thomas was homeless.

Calder gritted his teeth through the pain and looked at the coyote. "What's your name?"

"Patrick."

"You're not here because you wanted to be?" Calder wanted to be a hundred percent sure of that.

Patrick shook his head. "I was glad the council took away those carriers. I didn't know they were there, but they're about my age and the way they were treated . . ." His voice trailed off. He cleared his throat. "I never wanted to hurt anyone. That's why instead of following Roger to set up the bomb, I came to find you. I realized someone was in the living room because of the shooting. I didn't want you to die or get hurt."

"So you risked a lot to get to Kari and me."

Patrick shrugged. "Karl is going to kick my ass anyway. He's never happy with what I do. I might as well get beaten because I did a good thing."

"You won't be." If Patrick was telling the truth, Calder would make sure he didn't have to go back to the band if he didn't want to. Not all coyotes were like Karl, and they were doing their best to survive around shitty alphas.

Calder didn't know if he could do anything to help Patrick and the other coyotes who didn't want to stay under Karl's thumb, but he could talk to Thomas and see what he might be able to do. The alpha might have lost his house, but the cete would rebuild it, and hopefully, it would be with Patrick's help.

Kari was pissed. He was mad enough he really might slit that coyote's throat if something happened to Calder. Well, something more. Calder had already been hurt, and Kari didn't like that one bit. If he'd had any doubts he cared for Calder, they were gone now. It was more than that. Kari was in love with Calder, and the thought of losing him was terrifying.

Calder had shielded him during the explosion. No one but Kari's father would have done that, and Kari didn't know what to do. He wanted to run back to Calder and make sure he was okay, but the best thing he could do for Calder was to find him a healer.

If only Kari *could* find her. The area around the house was a mess, coyotes and other shifters still fighting. The fights had decreased after the explosion, but they were picking up again now that people had gotten over the shock. Kari had no idea where to start to find a healer, so he stopped running and looked around. He ignored all the fights until his gaze stopped on a specific one.

Thomas and Karl were still fighting. Thomas was in his human form, and to Kari's surprise, he was standing up to a coyote Karl. One of Karl's legs didn't work, so he kept hobbling around as he tried to rush Thomas and take him by surprise.

Kari went to them. He needed to find a healer, but that didn't mean he couldn't hurt Karl for what he'd done. Calder was wounded, and Thomas and his wife had lost their house. They'd been nothing but welcoming to Kari, and he wanted Karl to pay for what he'd done to them. It might not be his place, but that wouldn't stop him. The sooner Karl was taken out, the sooner the other coyotes would stop fighting for him. They needed to see he was a weak coward, and Kari wouldn't mind being the one showing it to them.

He got there just as Thomas threw Karl towards him. Kari stepped aside and watched Karl hit the ground. It wasn't enough to keep Karl there, so Kari stepped forward and punched him.

Punching a coyote was awkward, but Kari aimed for the face just like he would have if Karl had been in his human form. Karl whimpered and jerked back, and Kari hit him again.

Karl slumped to the ground, out for the count. Kari smiled smugly, took out his second gun since he'd had to leave the first one in the house that had exploded, and shot Karl in the knee.

Karl probably wouldn't have gotten anywhere anyway, but Kari wasn't taking any chances.

Karl screamed and started shifting, but Kari was done with him. He moved to leave only to change his mind and crouch next to Karl. He waited until Karl was in his human form and glaring at him to grin. "You shouldn't have come here," he said.

Karl gritted his teeth, but it was obvious he was in pain. "Since when does Thomas let others do his job?"

"Since you're not worth his effort." Kari thumped the gun against Karl's leg, satisfied when Karl tried to jerk away. "You think carriers are weak."

It wasn't a question, but Kari wasn't surprised that Karl felt the need to answer it. "They carry children. That's all they're good for."

Kari's smile widened. "They're also good for something else, like shooting you in the knee and punching you. I have to say that was satisfying as hell."

Karl's eyes widened, but Kari was already done with him.

He rose from his crouch and turned to find Thomas looking at him. The alpha was smiling even though he was wounded, and he gestured at two guards to grab Karl. "The bullet in the knee was a nice touch," he told Kari.

"I wanted to make sure he wouldn't leave."

"It was a good call."

"Good, because I don't feel guilty. He's an asshole, and he deserves a lot worse."

Thomas' expression sobered. "And he'll get it. He's not going back to the band, that's for sure."

Kari looked at the house, or rather, at what had once been a house. "I'm sorry. Calder and I managed to stop one of the two coyotes who did this, but I have no idea what happened to the second one." And he didn't think the boy who'd warned him and Calder actually had anything to do with it. He might have threatened the kid he'd slit his throat, but he wouldn't. He wasn't as good a man as Calder, but he could see that the kid didn't want to be here.

It wasn't surprising that Karl forced his people to come with him and to fight for him even when they didn't want to. Most people would have realized he was in the wrong, and the only reason they were there was that they were afraid for themselves and their families. Kari could understand that. He was angry and frightened for Calder, but he wouldn't let those feelings influence him, or at least, he'd try not to.

"You and Calder made it out okay?" Thomas asked.

Kari swore. "Calder is wounded. He shielded me when the house exploded, and I was looking for a healer when I noticed you and Karl. I need her."

Thomas was already moving. He waved two guards closer and gave them the order to look for Estelle. The other guards and the shifters who'd helped were gathering the wounded coyotes. All those who'd been able to run away had, and again, Kari wasn't surprised. If they hadn't been here for their loyalty to Karl, they no doubt wouldn't want to pay for what he'd forced them to do. They were cowards who were abandoning their wounded behind, but Kari knew Thomas well enough by now to be sure he wouldn't hurt those people if they didn't deserve it. He'd probably talk to every single one of them and ask them why they'd come before making any kind of decision about their future.

Kari pointed at the spot next to the house where he'd left Calder. "He's there. I'm going back to him to make sure . . ." Kari didn't want to say he wanted to make sure Calder was still alive. He knew Calder was. His wounds might be bad, but they weren't lethal. Calder was burned, and it would take him a while to heal, but he'd be okay.

He had to be.

Kari expected the coyote to be gone, so he was stunned that the boy was still with Calder when he got there. The boy was talking, distracting Calder and making sure he didn't pass out. Calder seemed to be having trouble staying in a sitting position on his own, but the coyote was there, holding him up.

Kari had to sit down. Now that the adrenaline was slowly leaving his body, he felt nauseous, and his head was spinning. Calder jerked when he felt Kari next to him, his expression shifting to worry as soon as he recognized Kari. He reached for him, wincing when the movement no doubt pulled on the wounds in his back.

"Are you okay?" Calder asked.

Kari snorted and leaned against Calder's shoulder, careful not to hurt him more than he already was. "I should be the one asking you that."

"I think we should agree that we're both in need of a healer."

"I told Thomas. Someone is coming." Kari looked at the coyote. "You should probably run before someone gets here."

The boy's eyes widened. "I'm not going anywhere."

"Why not? All the others who could are gone. Your alpha is out for the count, but since you helped Calder, I won't tell anyone you were here."

The boy shook his head. "What happened was my fault. I deserve to be punished for it."

"Patrick, I already told you nothing would happen to you," Calder said.

Kari cocked his head. "Patrick? Are you two on friendly terms now?"

"Patrick had nothing to do with this. He could have run away without telling us there was a bomb, and we'd both be dead. He never wanted to be here. Karl forced him."

Just like Kari had expected. "What did you promise him?"

Calder shook his head. "Nothing. But I told him I'd make sure Thomas and the others knew he wasn't here because he wanted to be. Karl threatened his family, and you, better than anyone, understands the length he was ready to go to in order to protect his mother and his sisters."

Kari did. He might not have been as understanding if Patrick had allowed Calder to get hurt even worse than he was, or if he'd run instead of helping him. But he was still there, ready to face the consequences of what he'd done. Kari might not be as eager as Calder to forgive him, but he'd give him a chance.

He'd earned it.

Kari was back. That was all that mattered for Calder, even with the pain in his back.

"Are you okay?" Patrick asked Kari. Calder had wanted to ask that, but Kari had distracted him.

Kari shrugged. "I'm fine. I'm not hurt."

He wasn't wounded, but he was pregnant, and between

the explosion and running away from the fire, something might have happened to him or the baby. "You need to have a healer check you," Calder said.

Kari narrowed his eyes. "There's no way I'm allowing her to touch me until I'm sure you're okay."

Patrick got up. He looked between Calder and Kari, clearly hesitant. "I'll be right back," he said.

Kari and Calder watched him walk away. "What are the odds he's going to come back?" Kari asked.

"You won't distract me. Whether Patrick comes back or not doesn't matter. You need to allow Estelle to check you. Something might have happened to the baby."

Kari pressed a hand to his stomach. "The baby is fine. I'm sure of it. You, on the other hand, are not. It's obvious your wounds are more serious than anything that's wrong with me. I can wait. You can't."

Calder tsked. "Don't you realize I won't be able to relax until I'm sure you and the baby are okay?"

Kari gently slapped Calder's knee. "The same goes for me, and I can see blood on you. That means you're worse off than me." He bit his lower lip. "Look, I'm okay. A bit lightheaded, but that's not surprising after what I've been through. I'm not in any kind of pain, I promise. I'll let the healer check me once she's done with you, I promise. But your back is badly burned, and it's obvious you're in pain. You have more need of medical help than I do. Let her do her job, and I won't protest when she tries to poke me."

Calder wanted to protest, to insist, but he knew better than to do that. Kari was stubborn, and he wouldn't change his mind, not when he was sure he was right.

Calder blinked when Patrick appeared in front of them. Like Kari, he hadn't been sure Patrick would come back. The boy had explained why he was there, and it would have made sense for him to go back home. He didn't know if he'd be allowed to see his family again, and he no doubt wanted to talk to them one last time. Instead, he was there, hovering in front of Calder while holding out a bottle of water.

Patrick shuffled. "Here. I found you some water. I don't know if it's going to help much with the lightheadedness, but it's better than nothing."

Kari blinked at Patrick and accepted the bottle. "Thank you."

"It's the least I could do."

Kari looked up at Patrick. "You helped Calder. You didn't have to."

"I would have even if what you're saying was true, but we both know it isn't. I did have to. It's partly my fault if he got hurt."

Calder started shaking his head, but even that hurt. He should remember it for the next time he wanted to try this. "It's not. You told Kari and I what was happening, and you gave us enough time to leave. We'd both be dead if it weren't for you."

"I shouldn't have been here, to begin with. It's not right."

"And we both understand that. I'll talk to Thomas, I promise." Calder didn't think Thomas would hurt Patrick anyway. From what he could see, he'd only told the guards to gather the wounded coyotes and to help them as much as they could. The cete only had one healer, but Calder knew that the bears had sent theirs to help, and maybe some of the other alphas had, too. He didn't think any of them were eager to treat coyotes, but they'd do it. They were healers. It was their job.

Calder looked up when he heard footsteps. He wasn't surprised to see Thomas walking towards him, the cete healer next to him.

"I'm sure there are people who need help more than I do," he grumped.

He wasn't surprised when Estelle didn't listen to him. She

was about two hundred years old, or at least, that was what it felt like. She'd already been the healer when Calder had been born, and she didn't take shit from him. Today was no exception.

She didn't even look at Calder in the face as she gently pushed him forward so she could examine his back.

"Kari isn't feeling well, and he's pregnant," Calder said anyway.

Estelle slapped the back of his head. "Shut up. I'm pretty sure talking hurts, so I'm not sure why you're flapping your mouth."

"Because Kari is sick. You need to check him and the baby."

Estelle looked at Kari, who shook his head. Estelle turned her attention back to Calder's wounds. "See? He's okay. He'll still be okay once I'm through with you."

"The baby—"

"Are you in pain, Kari?" Estelle asked. "Any bleeding?"

Kari's cheeks flushed. "No, and I don't think so. I haven't checked yet, though. "

"I'm pretty sure everything is good with you and the baby, but I'll check as soon as I'm done with Calder. Of course, that will happen faster if Calder shuts up and allows me to do my job."

Calder knew when he was beaten, and he was in this case. Estelle wouldn't focus on Kari until she was done with him, and that meant Calder needed that to happen as soon as possible.

He allowed her to poke at his back, doing his best not to whimper and yell at the pain. He had no clue how bad his back was, but he had a good idea from the pain. He was burned and probably had bits and pieces of the house embedded in his skin. It would be hell to get out, but it needed to be done. His back would get infected otherwise, and Calder couldn't allow that to happen.

He needed to be there for Kari. Kari's pregnancy was still in the beginning, but Calder knew how fast time could pass. He wanted to help with anything Kari might need, every step of the way.

"Okay. I need to get you home," Estelle said.

She looked at Patrick. "Do you have any experience in healing?" she asked him.

Patrick's eyes were wide as he shook his head. "No."

"Good. That way, I won't have to make sure you forget all the wrong things you might have learned. Come on. I need help to get Calder to his feet, and I doubt he'll allow Kari to do that since he thinks Kari is a delicate flower that might break."

Calder wanted to argue he didn't think that, but he didn't have the energy.

He allowed Estelle and Patrick to get him up, whimpering only a few times at the pain that seared his back. He felt like he couldn't walk, but he forced himself to put one foot in front of the other, then again. He could hear and feel Kari close by, following them as they awkwardly stumbled toward their house. Calder wanted to reach for Kari, but his arms were around Estelle and Patrick, and he knew he'd fall on his face if he let go.

He might be in pain, and he might be looking at weeks before he got back to normal, but this was over. Karl had lost, and he wouldn't make it through the night alive. Thomas and his allies would make sure of that.

Things would be awkward in the forest for a bit, and the coyotes would have to learn to live without their alpha until they managed to get their shit together and find a new one. Karl hadn't had the time to get married and have children after his father had died. Technically, the next in line to the position was Josiah, but he was a carrier, and there was no way to tell if the band would accept him, or even if he'd want to do that for them.

But Calder didn't have to worry about that right now.

CHAPTER FIFTEEN

Calder was going to be the death of Kari. Kari knew it, just like he knew he wouldn't have it any other way. If it had been anyone other than Calder, Kari would have already run and left him behind. But it *was* Calder, and there was no escaping him. Kari was in love with him, and they were going to have a baby together. Their child deserved both their fathers, and Kari wouldn't deny them that, no matter how much he wanted to strangle Calder.

At least Calder was asleep now.

He'd tried getting up to get breakfast ready for Kari that morning. It was ridiculous, since he'd been wounded yesterday. Estelle had been clear — she wanted Calder to stay in bed for at least a few days while the wounds started healing. Calder had disobeyed her, and Kari had found him in the hallway, leaning against the wall because the pain was too much for him to walk downstairs to the kitchen. Kari had ushered him back to bed after a stop in the bathroom, and he'd threatened to move back to the cabin he'd shared with his father if Calder didn't do what Estelle had ordered.

Calder had protested. Kari had expected it, of course. They were both stubborn, and Calder felt he had to protect Kari. Kari would have been offended in any other situation or with anyone else, but he knew Calder was aware of how strong he was. The reason he wanted to take care of Kari wasn't that he thought Kari was weak. No, he wanted to do it because he was in love with Kari, and he wanted Kari to be safe and protected and happy.

It had been hard for Kari to understand that in the beginning. His first instinct was always to lash out and show how strong he was, but he was starting to get used to this. Besides, he wanted the same for Calder. He wanted Calder to be safe and to heal. He hated seeing Calder in pain.

That was why he'd dumped some of the sleeping powder Estelle had given him on the down-low into the glass of water he'd made sure Calder drank. She'd known Calder would try to get up, and she'd told Kari to make sure that didn't happen. Calder needed sleep, much more than Kari did.

Calder wouldn't wake up for at least a few hours, and Kari was going crazy inside the house. It was probably stupid, since he'd been outside just last night, but he needed some fresh air.

Knowing Calder was safe, he left him in the bedroom and headed toward Thomas' house, or rather, toward what was left of it.

It was even worse in the daylight. The fire had been put out, but the house was still smoking. There wasn't much left of it. The explosion had made sure of that, and the fire had finished it off.

Thomas and his wife were already there, talking with some of the cete members and ordering others around. A team was already cleaning the area, and Kari suspected it wouldn't be long before it looked like nothing had happened and like the house had never been there.

"Kari. I didn't expect to see you today," Thomas said as he walked toward Kari.

Kari shrugged. "Calder is asleep. I wasn't about to spend my day watching him."

Thomas chuckled. "You're not afraid he'll sneak out of bed?"

"He can't. Estelle gave me a powder to make him sleep, and I didn't hesitate to use it."

Thomas laughed. "He's always worked too hard. I'm glad he found you. You're good for him."

"Why? Because I made sure he was asleep?"

"Pretty much. If you hadn't been there, he would already be out of bed trying to help here. Trust me. We've been friends for a long time, and I know him."

Kari suspected he was right. Even though he hadn't known Calder as long as Thomas had, it was long enough for him to know how Calder would have reacted this morning. Hell, he'd tried to get out of bed to take care of Kari even though Kari was fine. He didn't have as much a scratch on him.

Kari cleared his throat. "I'm sorry about this," he said, tilting his chin toward what was left of the house.

Thomas sighed and looked at what had once been his house. "We'll rebuild."

"I'll help."

"If Calder allows you to."

Kari would have been offended if he hadn't heard the amused tone in Thomas' voice. "He knows better than to try forbidding me from doing anything."

Thomas chuckled. "That's what I thought. But you know he's going to try, and not because he thinks you're weak. He worries about you."

"I know." Kari had been thinking that earlier, and he was glad that someone who knew Calder better than he did was confirming it.

"You'll be staying with him, then?"

Kari looked at his stomach. "I don't think I have much of a choice."

Thomas frowned. "You do. You don't have to be with him just because you're having his child. I can make sure you find another place to stay if that's what you want, and even keep Calder away from you for a bit."

Kari was more touched by Thomas' offer then he liked. He

wasn't used to people worrying about him and offering him that kind of possibility. He'd always been the one who worried about his safety and his father's. No one else had cared. Things were different now, though. Kari was going to have to get used to the fact that along with Calder, he'd gotten a family. He'd let love in with Calder, and now he was surrounded by different kinds of love, and he had to learn to live with it. "I'm fine. I wanted to be with Calder."

"Good. I think you'll both be happy with each other. You certainly deserve it."

Kari hesitated. He didn't particularly want to talk about his feelings, especially not with a man he didn't know well, but he wasn't sure Thomas would answer his questions about the coyotes and the carriers if he asked. He supposed he might as well try. "What's going to happen to the band? Who's going to be their next alpha?" It was something everyone was wondering, and everyone was afraid of knowing the answer.

Kari didn't know much about the coyotes. He'd always avoided them because both the old alpha and Karl had been assholes. Kari knew that didn't mean all coyotes were like them, but they had to obey their alphas. Now they didn't have one anymore, but maybe they still had at least a beta. If the man was anything like Karl and his father, things wouldn't go well, though.

"You know what will happen to Karl?"

"Not for sure, but I can imagine." It was the law of the forest. Karl had invaded cete territory. Thomas was allowed to choose his punishment, since he'd won that fight. Kari might not have been part of the cete for long, but he knew Thomas would do the right thing, no matter how hard it was or how distasteful he found it. That meant getting rid of Karl so the band would have at least a chance to make it. It would keep the rest of the forest safe, and that was the best thing anyone could do.

Thomas nodded. "As far as I know, Josiah, Karl's brother, should be the next in charge. We caught Karl's beta along with him, so right now, the band doesn't have a leader. But Josiah is a carrier, and he was terribly abused by his father and his brother. I haven't talked to him yet, but I'm going to go today, and I don't know if he'll want to step up. I'd understand if he didn't, and even if he does, we have no way to know if the band will accept him as alpha."

"And if they don't? If he doesn't want to?"

"Then the council might have to step in. We'll try to work something out with the band, of course, but we can't allow it to stay without an alpha."

"What about the carriers?" Because even though they hadn't yet found a second coyote carrier, Kari was convinced more of them were hidden in the depth of coyote territory. Karl was an idiot, but his father hadn't been.

"They can stay at the Bishop house for as long as they want to, of course."

"Is the council team going to enter coyote territory again to search it now that they can?"

Thomas arched a brow. "Do you know something I don't?"

"Not for sure. But Karl kept those three carriers hidden. I wouldn't be surprised if he had more stashed deeper in his territory. I doubt he'd admit it if you asked him, but without an alpha, exploring coyote territory shouldn't be a problem."

"I'll mention it to Terrence. You're right, of course. We should take this opportunity to make sure no one else is getting hurt. I should have thought about that."

He should have, but Kari couldn't find it in himself to be angry. "You have a lot to think about right now. Besides, that's why you have Calder and me, isn't it?"

Thomas laughed. "I suppose it is. You'll be a good fit with the cete, Kari. I'm glad Calder found you, and that you're staying."

To Kari's surprise, Kari was, too.

Something was vibrating.

Calder reached out to grab his phone from his bedside table and swore at the flash of pain in his back. How could he have forgotten about the wounds even for one second? The only explanation was that he was still half-asleep.

He groaned and opened his eyes. His phone was still vibrating, and he looked around, hoping Kari would hand it to him.

But Kari wasn't there.

Calder didn't allow himself to panic. Kari was no doubt downstairs having breakfast, or maybe lunch, depending on what time it was. He wasn't Calder's keeper, just like Calder wasn't his. They didn't have to be together all the time, even though not being with Kari freaked Calder out. That was only because of what had happened last night. Calder hoped that in time, he could forget the fear that had filled him when he'd realized he and Kari might be about to die after Patrick had told them about the bomb.

He'd never felt like that. Calder knew fear, had felt it just like everyone else, but last night was different. He hadn't been afraid for himself.

He'd been terrified for Kari.

Loving someone this much was new for Calder, and he needed to learn to deal with it. Maybe being hurt and having to rest would help.

Since it was apparent Kari wasn't coming, Calder shuffled to the edge of the mattress and grabbed his phone. It had stopped vibrating during the time Calder had needed to think, but it started again once he had it in his hand. It had to be urgent for whoever was calling to insist, so Calder didn't waste time answering.

"Yes?" His voice sounded weaker than usual, but he suspected most of the forest already knew he was wounded, so the person calling wouldn't be surprised.

"Calder, thank God. I wasn't sure you'd answer considering what happened last night," Abel said.

Calder started rolling to his back before remembering he shouldn't do that. He flopped back on his stomach. "I'm fine, I promise."

"I know. Thomas called me earlier. He told me you were resting and that you'll make a full recovery. I'm happy to hear that, but that's not the reason I called."

Calder could hear something was wrong from Abel's tone. "Tell me."

"The humans contacted us."

That wasn't what Calder had expected. He probably should have, though. "What did they want?"

"Someone noticed the explosion last night. They wanted to know what had happened and if we were a danger to the humans who live around the forest."

"What did you tell them?"

"That we weren't, of course. I'm not sure they believed me, though. They weren't happy about the explosion, and they want to know what's happening in the forest. They're sending a team to check in on us."

Calder sat up, swinging his legs off the side of the mattress even though his back protested at the movement. "Shit. When? How many of them? And why?"

"They talked about sanctions."

Knowing what he did of the humans who'd locked shifters in the forest, Calder suspected they'd find an excuse to give out sanctions even though they didn't have a reason to. Thomas' house might have exploded, and Karl might have rebelled against the council, but that didn't mean the council didn't have the forest under control anymore. They were still doing their job, and Calder thought it possible to spread their power now that Karl had been dealt with. The forest would be a safer place for all the shifters who lived there, and that meant the humans didn't have to stick their noses into shifter business.

Not that that was going to stop them.

They did what they wanted. They had the numerical advantage and not only that. They had weapons shifters would never be able to get their hands on, and while the shifters in the forest might fight against them, they wouldn't win. They didn't have the resources.

"The council needs to meet," Calder snapped.

"I know. I already organized something for tomorrow. I wanted to do it today, and I called everyone, but like you, some of them are busy."

Calder's thoughts went to Jacqueline. She was the coyote council member, and while he'd never liked her and thought she didn't belong on the council, he couldn't help but be sorry for what she was going through. She didn't deserve him to feel that way, but he did anyway.

He wanted the meeting to be today, but he knew that wouldn't change anything. The humans were coming. Giving the council members a day to think things over and possibly talk about them with people they trusted would help. They'd come to the meeting with more ideas, and hopefully, a way to help.

Calder was still freaking out when he hung up, even more than he had been earlier. He needed to find Kari as soon as possible. Even though he knew Kari hadn't left the forest and that the humans weren't there yet, Calder wanted to see him and make sure he was okay.

He was halfway down the stairs when the front door opened. He almost fell on his face in his rush to get to Kari, who walked in looking unworried. He jerked when he heard

Calder, and he rushed to Calder's side, helping him down the last steps. "What are you doing on your feet?"

"I had to find you," Calder answered.

Kari rolled his eyes. "I'm fine. You have nothing to worry about. I was with Thomas."

Calder should have known. Still, he touched Kari's face, reassuring himself that Kari was in front of him and that he was safe.

Kari frowned. "What happened?"

Of *course* he realized something had happened. "I just got a phone call. From Abel."

"Don't tell me there's a council meeting. I'll go with you if you have to go, but I'm not happy about it. I don't want you to exert yourself too much. You're still healing, and you need rest."

"We're meeting tomorrow. You can come with me if you want to, but I don't think you'll be allowed inside the room." Not when this meeting was about humans coming to the forest. But that didn't mean Calder shouldn't tell Kari. He wanted Kari to know what was going on so he'd be ready to act if he needed to. "The humans noticed the explosion."

Kari leaned back. "I'm not surprised. Karl was an idiot. He shouldn't have done that. What did they say?"

"They're sending a team. They're talking about sanctions and making sure we're not a danger to the humans outside the forest."

"That's bad."

"It is. Depending on what they find and what they decide, this could be a disaster for the forest."

"You're going to try to reach out to them before they come, aren't you?"

"We'll contact them. We'll try to find a way out of this, but I doubt they'll listen."

Kari sighed. "Come on. I'm walking you back to bed.

There's nothing you can do right now anyway. You might as well rest so you'll be stronger tomorrow."

He was right. No matter how much Calder wanted to go out there and help, he couldn't, especially not in the state he was in. "Only if you stay in bed with me. You might be okay, but you're pregnant, and I know you're exhausted."

"I'd be angry with you for always mentioning the fact that I'm pregnant if you weren't right. I *am* exhausted."

Calder moved slowly. His back hurt more than it had when he'd woken up, and it was his fault. He should have waited in bed for Kari to come home, but he'd let his emotions take over and have the better of him.

Kari was Calder's weakness. Calder didn't mind, and he didn't care, but he would have to learn to live with it. He'd always tried to do the right thing for the cete and for Thomas, but now, they weren't his main concern anymore. He knew Thomas wouldn't care and that he'd approve, but hard times loomed over them, and they'd all have to work to get the humans to leave the forest and make sure they didn't destroy it on their way out.

Shifters didn't deserve to be stuck in a limited amount of space, but it was their life. They'd been in the forest for long enough that some of them knew nothing of the world beyond it, including Calder. He'd been born here and had never left. He didn't want to know what the rest of the world was like. He wanted to be left alone, and he'd fight for it.

He'd fight for the forest, for the cete, and for Kari and their child.

YOU MAY ALSO ENJOY THE FOLLOWING FROM EXTASY BOOKS INC:

Justin
Catherine Lievens

Excerpt

Yedley was happy. He hated that it had taken him being kidnapped to find his brother, but it was better than not having Pryderi at all. He could do without having to help his brother move, though.

"I thought you were going to help me?" Pryderi asked when Yedley opened the door of Calvin's room.

Yedley grinned at him. "I'll help you unpack." There was no way he was walking up and down the stairs, not when he knew Calvin was uncomfortable with having someone who wasn't part of their small family in the apartment. Pryderi had asked his best friend to help him move, and while Yedley didn't blame him since it meant he didn't have to help, he wished something could be done to make Calvin more comfortable.

"I suppose it's better than nothing. Lunch is ready."

"We'll be right there."

Pryderi walked away, and Yedley closed the door and turned toward Calvin. Calvin was on his bed, curled up with his back against the wall. It was his usual position, as if he expected someone to attack him. He probably did considering what had happened to him. "You heard Pryderi. Lunch is ready."

Calvin looked like he might decide not to have lunch, but he knew better than to suggest that to Yedley. Calvin needed to eat after all the time he'd spent between labs and the Beasts, and Yedley wouldn't allow him to stay in his room only because Pryderi's friend was there.

"He's my brother's best friend," Yedley said. "Pryderi wouldn't have asked him to help if he didn't trust him."

Calvin sighed. "I'm not trying to make this difficult, I swear."

"I know you're not. Come on. You can peek inside the kitchen and decide if you want to eat with us or bring your lunch back here."

Yedley hated the thought of Calvin eating alone in his bedroom, but he didn't want Calvin to freak out because a stranger was there. It would take him some time to get used to having people who weren't planning to hurt him around. Yedley didn't want to push him too hard.

Pryderi was leaving the bathroom when Yedley and Calvin got there. He waited for them to wash their hands, keeping his distance from Calvin. Yedley was grateful his brother did that without having to be asked. The three of them—Yedley, Pryderi, and Nate—might not know what Calvin had been through, but they were aware it had been hell for him, and they all wanted him to be happy sharing the apartment with them as a family. There was a lot of walking around on eggshells and making sure he wasn't freaking out, but it was a small price to pay.

"Are you sure your brother's friend is okay?" Calvin asked, leaning close to Yedley as they walked toward the kitchen.

"Well, I've never met him, but I trust my brother, and if he trusts this guy, then I do, too."

The corner of Calvin's lips curled. "That's a lot of trust."

And it was precisely what Calvin was missing in his life, but Yedley didn't say that. Calvin was aware of it, and there was no need to hurt him more than he already was.

Yedley followed Calvin into the kitchen, but he froze as soon as he saw the man already in there. *Justin.* It couldn't be anyone else since he was the only one helping today.

He was also Yedley's mate.

What was Yedley supposed to do? He wanted to talk to Justin. He wanted to run away.

He'd never imagined he'd meet his mate. He probably should have, but he'd been so busy and worried over his kidnapping and the time he'd spent with the Beasts, and of course, possibly having to come out to his parents if he ever got free, that the thought hadn't gone through his mind.

And now he was staring at his mate. As far as he could see, Justin hadn't realized something was happening. That was good. No matter how much Yedley wanted to talk to Justin, he had no idea what he'd say to him, or even if he'd be able to get a word out of his mouth. "He's single," Pryderi murmured. He tried to push Yedley into the room, but Yedley wasn't moving. He *couldn't* move.

He forced himself to swallow. "You're sure?" He was confused, but knowing that his mate didn't have a boyfriend made him feel better.

"Yeah. He's one of my best friends. I'd know if he had someone, even though I haven't been spending a lot of time in Whitedell lately."

Yedley nodded, mostly to himself. He was relieved he wouldn't have to take his mate away from someone else, but that didn't mean he had even the slightest idea of what to do now. "Good."

"Yeah?"

God. What would Pryderi think about this? Would he be happy that his brother and his best friend were mates? Or would he get angry? Yedley supposed there was only one way to find out. "Yeah. I'd hate to think of my mate with another man." Or woman. Yedley didn't know Justin. He didn't even know if Justin was gay, or if he liked men at all.

"What?" Pryderi looked nonplussed as if he didn't quite believe what Yedley had just told him.

Yedley didn't blame him. "He's my mate." Yedley didn't want to analyze his feelings about this too closely. They were a jumble of hope that Justin would want him in his life and they could be happy, fear that Justin *wouldn't* want him, happiness at having found his mate, and a whole bunch of other things Yedley hadn't even been aware he could feel at the same time.

Pryderi blinked. "Justin?"

Yedley understood being shocked by the news better than anyone, but was Pryderi serious? "Who do you think? Calvin? I would have told you already if that were the case." And since the only other man in the room was Nate and he couldn't be Yedley's mate since he was Pryderi's, it shouldn't take long for Pryderi to realize Yedley wasn't lying.

Pryderi looked from Yedley to Justin, then back at Yedley again. "I didn't expect this."

"I didn't either, trust me. I have no clue what to do with a mate. I don't even know what to do with my *life*."

Pryderi's expression twisted. "He won't push for anything. I know Justin. He's a good guy."

"I hope you're right."

"I've known him for years. If there's one thing I'm sure of, it's that he's a good guy."

Yedley nodded. He wasn't sure what else to say. He knew the others in the room expected him and Pryderi to sit at the table and have lunch, but he didn't think he could do that. How was he supposed to face Justin and not blurt out that they were mates? Besides, Yedley was pretty sure Justin was a shifter, and that meant that once he got close enough, he'd realize Yedley was his mate.

"I know you're not ready for this," Pryderi said. "It's understandable. You don't *have* to be ready for it."

Yedley wrinkled his nose. "He's going to find out if I sit at the table with you and the others."

"It's not a bad thing. Or were you planning on keeping it a secret from him?"

Yedley shook his head. "I have no idea."

Pryderi looked around the room again. "You should probably talk to Justin alone. I doubt either of you wants to be this exposed for this conversation."

Yedley certainly didn't want to. He wanted to go back to his room and hide away, but also to crawl into Justin's lap and ask his mate to keep him safe.

Pryderi cleared his throat. "Why don't you go downstairs to the bar? It's closed right now, so you won't be disturbed. I'll tell Justin to follow you there, and you can tell him whatever you feel up to." He squeezed Yedley's arm. "Everything will be okay. I promise."

Yedley wanted to believe his brother, but he wasn't sure he could.

About the Author

Catherine lives in Italy, country of good food and hot men. She used to write fantasy as a child, but it was reading her first gay erotic romance novel that made her realize that that was what she really wanted to write.

After graduating from college in English language and translation, she divides her day between writing, reading, taking care of her son and reading some more.

Connect with her:

lievens.catherine@gmail.com
BookBub
Website
Facebook
Facebook Group
Twitter
Newsletter

www.ingramcontent.com/pod-product-compliance
Lightning Source LLC
Chambersburg PA
CBHW070606130626
46556CB00001B/287